DEMONIC
INDEMNITY

DEMONIC INDEMNITY

CRAIG McLAY

DEMONIC INDEMNITY
Copyright © 2019 Craig McLay

Edition: 2019
ISBN: 978-1-9990837-2-4

Cover Design By: Carl Graves (www.extendedimagery.com)
Book interior: 52 Novels (www.52novels.com)

GLOSSARY OF INSURANCE TERMS

Frankenstein Exclusion
All damages caused by a reanimated creature, sentient being or other life form created by the insured are excluded from coverage (unless you have the Prometheus Endorsement, which requires Level 3 underwriting approval).

Amityville Settlement Amendment
Damage awards will be reduced by this amount in cases where the insured knowingly bought/leased haunted property or artefact.

Additional Personality Expense
In the event that an approved exorcism has been totally or partially ineffective, the insured will be paid a flat payment for future loss of income/damage expenses and be ineligible for Identity Theft Endorsement for at least six years.

Summoning Exclusion
Whereby the insured does knowingly summon a ghost, demon or other supernatural entity by Ouija board, séance or other means, all resulting damages are excluded from coverage.

Multi-Spectrum Indemnity Clause
Insured shall be covered for all damages caused by possessed property (including cars, appliances and prosthetic limbs) regardless of supernatural origin (meteor shower, ghost, etc).

Djinn Rider

Damage caused by djinn is excluded from all policies unless this coverage is present. This rider does not include damage to plumbing or heating systems caused by water or fire variants.

Identity Theft Endorsement

Coverage for loss or damage caused by possession by supernatural/paranormal entity. Includes loss of income if insured is terminated from their job due to compromised reputation while possessed (limit of $5,000 for public nudity or sexual impropriety).

Pitchfork Rider

Covers loss/damage caused by angry mobs who storm your house/castle/business in the belief that you are building a creature or involved in a satanic ritual or demonic worship.

Poltergeist Exclusion

Any property built on land that was at one time a graveyard, portal, site of a massacre, celestial calendar or staging ground for ritual sacrifice is excluded from coverage. If this becomes known after coverage is bound, then policy will be cancelled on the grounds of misrepresentation with 30 days' notice by registered letter.

1

As the first human in the company's 3,200-year history to work in the Special Investigations Unit of Crimson Seal Property & Casualty, LLC, it would be fair to say that Tim Lovecraft was more nervous than usual reporting to work on his first day.

It wasn't his first day with the company—Tim had started on the phones at the client contact centre right after graduating from university 10 years earlier with a degree in demonology and a minor in folklore before moving on to work as an assistant underwriter and then claims adjuster—but this was a bigger step than either of those. The SIU was a small department with only nine employees made up of eight investigators and a director. Its mandate was to investigate all potentially fraudulent activity, whether internal or external. Because they might end up investigating anybody, right up to the CEO, it did not exist within the regular corporate hierarchy and instead reported directly to the audit committee of the company's board of directors.

When the posting had first appeared on the board, Tim had never imagined that he would in a million years manage to get it. He had all the qualifications—his Chartered Supernatural Insurance Professional (CSIP), Certified Infernal Auditor (CIA) and Licenced Paranormal Insurance (LPI) designations—but didn't think that would do much in his favor. All of the other applicants would have those, too. The SIU was secretive. It was small. Jobs almost never came up in there. The last time they had hired was 12 years before, when one of their senior investigators had been possessed by a djinn and didn't survive the exorcism. Tim knew about djinn. They were nasty little buggers. Almost all policies excluded them, and with good reason. According to actuaries, djinn alone were responsible for 37 per cent of the loss ratio on an industry-wide basis. Not even all the werewolf damage caused by the infamous once-in-a-century blood moon of the previous quarter could touch them for their sheer malicious ferocity.

The other thing Tim had going against him was that he was a human. The SIU had never had one before. Humans were thought to be extremely ill-suited to that kind of field work. As adjusters? Sure. Tim had done that job for five years. It was only when adjusters thought that there might be something funny going on that they called in SIU, and that was where things could get a bit messy. Humans were not considered to be good at messy, at least not by the wider paranormal community, who considered them weak, easily scared and far too vulnerable to even the mildest threats, like fairies and slow-moving zombies.

As the third-largest supernatural insurer (based on Gross Written Premium) in the country, Crimson Seal was no different than many of its competitors in taking an extremely conservative view of who was best suited to what jobs.

Times, however, were changing. The company now had three humans in senior management positions and had just appointed one of them, Lilith Warwick, to the position of executive vice president of claims. One of her stated aims was to "foster greater diversity and inclusion" in the ranks so that more people and entities of all kinds could break into departments that had been previously closed off to them. There had been a lot of grumbling about that, most of it in voices slightly lowered in hallways or on the other side of plastic cubicle walls, but some of it was more overt.

"Sounds like a load of PC malarkey to me," said one demon to another in the break room on the day after the communication went out. "Everyone knows humans can count, but they're really not much good for anything else."

She had apologized when she noticed Tim refilling his water bottle within earshot.

"I didn't mean you, dear," she said, looking more alarmed that she might be the subject of an HR complaint than anything else. "You know how it is."

Tim did know how it was. He had heard most of it before. He had applied anyway and was amazed when he received more than just the standard email acknowledgment in reply. When they called to tell him he had gotten the job, he had been so stunned that he dropped his cell phone in the document shredder which, fortunately, was not turned on at the time.

In addition to its hierarchical outlier status and aura of secrecy, the SIU was cool in one other major respect—it wasn't located in the main Crimson Seal building, which was a hexagonal red sandstone tower on Sixth Street. The SIU operated out of its own space on Morningstar Avenue, the address of which was officially a secret. Tim had done his first interview by videoconference, which wasn't unusual. For his second interview, however, he had been asked to stand on the corner next to his apartment and wait. At the appointed time, two SIU employees in masks had pulled up and handed him a hood, which he was forced to wear for the duration of his ride. It was only after he had gotten the job that they had told him where he would be reporting to work every day.

Standing in front of the building, Tim couldn't help but think that his new boss had been putting him on. The sign out front identified it as Asgaroth's Relics & Ritual Supply. The place sold a variety of supernatural and cursed objects, the vast majority of which were fake. Their clientele was mostly fake witches, warlocks and phoney fortune tellers looking to boost their credibility with a few well-chosen accessories. Tim knew the place had lost its licence to sell supernatural artefacts twice in the last 18 months alone, most recently for selling what it claimed was John Dillinger's cursed penis to a private men's club in the old Distillery District. Unfortunately, one of the members of that club was the former mayor, and he did not take kindly to the discovery that his membership fees had been spent on a member that was not exactly genuine. A subsequent investigation revealed that the origin of the organ went back only to a Belgian tourist who had made the mistake of failing to tip his table dancer at a strip club in Little Olympus. Tim had never been there himself, but even he knew that it was a bad idea to piss off the Bacchante, who made up the majority of the dancers in those places. They were beautiful, never aged and would usually work for wine, but they were also prone to uncontrollable fits of rage and cannibalism.

Tim opened the door and stepped inside. He was immediately hit with the strong smell of incense, which he recognized as Essence of Mercan. It was rumored to weaken a person's willpower, making them less sales resistant. Half the businesses in the city used the stuff. Federal consumer protection law prohibited them from burning it in concentrations greater than .025 per 100 square feet of retail space, but many of them ignored that rule. They knew the chances of a ministry employee showing up unexpectedly with an air monitor were almost zero. And even if they did get caught, the fines were minimal.

Tim breathed through his mouth and made his way to the back of the store. There was a black cat dozing in a basket on the counter next to a bored-looking girl in a red cloak. The girl was scrolling through something on her phone and barely lifted an eyebrow to acknowledge his presence. Tim passed shrunken heads, Ouija boards, wands, ankhs and other touristy bric-a-brac before reaching a door in the back left corner. It was a plain black door with a handwritten "Staff Only" sign hanging from a nail. The only unusual thing about the door was that it had no handle. Instead, it had a magnetic card reader built into the wall next to it. The reader blended in to the frame and wasn't immediately visible.

Tim looked around to make sure that nobody was watching and then took out his employee ID card and held it up to the reader. It beeped and flashed a red light. Tim tried the door, which did not budge. He tried the card again and got the same result.

"Damn it," he muttered, looking over his shoulder again to make sure no one else was watching. The girl behind the counter, however, had not looked up from her phone. There was no other door. This was the one. Had he gotten the date or time wrong? No, he knew that this was where he was supposed to be. Were they messing with him?

He looked more closely at the door. There was no bell, knocker or anything else on it that he could see to alert the people inside that he was stuck out here.

Oh well, Tim thought. I guess I'll have to do this the old-fashioned way.

Tim knocked on the door. Ten seconds passed that felt like ten minutes. He counted off 20 more seconds and then knocked again. Were they even back there? Maybe everyone had gone for coffee at the same time. He had just finished counting off another minute and was about to knock again when the door was opened by a pudgy man with yellow-brown hair and a sallow complexion. He had a large bandage on his cheek just above his beard, which was scraggly and unkempt. His most striking feature, however, were his yellow eyes.

Werewolf, Tim realized, taking an involuntary step back.

"Yes?" the man growled.

"Uh, hi," Tim said. "I'm, uh, Tim Lovecraft. I'm supposed to be starting today."

"Right then, uh Tim," the man said, waving him inside. "This way."

Tim stepped through the door and followed the man down a sterile and neon lit carpeted hallway that stood in sharp contrast to the eccentrically bohemian store he had been standing in a moment before. The air in the hall was crisp and free of Mercan. Tim could feel his urge to buy dismembered genitalia fading with every step.

"Vol mentioned that you'd be coming in today," the man said, moving with surprising grace and speed for somebody of his body shape. "I'm Lonnie Fuhrman. Been a case worker for 32 years."

"Nice to meet you," Tim said.

"Before you ask, no, I didn't cut myself shaving," said Lonnie. "I'm a werewolf. You got any problems with that?"

"No," Tim said hurriedly. "Not at all."

"Good," Lonnie said. "Feel free to get all of the jokes out of your system as quickly as possible."

"Jokes?" Tim said.

"Yeah," Lonnie said. "Fuhrman. Fur man? Bush boy? Crotch sniffer? You know the deal."

"Oh," Tim said. "I would never-"

"I could take the Narlune," Lonnie said, referring to the popular medication that prevented werewolf transformations. "But I spend so much time cooped up here or in my apartment that it's nice to get out and run around for a bit, you know?"

"Yeah," Tim said. "I can totally understand that."

Werewolves were allowed out provided they stayed within the walled enclosure of Chaney Park during their transformations. Any caught outside that area were tranquilized and held in what police referred to as the "Wolf Tank" overnight. More than two such incidents in a 12-month period could theoretically lead to the subject being chemically de-lupinized via Narlune subdermal implants, but only in the case of death or serious injury.

The two of them got into an elevator. The doors closed and Tim felt them begin to descend. He wondered for a moment how on earth anyone could have heard him knocking on the door before he remembered that werewolves had exceptional hearing. The doors opened and the two of them stepped out into a bustling office space. Tim counted about ten desks arranged throughout the room, some of which had individuals busy at work typing on laptops.

"Open concept office as you can see," Lonnie said, gesturing to the space. "No windows, of course. We've got George to thank for that."

"George?" Tim said.

"Over there," Lonnie said, pointing to an extremely pale man sitting at a desk in the back corner. He had a white face that was almost entirely hidden by sunglasses. The part of his body that Tim could see was covered by a black sunbreaker jacket and he was wearing black gloves. "That's George Sticker. He's our resident vampire. I'd introduce you, but he's a little hungover today. Went to that new blood bank on Amsterdam and had himself a little too much fun last night. Had a few too many of those new signature cocktails where they hang the bag right up over your table. Ain't that right, George?"

The vampire lifted his hand and slowly extended his middle finger, causing Lonnie to break out in laughter.

"He's not so bad," Lonnie said. "But if you cook with a lot of garlic, you might want to give him some space."

"My brother's a vampire," Tim said. "I'm used to it."

"And this is Carmilla von Karn," Lonnie said, gesturing to the woman at the desk closest to them. She was dressed in a black leather jacket over a white T shirt and jeans. She had coal-black skin, shoulder length hair and piercing eyes. Both of the latter two features were the same infernal shade of red. "Whatever you do, don't fall in love with her. She will suck your soul straight out of your body, chew it up and spit it out again."

"Very funny, furball," she said. "Who the hell is this?"

"This is Tim Lovecraft," Lonnie said. "And it's his first day."

"Hi," Tim said, stepping forward and reaching out his hand. He felt a strange buzz that was not unlike the one he had felt in the store, only much more powerful. "Nice to meet you."

She looked at his hand like it was a snake that had slithered out of her fridge. "Oh good. A white male normie who got the job ahead of somebody much more qualified courtesy of our new dumbass inclusion policy. Do me a favour and don't introduce yourself, okay, Timmie? That way, I won't have to say anything at your funeral about what a privileged dick you are. Because you aren't going to last five minutes out there."

"Uhhhh…" Tim stuttered.

"Relax," Lonnie said, steering Tim away. "She says that to everybody."

Tim realized that he was still holding out his hand and dropped it. "She does?"

"She's half-succubus," Lonnie said, dropping his voice slightly. "Little sensitive about, you know, the assumptions people tend to make about that."

"I see," Tim said, relieved. That explained the sudden burst of attraction that he had felt for someone who had just told him to his face that he was an entitled dickhead who deserved to (and probably would) die on the job. He could feel his head starting to clear as Lonnie pushed him towards a black office door on the far side of the room.

"Hey Vol!" Lonnie called, knocking on the door. "New guy's here. You busy?"

There was a rumble of what sounded like thunder from the other side of the door. Lonnie rocked back and forth on his heels and hummed what Tim recognized as the first few bars of the theme to *Wolf on the Beat*, a popular sitcom about a werewolf detective and her prissy human partner. Tim looked down to see that said heels were not encased in shoes.

"Flat feet," Lonnie said, noticing Tim's gaze. "Hazard of the condition. Although it took the company a while to agree. Had to wear these stupid sandals for a year before they finally adjusted the dress code. Usual HR committee bullshit. Zombies get their own fridge in the cafeteria for brains just like that, but asking to go without shoes? You'd think I asked for an office with a moonroof."

Tim jumped when the door flew open and a deep voice growled: "Enter and be damned!"

"Catch you later, Tim!" Lonnie said, nodding. "George and I are heading to that new Transylvanian place for lunch later if you're interested. It's a skewer-it-yourself thing. Very in with the hipsters."

Lonnie sauntered barefoot back to his desk as Tim took a deep breath and entered the office of the SIU's director of operations. He had met his new boss once before during the interview process, but had been too intimidated to take anything in. The first thing he noticed was the overwhelming smell of sulphur. The whirring of seven separate electronic air fresheners did their best to ameliorate the stench, but its power was such that even sucking every last molecule of air out of the room wouldn't be enough to dampen it. Tim made an effort to breathe through his mouth and appear unaffected. He wanted to make a good first impression.

At only 988 years old, Volkerps the Foul was the youngest demon ever to be named director of the department in the history of the company. From his research, Tim knew that Volkerps had started as a simple claims processor back in the days when policies were still being handwritten on parchment. From there, he had risen to adjuster and then investigator and finally to director, taking over the job from his own father, Cthollor, who had retired to an aging demon's home in Florida. Demons were a rarity on the claims side—most of them tended to work in the wealth management or finance divisions.

Volkerps was a massive red torso floating over a rumbling swirl of storm clouds that flickered with lightning. He had no legs but did have four massive arms, each one tapering to scaly, thirteen-fingered claws that looked capable of ripping the hide off an armoured rhino. On top of his shoulders were two heads: one consisting of four horns and a massive mouth full of sharp teeth; the other, nothing but blinking eyes.

As Tim entered, the head with the eyes was scrolling intently through a spreadsheet of numbers on one of his six large monitors while the other was gulping down what looked like (and probably was) boiling tar out of a large mug with the slogan "Underworld's Best Boss" on the side.

"Lovecraft!" a voice boomed. It seemed to be coming from the swirling mass of clouds, which lit up as it spoke. "Have a seat. I'm just taking a quick look at the latest loss ratio numbers before we post them to the company intranet. Coffee?"

"No thanks, sir," Tim said, eyeing the carafe warily. "I'm good."

"No trouble finding the place, I see," Volkerps said. "Meet everyone?"

"A few," Tim said.

"They'll come around," Volkerps said, waving one of his claws. "Now, you ready to get to work?"

"Sure am," Tim said.

Volkerps switched his attention to one of his other monitors. "Now where the hell did I put that file? With three heads, it should be easier to find this stuff."

"Three?" Tim said, confused.

"Yeah," said Volkerps. "I'm not allowed to talk about the third one, though. Last thing this department needs right now is a harassment claim. Ah, here it is. Thought we'd ease you in with a nice identity theft."

Identity theft was the official term for a possession of a person (or similar sentient being) by a supernatural entity. It was extremely common for certain types of spirits and demons to take possession of an individual for varying periods of time. Generally, these things were purely profit-driven—grab a rich person and have them empty their bank accounts into the coffers of an accomplice—but in some cases (most often involving djinn) they were done for sheer malevolent fun. Anyone carrying Identity Theft coverage would be indemnified against any financial loss up to the policy limit as well as any property damage or liability expenses incurred during the period of third-party supernatural control. This included any medical costs for the insured or other, non-possessed individuals injured as a result of possessed action/inaction, loss of reputation costs (demons loved to be filmed taking control of celebrities in particular—one social media share of a djinn named Beuthelas forcing *Naked Bridegroom* star Tor Vanderblat to set fire to his own testicles had been viewed 80 million times), loss of employment, and other associated expenses.

Identity Theft coverage was different from the Monkey Paw Rider, which covered cursed and possessed items, such as cars, appliances, prosthetic limbs, instead of people. Those were generally much easier to deal with, unless the insured knowingly purchased or otherwise acquired said item with the intent of using it for some supernatural purpose, in which case, any resulting loss or damage was excluded.

Because it would have been all too easy to claim demonic possession for anyone committing any kind of crime intentional or otherwise, or publicly embarrassing themselves by say, posing with an animal they had just killed for fun and posting the pictures online, insurance companies like Crimson Seal had strict guidelines covering how they processed such claims. Anyone who knowingly encouraged demonic possession through ritual or incantation, like seers, occultists, or séance runners, was ineligible for coverage under the Summoning Exclusion. Claims had to be submitted within 24 hours of dispossession or abandonment. Demons tended to leave traces behind in their hosts that only lasted a short time, so it was imperative that the victim was seen by an adjuster within that period. The adjuster would run a simple psycho-kinetic energy scan to verify the presence and type of entity–a blood sample was often enough– before submitting the claim.

"Potential faker?" Tim guessed.

"Professional faker," Volkerps said. "And that's the problem."

Tim was confused. The company didn't underwrite known fakers and kept a large database of their names and various identities, as some of them applied multiple times under various aliases.

"Madame Zoudini," Volkerps said, spinning one of his monitors around so that Tim could see the claim file. In the top right-hand corner was an image of a woman in her fifties who was wearing a gold turban and rather an excessive amount of eye makeup. "She runs a tarot and palm place down on Purgatory. No summoning capacity whatsoever. Sells a few knicknacks. Dice, crystals… you know. Standard business model for a regular clientele of bored housewives and the occasional tourist."

"Right," Tim said, nodding. His own mother was the proprietor of a place that was similar, although more boutique-y and upscale. Sort of a high-end supernatural salon. She made most of her sales and did most of her "readings" online now.

"Last week, she had a client come in who wanted to have her monthly chat with her dead husband," Volkerps said. "Zoudini's a former actress. Nothing big or professional, you understand. Did some community theatre and what have you. But she's good with voices. She'd done some research on the husband, so she knew what to cover. She doesn't do any of that possessed person sex. Most of that happens down at those dive boutiques in East Hades, as you know."

Tim nodded. East Hades was well known for its succubus houses, demon bars and curio shops. Most of the stuff was fake, but some of it was very real, and sometimes it was hard to tell the difference. It used to be an absolute no-go zone after dark, with its scraggly lines of junkies in front of wolfsbane clinics and blood banks, but, like many other parts of the city, was slowly gentrifying. His mother had even opened a pop-up store out there last month and had been talking about permanent expansion.

"Anyway," Volkerps said. "She's about halfway through her 15-minute session when something goes wrong."

"What?" Tim asked.

"Well," Volkerps said. "According to the claim file, she suddenly became possessed by something else. Something real."

"What?" Tim asked.

"Unknown," Volkerps said. "But whatever it was, it was a hell of a lot more fierce and powerful than the late Gerald Browdley, CPA. It caused a level 3 spectral fire that incinerated most of her stock and did a significant bit of damage to her fixtures as well. The building itself was mostly unharmed."

"Lead paint on the walls?" Tim asked.

"Very good," Volkerps smiled, which made him look even more terrifying than usual. "See? I knew you knew your stuff."

"That means, whatever it was, it was probably generating real Hellfire," Tim said.

"Right," Volkerps said. "Unless somebody's found a way to fake it that we don't know about yet. Trashed her stock and melted most of her crystals. Not to mention scaring the hell out of her client."

"So why is the SIU getting involved?" Tim asked.

"Automatically flagged," Volkerps said. "She signed a release certifying, to us at least, that it's all an act. That's why there's no Summoning Exclusion on her policy. The fact that she somehow managed to really summon something that did a tremendous amount of damage that Crimson Seal is now on the hook for is, needless to say, inherently suspicious."

"Gotcha," Tim said.

"Seems like the business might not have been doing so well, either," Volkerps said. "So she might have had a financial imperative as well."

"Right," Tim nodded.

"I'll email you the case file," Volkerps said. "Look it over and then head out there and check it out. Report back to me when you've got something."

"Yes sir," Tim said.

"Ask Lonnie or George if you need help with anything," Volkerps said. "I'll be out of the office this afternoon. Doctor's appointment. Got some horn rot."

"Right," Tim said, uncertainly.

"Should be pretty straightforward case," Volkerps said. "Nice easy one to get you started. Lot of beings around here will be rooting for you to screw up. Try not to."

Tim swallowed nervously. "I'll do my best."

2

Tim stepped through the door marked "You Are Now Entering the Realm of the Spirits!" and flicked on the lights.

Madame Zoudini's parlour reminded him of pretty much every other spiritual hustle parlour he had ever seen: lots of lacy curtains, candles, shelves full of tacky nick-knacks, incense sticks and other hokey paraphernalia. The only thing missing was a crystal ball, and it wasn't really so much missing as it was partially melted on what was left of the table.

Tim clipped the Bluetooth camera to the side of his glasses and activated the recorder on his phone. This was his first official investigation as a member of the SIU and he intended to do it 100% according to the Special Investigations Process Guide so as not to miss anything.

Emily Russenberger, aka Madame Zoudini, had taken out her policy 14 years before, shortly before opening her business at its present location. She was not a licenced spiritualist, which meant that she was not eligible for some of the additional coverages offered to real mediums, like the Exorcism Extension, which came into effect when a banished supernatural entity refused to stay banished, but also not subject to some of the exclusions, either (like the Summoning Exclusion, which essentially said that an insured was personally liable for any demon or other entity that they called up deliberately).

Being unlicensed meant that she was unable to refer to herself as a medium or spiritualist on any of her correspondence, advertising or signage. That explained why she referred to herself as a "Portal to the mystic dimension!" on the sign out front and her social media pages. This prevented her from joining the spiritualist's union, which in turn prevented her from being awarded any government contracts. Spiritualists were in heavy demand as they were always part of the feasibility study teams brought in to determine if a potential building site could be granted a construction permit. The city had a high demand for new residential and commercial facilities but was legally prevented from building or renovating on land that was deemed to be cursed.

Crimson Seal had a similar embargo on insuring such sites. The Poltergeist Exclusion wording was included with every single policy they bound. Any property found to have been built on the site of a previous massacre, graveyard, temple, portal, celestial staging ground or place of ritual sacrifice was ineligible for coverage. If such information came to light after the policy had been bound, then said policy was subject to cancellation within 30 days by registered letter.

The risk management department had extremely detailed territorial maps outlining exactly where the company would and would not underwrite certain risks. It was a big reason why large chunks of the city had failed to gentrify as quickly as others. It was possible to spiritually remediate a site to make it eligible, but it was expensive and the results were not always guaranteed. The city had found that out the hard way the previous year after greenlighting the construction of a new recreation centre on the site of an old insane asylum that had burned down almost a century before. The contractor had assured them that the site had been scrubbed, but that turned out not to be the case—something glaringly evident when the Olympic-sized swimming pool suddenly filled up with blood and screeching ghouls began showing up during senior's salsa dancing lessons.

The lawsuits were still flying on that one. The city had sued the contractor for negligence, alleging that no spiritual mitigation had been done. The contractor then countersued the city for failing to certify that the mitigation had been licenced. It was a mess that would take years to make its way through the courts. The city had tried several more rounds of mitigation, but it wasn't unusual to see the odd Chupacabra pop up in the middle of a hotly contested girl's under 14 ball hockey tournament.

Madame Zoudini's House of Spiritual Awakening sat right in the middle of two different exclusion zones. To the north was Pentangle Park, a park with a large earthen mound that had once been used for human sacrifices by a pagan clan of sun-worshipping cannibals. To the south was the Huisker Mansion, ancestral home of one of the city's most notorious serial killers and one of the most densely haunted buildings in the world. It was so popular with tourists that they had knocked down what had once been a greenhouse to make room for a bus parking lot.

Zoudini's had once been popular with those same tourists, but the lack of other sightseeing options in the vicinity and the rapid growth in other parts of the city meant that it had long fallen out of favour with everyone except for an aging (and diminishing) roster of regular clients. Russenberger had missed two policy payments in the last 12 months. Although she had made the payments up within the required ten days, she was only one more NSF away from having her policy cancelled. That was just one more reason to suspect that the fire may not have been exactly what she had been claiming it to be.

Tim looked around the room carefully. Real Hellfire wasn't like ordinary fire. It didn't burn things indiscriminately. And it left clear signs behind, provided you knew what to look for.

The table and crystal ball were melted, but the floor and ceiling appeared to be untouched. Tim knelt down to look at them more closely. The table was cheap pine with metal legs, covered with a red damask cloth. All three had oozed together to form a puddle on the floor. Hellfire didn't scorch and burn like regular fire. That was why the table hadn't actually burned and there was no smoke or scorch mark on the ceiling. It existed on a slightly different, ethereal plane. When it poked through into the physical universe, it tended to destroy the structural integrity of what it touched but didn't cook them in the way that more traditional fire did.

The table certainly appeared to corroborate that hypothesis, but Tim reminded himself to be careful. There was no shortage of arsonists out there who were more than capable of mimicking the physical effects of Hellfire, but there were other telltale signs to look for.

The overhead light was a plain fluorescent tube. Chances were, Tim knew, that Madame Zoudini didn't use it. That kind of lighting wasn't generally conducive to making clients think that they had entered a mysterious spiritual realm. There were a few candles around the room, some of which showed evidence of having been lit, but there weren't enough of them to do the trick without causing a legitimate fire hazard.

Tim crossed the room and found a small lamp on a side table. He unplugged the lamp, the shade of which was covered with a sheer white cloth. Tim lifted off the cloth and unscrewed the bulb from the lamp. He took his case bag off, unzipped it and removed what looked like a freezer-sized grey Ziplock bag. Tim put the bulb in the bag and sealed it up, then put the bag on the floor. Taking a quick glance around to make sure there was no one else, he lifted his foot and stomped on the bag. There was a muffled popping sound as the bulb broke under his heel. Tim attached a spray canister to a special valve on the side of the bag and turned it. There was a hiss as the bag began to fill with gas. Tim allowed it to inflate roughly halfway and then checked his watch, counting off 30 seconds. Once he hit the allotted time, he opened the bag.

Inside were a dozen wriggling white larvae moving between the broken pieces of the glass. As the air hit them, they rapidly began to swell from maggot-sized to finger-sized.

Tim sealed the bag again quickly. The last thing he wanted was to be stuck in a room full of giant writhing slugs. He pulled out a sharpie and scribbled the case number, date and time on the side of the bag, then dropped it into his case bag.

"Maggot test positive," Tim said for the benefit of the camera.

Okay, he thought. Let's see what else we can see.

Tim made his way through another door at the back, this one labelled "Seers Only!" and found what looked like a small kitchenette and a bunk. He knew from the policy documentation that Madame Z had recently changed her residential address to match her business address—another sign that things were not going well financially.

The small bar fridge was empty except for some carrots and a desic-cated avocado. Tim checked the cupboards and found a small coffeemaker in the one next to the sink. Tim moved the espresso pods aside and pulled it out. He lifted the lid and saw that there was still water in the reserve tank.

Perfect.

Tim reached into his case bag and pulled out a small plastic sam-ple jar. He unscrewed the lid and half-filled it with water from the tank, then grabbed a plastic playing-card size sheet of pills sealed with foil. He popped one of the small white pills into the water and replaced the lid, shaking it around a few times. The pill dissolved and a moment later turned cloudy and then bright red.

"Standing water blood test also positive," Tim said. "Hellfire appears to be confirmed."

Tim got out his marker and wrote the case file, date and time on the bottle before depositing it in his case next to the writhing maggot bag. He did not relish the thought of driving back to the office with those things, but that was part of the job. He got out his laptop and made a few quick notes. They would need to do a complete flush on the pipes and all stand-ing water in the unit before the occupant could return. That was included with the standard settlement agreement. Drinking residual demon blood was known to have some nasty side effects.

The presence of real Hellfire strongly suggested that the claim was valid, but he would still have to interview the client and the witness before he could sign off on the claims approval. This was his first case and he didn't intend to cut any corners.

Tim finished typing and packed up his laptop. He shut off the lights in both rooms and headed out to the front of the shop, which had a few chairs in a makeshift waiting area and a couple of shelves full of supernatural bric-a-brac. He was about to close up and head out the door when something unusual caught his eye.

One shelf was made up entirely of crystals and beaded jewellery—necklaces, brooches, rings and tiaras galore—while the other appeared to be stacked with more esoteric items.

Or it had been.

Now all Tim could see were the outlines of things—cups, plates, small square things that may have been paperweights—each one evidenced by a singed outline of black on the scuffed white wooden surface. What could have possibly happened? It looked like every single item on the shelf had just suddenly spontaneously combusted.

All except one.

Tim bent down to look at the stone statue on the lowest shelf. It depicted a fearsome looking demon with large horns and a mouth full of teeth that appeared to go all the way around his head. In one hand, the demon was holding what looked like a spiky hammer and in the other, what was unmistakably a severed human head.

Charming, Tim thought.

It definitely did not seem to be in keeping with the supernatural earth mother vibe of the rest of the impulse items. Had Russenberger really put this thing out for sale? And if so, what had happened to the rest of the things on the shelf? He didn't feel like getting the laptop out again and made a mental note to ask her during the interview.

Tim didn't recognize the demon in the statue. Often, their names were engraved on the underside of the base. He reached out to turn the statue over and yelped in pain as soon as he touched it.

"Yow!" Tim shrieked.

It was blazing hot to the touch, but not radiating any heat. Tim checked his fingertips and saw that they were already starting to blister. He pulled off his case bag and reached inside for his emergency medical kit, cursing himself for making such a rookie mistake. The statue just smiled back at him in an almost taunting way as he squeezed some of the balm onto his hands and rubbed it in.

"Dumbass," Tim muttered, partly at the statue and partly at himself. He made another mental note, this time to edit out that portion of his video report before he submitted it. Once he had tended to his fingers, he took a high-res series of pictures of the statue and the surrounding scorch marks. It probably wasn't connected to the event and was therefore unrelated to his claims investigation, but he figured that it was better to cover all his bases.

Tim closed up the shop and headed back out onto the street. It was too late to interview the client today. He would finish with his site report and track her and the witness down tomorrow. Tonight, he had other things to contend with.

His parents were coming over for dinner.

3

Tim stepped into the lobby of his apartment and got out his keys to check the mailbox.

At 624 years, the Decameron was one of the oldest buildings in the city. It had originally been built as a luxury hotel, although many of its more elegant touches—the mosaic tile floor in the central atrium, the gold-embossed rails—had long disappeared under years of abandonment and neglect. The place had only been a hotel for eight years before the owner, a steel tycoon named Dyson Pulliver, was shot and killed in the penthouse suite by the husband of one of his many mistresses. The building fell into disuse before being converted into a theatre, a casino, and then eventually back into a hotel. Like the Chelsea Hotel in New York, the Decameron had served as a flophouse for vagabonds, artists, musicians and everyone else who couldn't afford the four and five-star places in Upper Styx. Overdoses, suicides and various crime of passion were a regular occurrence, and as a result the place was seriously haunted.

Some of the most famous—or notorious—rooms included 409, where the renowned stage actor Domenic Tufts had thrown himself out the window only to bounce off the marquee and land in the middle of the street (where he was run over by a milk cart). Celebrated opera singer and closeted werewolf Dorothea Langer's true nature was finally revealed when she broke through the door of 715 and mauled a chambermaid. Austrian Crown Prince Heinrich Von Tepes was a regular occupant of the top floor penthouse suite, where, rumour had it, he had the plumbing rigged up to run with blood (his family never officially admitted that he was a vampire, as this was considered a great dishonour in those days).

The Decameron had survived it all. One force that was harder to resist was the change in the city's fortunes and subsequent flood of development that was rapidly changing the face of the neighbourhood. The fact that it was a designated historical landmark had kept the Decameron from being knocked down or modernized like many others, as developers and speculators were prohibited from ripping out the old fixtures to replace them with the latest solid titanium countertops, voice-activated taps and other faddish design touches that fickle new condo buyers demanded.

Tim had been living in the place for eight years, having moved in shortly after he started work at Crimson Seal. He liked the place. It had leaky pipes, creaky walls and extremely spotty WiFi, but it also had a lot more character than the gleaming glass-walled shoeboxes being thrown up with alarming speed along the shores of the Acheron River on the city's east side. Sure, it had ghosts and other so-called shifty supernatural types, but most of them were totally harmless. They just wanted someone to talk to, mostly.

Tim unlocked his mailbox and pulled out a stack of letters. Only two were for him—a renewal notice for his tenant policy and an offer to upgrade the spending limit on his credit card, which he had no intention of doing. The rest were an agglomeration of brightly-coloured junk mail mostly addressed to his brother, Keef.

Tim sighed. Most of the envelopes contained free samples of the latest synthetic blood products, some offering energy boosts ("Go all night with Plasma Pulse!"), while others made bogus-sounding health claims ("Clear your capillaries with Omega Positive!") or more dubious benefits ("Keep your fangs sharp with Virgin Cherry!"). Keef was always signing up for free trials and then forgetting to cancel them when the payment part kicked in. This explained the fact that the other half of his mail was mostly past due payment notices and letters from collection agencies. In the beginning, Keef had even given Tim's name and number to some of these companies, but Tim had quickly made it clear that, should he get one more call from a sales rep or collection agent, that Keef would be looking for a new place to live.

Keef (his full name was Keefer, but no one ever called him that) was two years older than Tim and had been a vampire for five years now, having been turned by one of his many vengeful ex-girlfriends. The irony was, it didn't really do all that much to change Keef's lifestyle. He had slept all day and gone out to clubs at night even before avoiding daylight had been a requirement of his condition. If anything, his diet had slightly improved as he was no longer able to subsist on junk food and beer, although he quickly found blood-friendly alternatives to both.

Keef had scraped through high school and managed only one year in the Business of Music program at Sagrada Sangre Community College before dropping out. A brief spell working as an apprentice in their father's supernatural pest control business had gone about as badly as everyone in the family might have expected. Keef had managed to release not one but four nasty poltergeists during a routine sweep of an elementary school, almost costing Thad's Spectral Removal Services one of its largest municipal contracts.

Keef had bounced through a variety of jobs since then. He had worked as a nighttime security guard at a parking garage (fired for sneaking off and allowing a roving gang of zombies to trash an entire fleet of food trucks); a bartender at a nightclub (fired for serving blood to non-vampires); a performer at Werner's Haunted Mansion & Waxwork Museum (fired when patrons caught him in a coffin with another employee who was playing a banshee); and the night shift at Bram's Convenience (fired for selling blood bongs to minors). He was currently employed as desk clerk at the Were Clinic, where he disbursed Wolfsbane to recovering werewolves.

Keef had been crashing at Tim's place for just over a year, ever since his last girlfriend, Lucy, had given him the boot. It was originally just supposed to be a couple of weeks, but his difficulties with employment and finding a place that was vampire-accessible had blown through that deadline. Tim was hopeful that the Were Clinic job would pan out so that Keef would finally be able to move out. Keef was extremely lackadaisical in his personal habits, tending to leave open blood packs in the fridge and junk all over the living room. Their opposing schedules meant that one of them was always trying to sleep when the other was up and about, which had caused no small amount of friction. Keef enjoyed throwing parties and liked to have lots of female company, although he claimed that he never turned any of them, no matter how keenly they pushed for it.

"I'm not big on long-term commitments," Keef said once, puffing philosophically on a blood bong. "And let me tell ya, bro, it doesn't get much longer than immortality."

Tim considered dropping the samples in the garbage—he would probably just find them stuffed down the side of the couch or lying on the kitchen floor a few days from now—but decided against it. He was trying to be optimistic where his brother was concerned. He closed up the mailbox and turned back to the lobby where he saw his landlady, who greeted him with a wave.

"Hello Tim," she said, floating just above the tile floor. "Just finishing for the day?"

"Hi, Dede," Tim said, smiling. "That's right."

Dede Diamond had been the landlady, or "Building Supervisor" as she preferred, at the Decameron for more than 50 years, and her dedication to the job had not waned even though she had been technically dead for the last 45 of them. In life, she had been an actress and had enjoyed a certain amount of success, having starred in a couple of moderately successful independent movies in the 60s. The jobs had dried up after that, however, although she did do a few foreign-language films and some TV. Like many others on the fringes of the entertainment business, she had drifted to the Decameron, where she became sort of an unofficial house mother.

Tim wasn't sure about the circumstances surrounding her death. There were a lot of rumours, naturally—that she had been strangled by a lecherous director after spurning his overtures or that she had overdosed in a bathtub after losing a role in a TV movie—but she had never elaborated and Tim didn't think it was polite to ask. That didn't stop her from talking about all the other residents, of course. Dede was the best source of gossip in the building, if that was your thing. And even if it wasn't. Being dead, Dede had a slightly more flexible notion about the importance of time.

"Missed an exciting morning, you did," Dede said, puffing on a ghostly cigarette.

"Oh?" Tim said. He wasn't sure how old Dede had been when she died, either. If he had to guess, he would probably put her at somewhere in her 50s, but it was hard to tell. It also seemed like the kind of thing that was impolite to inquire about, even if the person in question could not technically get any older.

"Police were here for Mr Patopoulis again," Dede said.

"Oh dear," Tim said. He assumed she was talking about Domenikos Patopoulis, who lived in 607.

"Seems somebody's been flashing women in the park again," Dede said. "Still, doesn't seem fair to pick on the guy. He's a satyr. Can't help himself at the best of times, can he?"

"I suppose not," Tim said. Mr. Patopoulis was an orthodontist, but that didn't seem to stop the cops from showing up at his door anytime somebody with goat legs waved his junk at passerby. "They didn't arrest him, did they?"

"No," Dede muttered. "Just the usual. I told him he should file a harassment complaint, but he thinks that'll only make things worse. Poor dear."

She was interrupted by a groan from behind. Tim looked over to see that maintenance guy, Mug, had entered the lobby. Mug was a zombie. No one knew his age or his real name. He got the name "Mug" because he was always wearing the jersey of famous undead baseball player Jerome Muglin, who had played shortstop for the Los Angeles Nightwalkers about a decade ago.

"Oh, there you are, Mug," Dede said. "Did you fix that toilet block in Mrs. Chaney's room?"

Mug groaned in what Tim assumed was assent.

"Good," Dede said. "Werewolves are wonderful people, of course. But good lord. The volume of hair in the drains! They're always gumming up. Can't keep up with it. Poor Mug's in there with a snake almost every other day. That reminds me, Tim. We'll be replacing the pipes in the unit under yours tomorrow morning, so you might hear a little more banging and moaning coming out of there than usual."

Mug groaned and held up an adjustable wrench.

"Thanks for letting me know," Tim said.

"He is so very handy," Dede said, looking at Mug fondly. "Oh! Did I tell you I had a visit from my fan club today?"

"Really?" Tim said. He happened to know that there was only one surviving member of the Dede Diamond Appreciation Society and that was a 102-year-old retired car salesman from Toronto. The only other member had died of renal failure two years earlier. "That's great."

"If anything, I'm a bigger star now than I ever was," Dede said, looking nostalgic. "That often happens only after we die, of course. They showed one of my movies on TV last night! *Donna Sfortunata*! Made that one with Donatelli. Wonderful role. I played a woman who murders her husband's mistress only to find out that she was her sister. Massive hit overseas. I would've won whatever the Italian equivalent of the Oscar is if they hadn't dubbed my voice. Did you see it?"

"Not yet," Tim said. "But I'll definitely track it down on Deadflix first chance I get."

"I will warn you, though," Dede said. "I am naked for a few scenes, so don't get any ideas!"

Tim chuckled nervously. "I promise."

"Mug's seen all my movies, haven't you Mug?" she asked.

Mug groaned.

"Course you have," Dede said, sending out some ghostly smoke rings.

"Sorry, Dede," Tim said. "But I've got to get going. Parents are coming over for dinner tonight."

"Well, don't let us keep you," Dede said. "I'm sure your mother will find a way to bring some young woman for you to date."

Tim winced. His mother was always coming up with flimsy pretexts to introduce him to single women, most of whom worked as part-time psychics in one of her salons and pop up stores. "You're probably right."

"Oh, and I know it's not you, dear," Dede said. "But could you make sure you don't put the empty blood bags in the regular garbage? They need to go out with the hazardous stuff. Poor Mug here has to separate them or the waste management people will surcharge us."

"Sorry about that," Tim said. "I'll make sure."

Tim made his way through the lobby and took the elevator up to his apartment on the 14th floor. He was relieved to get elevator #2, as #1 was haunted by the ghost of a former operator who got irascible if you didn't tip him. Tim almost never carried cash and had been the target of his ire more than once, including the time he had stopped the car between 10 and 11 and floated off, leaving Tim stuck. It had taken Mug almost an hour to get the elevator moving again.

Tim got off the elevator and unlocked his door, stepping inside. He flicked on the lights and took a quick look around. The curtains were all

closed, as usual. The sun was just starting to go down, so his brother probably wouldn't be up for a couple of hours yet. Keef was an extremely late
riser.

The apartment was a standard two-bedroom unit with a separate
kitchen and small dining area next to the living room. He had stopped at
the market on the way home and picked up everything he would need to
make tortellini, which was his mother's favourite. Everything except garlic, of course. Keef couldn't eat, but was hypersensitive to the stuff. Even
a single clove would send him charging out into the hall in a choking fit.

Tim put the ingredients in the kitchen and did a quick circuit of the
place. Keef had left a couple of blood packs on the table and a bag of Scabs
chips open on the couch. Tim deposited both in the garbage. Even most
vampires avoided Scabs, which were gross beyond belief, but his brother
absolutely loved them, especially the AB Negative flavour. Tim was always
finding Scabs crumbs in between the cushions and scattered on the floor.
It was after finding them in the bathroom sink that Tim had finally put
his foot down and ordered no more Scabs would be allowed in the apartment. It was one of many such edicts that Keef had obviously decided to
simply ignore.

And mom wonders why I'm reluctant to bring women back here,
Tim thought, shaking his head. The sooner I've got his place back to myself, the better.

Tim did a quick clean of the apartment and then headed for the
kitchen to start prep work for dinner. He'd been at it for less than half an
hour when Keef stumbled in wearing his usual look: long dark hair, shirt
open to the navel, black leather pants and bare feet.

"Hey, little bro," he said, yawning to reveal his overlong canines.
"Que pasa?"

"Just getting a start on dinner," Tim said. He decided not to mention
anything about the Scabs. It would only put his brother in a surly mood
and that was never ideal, particularly with their parents coming.

"Oh, right," Keef said, padding past to grab a Blood Blast from the fridge. "The parental units doth arrive imminently, do they not?"

"They doth," Tim agreed.

Keef popped open his drink and took a chug. Colour instantly flooded back into his pale cheeks. "Ahh! That's the stuff."

"Rough night?" Tim asked.

"No more than usual," Keef said. "How was the first day on the new job?"

"Good," Tim said. "Got my first case. Fairly straightforward identity theft, it looks like. Met some of my coworkers. One of them's a vampire. Guy named George."

"George what?" Keef said, letting out a burp.

"Shit, I forget," Tim said. "Pale skinny guy. Dark hair."

"Yeah, sorry man," Keef said. "But for a vampire, that doesn't really narrow it down. Who else?"

"Guy named Lonnie," Tim said. "He's a werewolf. Seemed really nice. And a succubus."

"A succubus!" Keef said, eyes widening. "Is she hot?"

"Half-succubus," Tim corrected.

"I met one of those last night at the club," Keef said. "Her powers don't work on me, but I can definitely see why they work on you dainty little blood bags. Woo."

"Wait," Tim said, halfway through slicing the veal into sections. "What do you mean?"

"I get it," Keef said. "They're like sirens, but more down and dirty and less singing."

"No," Tim said. "I mean, what do you mean you met one at the club? Weren't you supposed to be at work?"

Keef sagged. "Yeah ... there was a complication with that."

"You got fired *again*?" Tim said.

"Look-"

"For Christ's sake, man!"

"Don't be using that name in my infernal presence!" Keef said.

"The hell with that!" Tim said.

"That's better," Keef said.

"You promised me you were going to keep this one!" Tim said. "What happened this time? Actually, you know what? Don't tell me. I don't want to know."

"It wasn't my fault!" Keef protested. "This guy came in and said he was looking for a place he could do some animal sacrifices. I said-"

"You were supposed to be saving up so you could move out!" Tim said. "I need my own space!"

"I'll get it figured out, I promise," Keef said. "Just don't tell mom and dad, okay? Not until I've got something else lined up."

No sooner had he said those words than the buzzer rang. Tim put down the knife and went to the panel to buzz his parents in. They knocked on the door a few minutes later. Tim opened it to reveal the two of them. His mother Regina was short and dressed in a stylish brown leather jacket. As always, her hair was elaborately up-styled in a Bride of Frankenstein do. As the proprietor of several high-end boutiques, she could never be seen out in public looking less than ready for the cover of Cosmopolitan.

His father, Thad, couldn't have posed more of a contrast if he tried. Where Regina was short and elegant, Thaddeus was tall and ungainly. His suede jacket was old and fraying at the cuffs. His jeans were wearing at the knees and his shoes were scuffed at the toes and heels, the product of many hours of climbing through dark spaces as part of his supernatural pest removal business.

"There's my baby boy!" his mother said, pulling him into a hug.

"Hey ma," Tim said.

His father settled for a more restrained handshake. "How was the first day on the new job?"

"Good," Tim said, waving them inside.

Keef emerged from the kitchen and was pulled into a similar hug by his mother. It lasted only a half a second before she pushed him away, breathing deeply.

"You smell like a nightclub," she said. "Did you get fired again?"

"How do you do this?" Keef said in disbelief.

"I'm your mother, Keefer," she said. "I don't care if you've got mind powers now that you're a vampire. I'm a seer! You can't hide anything from me."

"Unbelievable," Keef said, shaking his head.

"Timmy," Regina said. "You got a promotion. Can't you get your worthless undead brother a job?"

"Thanks, mom," Keef said. "Technically, I'm immortal. But even I would die of boredom if I had to work for an insurance company."

"My son is a parasite," Regina said, shaking her head. "A literal, blood-sucking parasite. How am I supposed to explain this to the women at the salon?"

"I've met some of the women who work at your salon," Keef said, smiling in a way that bared his teeth. "They don't seem to mind so much."

"Don't you dare turn any of my staff!" Regina said, pointing an accusing finger. "You bite any of my girls and I'll put a stake through your heart myself, Keefer Eladio Lovecraft!"

The buzzer sounded again.

"Who's that?" Tim said, confused. Everyone who was invited was already here.

His mother put a hand on his shoulder. "Her name's Tiffany. She just started at my pop up. Wonderful girl. And before you say anything, she's getting her teeth fixed."

"Mom!" Tim groaned.

"Just be charming and try not to talk so much about demons and such," his mother said, pushing the button to let their new guest in.

"It's my job," Tim said. "My boss is, literally, a demon."

"Yes," his mother said. "Maybe save that stuff for the second date, okay? You're not getting any younger, Timmy."

"I'm only 28!" Tim protested.

"Exactly!" Regina said. "In a couple of years, your sperm'll stop swimming and that'll be that. No grandkids for me. Just ask your father."

"Ask him what?" Tim said, exasperated.

"Motility," Regina said. "It's dropping all the time. I read an article about it at the salon. It's a modern epidemic!"

"I don't believe this," Tim muttered.

"You're a good kid," Regina said, pinching his cheek. "You just need some help. Now why don't you go change out of that shirt? It's got black dust all over it. And you smell a bit like rotten eggs."

"It's sulphur residue," Tim said. "From a claims investigation I'm working on."

"Whatever," Regina said, reaching into her bag and handing him a small plastic tube. "Spray some of this on, too. It's a cologne sample I got from work. *Beast*, it's called. All the women love it. Chop chop! She'll be here any second!"

Tim groaned and headed for his room to change. There were times, although they were few, when he envied his brother.

4

Tim arrived at the Crowley Clinic first thing the next morning.

This was the first place that Emily Russenberger, aka Madame Zoudini, had been brought following the incident at her palm reading and tarot shop. This was where all possessed individuals in the city were brought. It was located in a former institute for the criminally insane and divided up into two wings. The inpatient wing was for those who were still possessed, or, to use the official term, "occupied." The outpatient wing was for those whose demon occupants had vacated but were still experiencing lingering symptoms.

As she had been unconscious at the time of her admission, Russenberger had been checked into the inpatient wing, where she had remained for the requisite 48 hours. Her case was reviewed by the demonologist on duty, who had ordered the standard tests—blood work, a pyscho-kinetic radiograph (or PKR), and an intravenous course of anti-inflammatories. Possession often caused organs to swell, although no one really knew why. After regaining consciousness, she had been assessed by the exorcist on call, who had decided to keep her in for an additional 24 hours before transferring her to the outpatient wing. Today, she was scheduled to be discharged.

Tim was meeting with the exorcist, whom, as luck would have it, was the same one who had done the initial diagnosis. That was lucky. There were a lot of exorcists on staff and the nature of the work often meant that they could be called away at a moment's notice, sometimes never to return. It wasn't unusual for supernatural entities to jump out of whomever they happened to be in at the time and right into the next most convenient host. Demons were especially lazy in that respect, so it was a high-risk occupation. The turnover rate was high. Most of the interns at the Crowley were only there to get their certification so that they could move on to more lucrative opportunities in the private sector, where they could move on to deal with fewer people and more cursed objects, like cars, boats, houses and sporting equipment.

Regan Blatty was in her final month of residency. She had studied at the Barker Institute, where she had graduated with a double major in entity remediation and demonology. She had spent a year abroad in Cairo after graduation, where she had been directly involved in the containment of the spectral outbreak that followed the opening of the tomb of Amun-Sat. She already had a job lined up with the famous Boothby Auction House, where she would be part of the team that would ensure all objects were curse and possession-free before they went under the gavel. The Boothby had made some very public and expensive errors in that regard in the last few years, having sold a 2,000-year-old chastity belt to the billionaire founder of Infernachat, an extremely popular app used by non-human entities for dating purposes. The owner claimed to have bought the belt as a publicity stunt to promote the app, but that didn't make it any less embarrassing when the spirit of the extremely angry castrated Egyptian prince who had been inhabiting it for all those years took up residence in the new owner's testicles.

"Thanks for meeting with me," Tim said as they sat down in the corner of the clinic's staff cafeteria. Blatty had just completed her night shift and there were dark circles under her eyes. Tim guessed her age at about

25 or 26. Like many people who spent most of their time indoors in a stressful job, her skin was pale and her frame skinny and undernourished.

"No problem," she said, yawning.

"Out of here soon?" Tim said.

"Yeah," she said. "I can't wait. I will actually manage to get out in daylight. No more spinning heads or projectile vomit. I can wear nice clothes to work for a change."

Tim could relate to an extent. As a claims adjuster, he'd seen a lot of the immediate aftermath of demonic interference, werewolf maulings and zombie attacks.

"I can imagine," he said, opening his laptop. "So how is Mrs. Russenberger doing?"

Tim had checked her file already but wanted to get the opinions of everyone on the scene. All clients signed a release allowing Crimson Seal access to their medical records as a matter of procedure. If they refused, then they didn't get coverage.

"Seems to be doing fine, now," Blatty said. "A lot better than when she came in, anyway."

"How was she when she was admitted?" Tim asked.

"Unconscious," Blatty said. "We ran a PKR. Showed nothing. Zip."

"Nothing?" Tim repeated.

"Not a blip," Blatty said. "No brain activity whatsoever. It's normal for that to happen in the moments during and immediately after a possession, but it only tends to last a few seconds. A couple of minutes at most. This was at least a half an hour after the event."

"That's unusual," Tim said.

"Extremely," Blatty said. "I've never seen it before in the entire time I've been here. If she wasn't breathing and didn't have a heart rate, we would have shuttled her to the morgue instead of the ward. I ran a PKR on one of the orderlies just to make sure the equipment was working properly."

"How long before she came back up?" Tim asked.

"Almost six hours," Blatty said. "That's why we kept her in longer than the standard 24. Needless to say, she doesn't remember any of it."

Tim knew that part wasn't unusual. Victims of possession almost never had any memory of the event itself. That was one of the reasons that corroborating evidence was crucially important.

"Did you get anything from any of the other tests?" Tim asked.

"Nope," Blatty said. "But whatever it was, I'm guessing it was big if it wiped her out for that long. Bigger than anything I've ever seen before, anyway."

"Any other marks or signs on the body?" Tim asked.

"The EMTs who brought her in said they thought she might have had some sort of scar or lesion on her upper abdomen," Blatty said. "But we didn't see anything. It's possible that it was some sort of paradermal hematoma, but like I say, there was nothing when we checked."

"Did she say anything at all during her unconscious period?" Tim asked.

Blatty shook her head. "Not a peep."

"Any levitation or telekinetic movement in the room?" Tim asked.

"None."

"And how was she when she woke up again?"

"Thirsty," Blatty said. "Drank about two liters of water in as many minutes."

Blatty's phone beeped. She pulled it out of her purse and studied the screen for a moment.

"Patient?" Tim asked.

"No," Blatty said. "My fiancé. We're in the middle of trying to plan our wedding. He's big into haunted houses, so he wants to do a destination wedding at the Black Hook. Have you heard of it?"

Tim nodded. The Black Hook Motel had been located just off the highway near a popular ski resort in Colorado. Travellers who got lost or stuck in bad weather on their way to the slopes had sometimes checked in there, but many never checked out—at least, not without passing through the digestive system of the proprietor.

"I see enough weird stuff in a day," Blatty said. "I don't need it on my wedding, too. I'd be happy with a nice quiet beach. I don't need to go and look at a place where a homicidal cannibal ate most of the customers, okay? Especially when some of them are still using the shower."

Tim chuckled. "I imagine."

"The place is booked solid for like, the next three years," Blatty said. "Now they've got a last-minute cancellation and he wants to move everything there." She groaned. "You married?"

"No," Tim said. "But it's not from my mother's lack of trying."

The surprise "date" with Tiffany the night before had gone about as well as many of the other dates that his mother had sprung on him at the last minute. Tiffany didn't really have much interest in books, movies or music and had spent most of the dinner talking about a reality TV show called *Demon in the Sack*, which Tim had never seen. Apparently, it was full of intrigue, which for Tiffany meant lots of humans cheating on their partners with satyrs and succubi.

Blatty moved to get up. "Sorry. I can't really add much. Do you mind if I get going? I better take care of this before my fiancé becomes the Black Hook's next victim."

"No problem," Tim said. "Just email me if you think of anything else."

Blatty made for the door, tapping angrily on her phone. Tim packed up his laptop and headed for the outpatient ward. He checked in at the nurse's station and was directed to a room at the end of the hall, where he found Madame Zoudini sitting up in bed reading something on her tablet. She was wearing her regular clothes and appeared healthy and alert. The room had two beds in it, but the second one was empty.

"Mrs. Russenberger?" Tim said, holding up his ID. "I'm Tim Lovecraft. I'm with Crimson Seal."

She squinted at his badge. "Special Investigations Unit?"

"I'm just doing some checking so that we can process your claim as quickly as possible," Tim said. "How are you feeling?"

"Fine," she said, shrugging. "I'm afraid I don't really remember a thing. Is there some sort of problem?"

"No, no," Tim said. "I just wanted to stop in and cover off a few details." He sat down on the chair next to the bed and pulled out his laptop. "How are you? Any headaches?"

"No," she said.

"No joint or muscle pain?" Tim asked.

"No," she said.

"Any pain of any kind?" Tim asked.

"No," she said. "They told me I could check out just as soon as the exorcist on duty stopped by. Has that changed?"

"No," Tim said. "Not as far as I know. Now, I stopped by your shop to take a look around and I just wanted to check a few things. It looks like the event destroyed most of the merchandise in the front room." He swung the laptop around so she would be able to see the pictures of the empty shelves. "Would you be able to provide us with a list of what was on there? Maybe attach an approximate dollar value to all of it?"

"Oh my," she said, studying the pictures closely. "It's all gone?"

"All except for this one," Tim said, flipping to a closeup of the statue of the demon holding the hammer. "Any idea why that one might have survived?"

Russenberger's face changed sharply as she looked at the image of the demon. All the colour drained out of her face and her eyes widened. Her body became rigid as she gripped the rails on either side of the bed. She began to breathe heavily and her body started to shake.

"Mrs. Russenberger?" Tim said, alarmed.

Russenberger opened her mouth and started to scream. The volume and pitch was so loud that Tim saw the screen of her tablet crack. He jumped back in shock. By the time the orderlies made it into the room, she was already floating two feet above the bed, which was on fire.

5

The last person Tim needed to talk to was Anita Browdley, the client who had been in Madame Zoudini's parlour when the identity theft had occurred.

Browdley was a 61-year-old widow who lived in a two-storey blackstone walkup in the now trendy Purgatorio district. The area had been home to a large number of middle-class, mostly immigrant families for centuries before most of them had upped stakes to the suburbs after the werewolf riots of the mid-80s. The area had been mostly ignored for decades, but that had changed in the last few years as it became the destination of choice for a new generation of zombie artists, musicians and performers. Where once there had been vacant lots and boarded-up storefronts, now you couldn't walk 20 feet without passing a trendy resto bar offering the latest in locally-sourced hippocampus apps and lobe tartare. Zombie nightclubs like The Romero and The Winchester were regularly packed with crowds there to hear the latest in Braincore and Groan Hop. Tim didn't mind some of it, although it tended to be pretty dirge-y.

Browdley and her husband had resisted the urge to leave. Gerald had run his accounting practice out of a small office on the first floor for 30 years before dropping dead of a stroke one afternoon right in the middle of explaining a complicated tax deduction about the refrigeration costs of storing expired blood.

"I've been going to Madame Zoudini every year since then," Anita Browdley explained. She and Tim were sitting at a small table adjoining her kitchen, which was near the back of the house and had a small window looking out onto the yard. "Just to check in and see how Gerry is doing, you know. If he's seeing anyone on the other side."

Tim resisted the urge to ask about the social life of the late Gerald Browdley. As Madame Zoudini was officially unable to actually communicate with the dead, she would be the last person to know if the deceased accountant had a girlfriend.

"I see," Tim said, sipping his tea. Browdley had used some sort of synthetic sweetener she had gotten at the Z-Mart around the corner and it tasted like motor oil, but he was doing his best to hide his reaction.

"I do it every year on the anniversary of his, you know, passing," Browdley said. "This year was a little different. I wanted to let him know that I met a wonderful man and I was getting married again."

"Congratulations," Tim said.

"Thank you," Browdley said. "I was sure Gerry would be fine with it. He's been seeing some woman named Charisse. She got electrocuted when her dog dropped her hair dryer in the bathtub. I've always been more of a cat person, myself. Gerry was never a big risk taker when he was alive. Hated taking vacations. Money down the drain, he said. My new fiancé is a bit of a wild man in comparison. My friend Ruth said he was only after my money. She's just jealous because he's so young. Only 52! We're going to Antarctica for our honeymoon! Do you believe that? It's the penguin mating season. He studies them, you see. They have a very interesting way of doing it. He showed me this movie-"

Tim felt the conversation was in danger of going dangerously off the rails.

"Sorry, Mrs. Browdley," Tim said, cutting in. "I just needed to ask you about your most recent visit to Madame Zoudini."

"Oh yes," Browdley said. "Very different than usual. Usually, the room would get chilly and fill up with this fog or smoke. After a few minutes, Gerry would sort of appear in this mirror and tell me the latest."

Tim nodded. All of these things were a simple matter of an air conditioner, a smoke machine, a projector hidden in the ceiling and some image manipulation of the subject in question. All of it was controlled by an app built directly in to Madame Zoudini's crystal ball. Practically every unlicensed medium in the city used the same one. People dropped so much information about themselves on social media that basic face-recognition software could identify a cold call and pull up all of the relevant information even before the subject sat down in the chair. Some complained that it was corrupting and diluting the psychic's art, but that certainly didn't stop them from using it.

"But this time was different," Tim said.

"Oh, my goodness, yes," Browdley said. "There was no smoke or anything. Well, it started. I could feel the room starting to get cold. But then, all of a sudden, there was this unearthly whooshing sound and the next thing I knew, Madame Zoudini was on fire!"

"Yes," Tim said, typing away on his laptop.

"She didn't seem to be burning," Browdley said. "It didn't feel hot or anything. At least, not to me. I just thought it was part of some new thing she had cooked up."

"New thing?" Tim said.

"Yes," Browdley said. "I'm not a fool, Mr. Lovecraft. I know Mrs. Zoudini is a fake. But all of my friends went to her and I'd been going there myself for so long. Leaving would have been like going to a new hairdresser. Especially after Gerry died. And I knew she was just barely getting by. Seemed like the least I could do."

"But this didn't seem fake," Tim said.

"No," Browdley said, shaking her head. "And I've seen some good ones in my time. Mrs. Zoudini, bless her, was not exactly up on the latest technology."

"What happened next?" Tim asked.

"Well, the table seemed to melt," Browdley said. "Including the crystal ball. That was kind of a giveaway right there, because I knew she ran most of the show using that. I was quite unnerved. I pushed my chair back all the way to the wall. Well, it's not a very big room, as you know. Poor Mrs. Zoudini levitated right up off the floor. Her mouth kind of dropped open and this terrible voice started roaring out of it."

"What did the voice say?" Tim said. "Did it sound human?"

"It certainly did not," Browdley said with a shiver. "It was very hard to tell what it was saying, though. It was this very deep, guttural growling sound. Words were hard to make out."

"Did you pick anything up?" Tim asked.

"Well, most of it was gibberish," Browdley said. "But there were a couple of moments where it almost seemed like she snapped out of it. Like she was sort of aware of what was going on."

"Did she say anything?" Tim asked.

"No," Browdley said, shaking her head. "It didn't seem like whatever it was, well … they weren't actually talking directly to me."

"How do you mean?" Tim asked.

"It seemed like it was just sort of making some general announcement," Browdley said. "It paid no attention to me whatsoever. Of course, I was probably screaming madly and trying to get out of the room, but I had backed right up against the door and couldn't seem to move."

"How long did this last?" Tim asked.

"Hard to say," she said. "You know how at the time it seems like it's going on for ages but in reality is probably only a few seconds? It was like that."

"Did you make out anything the voice said?" Tim asked.

"Well," she said. "It wasn't English. I took Latin in school, of course. Like everybody else. But I hardly remember any of it. I did think I might have heard the words 'return' and 'ocean of blood' and maybe 'destruction' in there somewhere, but I wouldn't swear on it in a court of law."

"Gotcha," Tim said, typing. "And then what happened?"

"Well, I guess, whoever it was, it said its piece and that was it," Browdley said. "The fire went out and poor Mrs. Zoudini dropped back to the floor. How is she doing, by the way? Have you seen her?"

"She's recovering," Tim said carefully. After he had shown Madame Z the picture of the statue, the orderlies had managed to put out the fire and get her back on the bed. She had lapsed back into a coma and been re-admitted to the clinic. Tim felt responsible for that, but how was he supposed to know that she would react that way? He had simply been trying to confirm the details on the property loss side of the claim.

"Poor thing," Browdley said, shaking her head sadly. "She has a daughter that works in marketing for one of those synthetic blood energy drink companies, I think. I don't know if they keep in touch, though."

There was no daughter listed as an additional insured or beneficiary on any of Russenberger's policy documentation, but that was all that Tim knew on the subject of her relatives.

"Mrs. Browdley," Tim said. "You said you've been going to Madame Zoudini's regularly for several years?"

"Yes," she said. "One of the few, I think. The new places are so much more popular nowadays. You know, like the ones in the Upper Styx with the built-in cafes and spa facilities?"

Tim was familiar, as his mother ran several of them.

"Most of the sales items in the front of the parlour appear to have been destroyed during the event," Tim said. "All except for one, anyway. If I were to show you a picture of it, would you be able to tell me if she just got it recently or if it's been there all along?"

Browdley shrugged. "Sure. She often kept clients waiting a little out there. I think it was partly for show—you know, to create a sense of anticipation and all that—but mostly because she was hoping that if she left you out there for long enough that you'd be more likely to buy something.

Most of it was pretty tacky. And dusty. That's part of the reason I never really buy them, myself. Crystals are such a pain to keep clean. You just have to dump them into a strainer and hose them off in the sink. But of course, you're only supposed to use purified water and all that. Just a nuisance."

Tim minimized his report and brought up the photo of the statue of the demon holding the hammer. He hesitated for a moment before turning the screen around. What if this woman reacted the same way that the last one did? This time, there would be no orderlies ready to rush in and bring the situation back under control. Still, he needed to know.

He spun the monitor around on the table. Browdley leaned forward and squinted at the image for a moment.

"Nope," she said. "Never seen it before in my life."

"You sure?" Tim asked, relieved that she had not caught fire.

"Yep," she said. "Madame Z never had anything quite so ostentatious or ugly on her shelves. The fiercest thing she ever put on them were fairies and some extremely ugly necklaces."

"Thanks, Mrs. Browdley," Tim said, closing his laptop. "You've been extremely helpful."

6

"Nice work on the Russenberger case file," Volkerps rumbled as Tim sat down opposite his boss the following morning.

"Thanks," Tim said. He had stayed up late the night before, proofreading his final report several times before hitting send. He had never read an SIU report before and didn't really know how they were formatted.

"We gave Claims the go-ahead on the payout," Volkerps said. "How are you doing? I heard she had quite the freak out at the clinic."

"Fine," Tim said. "The only thing I got was some singed fingertips from an object in the parlour. It's a bit odd. Witness said she'd never seen it before. Looks like it might have had some connection to the event."

"Don't worry about it," Volkerps said, waving one of his clawed hands. "Claim is valid, so that's our only concern. Other than that, it's none of our business."

"Right," Tim said. He still had an uneasy feeling about it, though. He knew that his job was just to focus on the insurance side of it. Once that was settled, his work was officially over.

But still…

"Got another one for you," Volkerps said, turning his second head to one of his many monitors. "Possible poltergeist. Problem is, client built the house directly on the site of an old research facility."

"What kind of research?" Tim asked.

"The mind control, weird surgical experiment and all-around horror movie kind," Volkerps said. "Sometimes it's Nazis or cults or just some whack job stitching one guy's mouth to somebody else's butthole. You know."

"Was it missing from our exclusion tables?" Tim asked. The risk management department had an extensive and detailed map of the country that included every known location where, in the manual's words, incidents of "excessive spectral distress" were known to have taken place. This was in turn linked to a GPS database that was built into the company's policy system that would prevent anyone in an agency office from binding coverage, although in some cases, the policy could be written with underwriting approval. The list was as comprehensive as possible, but new sites of historical horror were being discovered every day. Maintaining the database was a never-ending job. It was possible that a location was insured before the company found out what had happened there.

"No," Volkerps said. "Agent did the GPS pin drop in the wrong spot. By accident, he says. We might have a crooked agent on our hands. We're pulling in their entire book of business for review. This is just the first one down the chute because of the claim."

"Right," Tim said, sitting up a little straighter in his chair. The bigger agents wrote thousands of policies worth hundreds of millions of dollars a year. Investigating one of them was one of the largest and most sensitive investigations with which the SIU became involved. If word got out that your agents were crooks, it didn't look good for the company as a whole. That was the kind of publicity that tended to make business evaporate.

"Now," Volkerps said. "As you know-"

The office door opened and Tim heard a voice from behind him say: "Volkerps? Ah! You're both here!"

Tim spun around in his char to see a tall woman with blonde hair cut in a bob. She was wearing an expensive red pant suit and a pair of green-tinted glasses in designer frames.

"Hello!" she said, striding into the room and holding out her hand. "You must be Tim!"

"Uh, yes," Tim said, getting awkwardly out of his chair and shaking her hand.

"Lilith Warwick," she said. "I understand we have something in common!"

"We do?" Tim said, confused. He recognized the name from somewhere, but his head was so full of case details that he couldn't place it.

"We're both starting new jobs!" she said, smiling. She leaned forward to whisper in his ear: "And we're both the first humans to have those jobs in the history of the company."

"Lilith is the new vice president of claims," Volkerps rumbled.

"I understand that you just closed your first successful investigation," Warwick said. "Excellent work!"

"Thanks!" Tim said. In his entire time at the company, he had only met a vice president once before, and that was during a Halloween party.

"I'm happy to see that my new diversity initiative is producing such excellent results," Warwick said. "How are you enjoying it so far?"

"Enormously?" Tim said, sounding more uncertain than he intended. He never knew how to act around executives.

"Excellent," she said. "I'm just doing the rounds. Saying hello to everyone. People like us are the future face of this company. Keep it up and you'll have my job in no time."

Tim couldn't help but notice that as she talked, the cloud under Volkerps seemed to be getting darker by the second. He could tell from the fake smile on Volkerps's face that his boss was doing everything in his power to keep it from turning into a much more violent storm.

"Okay," Tim said.

"So what's next now that you've successfully closed your first case?" she asked, looking at Volkerps.

"Can't discuss that outside the department," Volkerps said. "As I'm sure you're aware."

"Of course," Warwick said, smiling thinly. "Well, whatever it is, I'm sure that Tim here can handle it. Right?"

Tim felt the room become suddenly smaller as he was placed between two obvious opposing interests.

"I'll do my best," he said, trying to smile.

"I don't doubt it," Warwick said. "I'd love to ask you a favour, Tim."

"Sure?" Tim said. How exactly was he going to say no?

"You know we do the monthly company newsletter, right?" she said. "We were going to put Lonnie on the cover of next month's issue, but I'm thinking it would be nice if we put you on there instead. Really let everyone know who you are and what you're up to. What do you say?"

Tim had never actually read the company newsletter. Every employee got one by email at the beginning of the month, but he would be amazed if more than one per cent of them actually opened it. The company also printed up paper versions that sat largely unmolested in break rooms and the main cafeteria, although the printed editions were being phased out as part of the company's attempt to reduce its carbon and sulphur footprint.

"Uh, sure," Tim said. "But I don't want to bump Lonnie off the front. Maybe I could just be on the inside somewhere or-"

"Oh, pish posh," Warwick laughed. "Such modesty! I'm sure that Lonnie won't mind at all. I'll have my assistant send you a meeting notice later today. Anyway, don't let me interrupt you, gentlemen!"

She shook Tim's hand one more time and then was gone. Tim noticed as she made her way out that she didn't really stop to chat with anyone else in the office. Tim was about to close the door when Volkerps stopped him.

"Don't worry," his boss said. Actual lightning was starting to crackle in the cloud he was floating on. "I'll email you the file. You're evidently busy."

"Sure," Tim said. He left the office and closed the door behind him. He was uncomfortably aware of all the eyes that were on him as he made his way back to his desk.

"Looks like you made a friend," Lonnie said as Tim sat down.

"Yeah," Tim muttered. *And a lot of enemies. Many of whom I have to work with on a daily basis.*

Tim scrolled through some unread emails while he waited for his next assignment. Most of them were fraud bulletins and claims alerts from his old job as an adjuster. The IT security department at Crimson Seal was notoriously slow and understaffed, which was probably the reason that they still hadn't removed his name from the old queue. He hoped that was also the reason he wasn't really getting emails from the SIU queue yet and they weren't just leaving him out.

His mind flicked back to the case he had just been working on. Something about it still bugged him. He knew that the SIU case file was closed, but what was the deal with that demon statue? He'd heard of objects and items disappearing in the wake of these kinds of events, but it was rare to have one popping up out of nowhere like that.

He decided to open up the case file and take another look through it. When he went to the directory, however, the file wasn't there.

Oh, that's right, he thought. Volkerps said they were paying it out already.

He opened up the paid claims directory using his old adjuster's logon access, which (no surprise) had not yet been deactivated. The file wasn't there, either.

What the hell?

He checked the unpaid directory. The file wasn't there, either. Tim paused for a moment. It was not possible that the claim had simply disappeared from the system. Claims did get misplaced, but it was surprisingly rare.

Having gone through the case file so many times in preparing his report, Tim knew the case file number off by heart. He did an all-directory search.

No results.

The identity theft claim related to Emily Russenberger, aka Madame Zoudini, did not appear to exist anywhere in the Crimson Seal claims system.

Okay, Tim thought. Something is very wrong here.

His first thought was to mention the file's disappearance to Volkerps but given his boss's evidently sour mood following their most recent meeting, that didn't seem like the most prudent course of immediate action. It was entirely possible that the whole thing was just a security level snafu, although he'd had no problem writing and accessing the report using his SIU ID up until this morning, when he had filed it. What could have happened to it in the six-and-a-bit hours between then and now?

"A few of us are going to Asphodel's for a drink after work if you'd like to tag along," Lonnie said, causing Tim to jump.

"Thanks," Tim said. "That would be great."

Tim had a follow-up date with Tiffany this evening, but he could squeeze a drink in before that particular bit of torture. His mother had insisted they meet again after the dinner and had even gone so far as to book the restaurant. Tiffany, who had talked so much that hardly anyone else had gotten in a word all night, had also seemed enthusiastic about the idea, which was surprising considering Tim doubted she even knew his full name, let alone what he did for a living or what his interests were. Tim knew he should have torpedoed the idea right then and there, but it would have been awkward and rude and he generally tried to avoid making those kinds of scenes. Now all he needed to do was find some sort of way to gently explain to Tiffany that he did not think that they were a good match. He figured he had a better chance of doing that at dinner with just the two of them as she would not be able to talk and eat at the same time.

Asphodel's was a real, old-school watering hole in that it was literally located in a hole. In 1875, a demonic portal had opened up under the Donovan Hotel, causing the northeast side of the building to collapse. The Donovan was a well-known spot in those days, serving then-illegal Firewater to a mostly demonic clientele. The part of the structure that had collapsed was home to the Donovan's brothel, and many of the more pious members of city council had seen it as a sign of some sort of divine retribution for the establishment's plentiful sins.

The portal was sealed and the building partially rebuilt, although the portion of the hole above the municipal water and sewer lines was left as is. Patrons entered down a long spiral staircase that ran along the inside of the rim and featured photos and articles detailing the place's colourful past. Asphodel's was in what would have been the sub-sub-basement and still retained some of the brimstone charm of its predecessor. It catered mostly to non-humans, serving up an array of appetizers and drinks strong enough to make even identity theft seem preferable to waking up the next day.

Tim had never actually set foot in the place before. The bar was in the middle and tables ringed the edges. There was no natural light, of course. The whole place was lit by simmering cauldrons of imitation Hellfire. Safety regulations naturally prevented the real thing from being used, even in a place like this. Tonight, the place was starting to get busy with the after-work crowd. Tim passed a rowdy pack of werewolves tearing into a platter of Buffalo Cherubs (deep-fried squirrels, breaded and heavily sauced) while they howled with delight at every on-court stumble in the National Undead Basketball Association game being broadcast on the nearby widescreen TV.

Behind them was a heavily-branded demon tossing back flaming coals next to his bored-looking girlfriend. He gave Tim a hard look as he walked by. Tim dropped his eyes and kept going. He felt a little self-conscious being pretty much the only human in the place, but he was going to have to get used to that feeling, especially in his new job.

He saw Lonnie wave and made his way over to the table where his coworkers were sitting. Lonnie had ordered a large platter of wolfsbane crudités, which he was washing down with a tall stein of amber beer. Next to him was George, who was tucking into a plate of blood sausage with a side of scabs. Also at the table was Xana Ctheruul, a demon, and Jasper Delphino, a ghoul. Tim didn't really know much about those two as he hadn't really talked to them before other than to say hello on the first day.

"Have a seat, Tim," Lonnie said, moving over to make room.

"Thanks for inviting me, guys," Tim said, sitting down on the booth's worn leather seat. "I've never been here before."

"Not too surprising," Xana said. "I'm not too crazy about it myself. This is where I met my ex-husband."

"How long have you guys been split?" Tim asked.

"Few years," she said. "He swore he'd stop with the identity thefts when we got together, but, like everything else, he was blowing smoke out his ass. It was mostly petty stuff. He'd take over seniors and tourists and get them to take money out of the bank. Few hundred bucks here and there. Told me he finally got a job. Should've known better."

"You kicked him out?" Tim asked.

"Not me," she said, popping a hot coal into her mouth. "He liked to work hotels. Who's gonna notice another demon bell boy, right? Dumbass jumped into a guy who turned out to be the keynote speaker at a professional exorcist's convention." She barked a laugh. "I mean, on the moron scale, that's hard to top."

"What happened?" Tim asked.

"Got his sorry ass cast right out," Xana said. "Left me to look after all 22 kids. Oldest ones are just coming up for college. I'm gonna have to work for like the next 500 years to pay for it. I told them, you wanna go? Better get yourself a job. Three of them already work for Crimson Seal down in the direct mail unit."

"Nothing wrong with a little nepotism," Jasper said. "Both my kids work for the company. And their kids. And on down the line."

"How long have you worked here?" Tim asked.

"Let's see," Jasper said. "It'll be 223 years next month."

"Wow," Tim said. "That's gotta be some sort of record for a non-demon."

"There's only one other ghoul who's been at the place longer than me," Jasper said. "Well, technically he died 63 years ago, but he's still coming into work. The problem is, the employee service recognition awards stop at 200 years. I really miss getting the gift certificates."

"Oh, boo hoo," George said. "You've got a better pension and benefits set up than all the rest of us combined."

"It's not my fault they grandfathered everything," Jasper shrugged.

"Is Carmilla coming, too?" Tim asked, looking around.

"Carmilla prefers to do her own thing most of the time," Lonnie said. "She doesn't usually make it out to these kinds of things."

"Because she thinks she's better than everybody else," Xana muttered.

"Now, Xana-" Lonnie said.

"What?" Xana said. "She totally does! She didn't exactly greet you with a fruit basket when you started, did she?"

"No," Tim admitted. She had actually said that she thought he was hopeless and would probably die on the job, which was not the most welcoming sentiment.

"She's got this massive chip on her shoulder because she's half-succubus!" Xana said. "Big deal! My husband's banished to the third circle and I'm stuck raising 22 kids, but you don't hear me complaining about it!"

"Other than now, you mean," George said, smiling.

"Bite me," Xana said, grinning.

"We actually do our best to stick together," Lonnie said. "SIU isn't like the rest of the company. We're in our own building. We don't report through the regular chain of command. We don't go to many of the big annual meetings or summer team events or anything like that."

"It can be a little isolating," Jasper said.

"Especially because we can investigate anybody," Xana said. "Inside the company or out. You won't make a lot of friends working here. You can't afford to."

"Which is why it's important that we at least look out for each other," Lonnie said.

"No argument here," Tim said.

"The new Claims VP seems to like you," George said.

"Yeah," Tim said uneasily. "I kind of wish she didn't. Quite so much."

"Don't worry about it," Xana said. "It's not like the SIU was exactly chomping at the bit to hire any of us. A female demon? A werewolf? A vampire? The department used to be nothing but ghouls back in the day."

"It's true," Jasper said. "They used to put it right in the job postings."

The waiter arrived and took Tim's drink order. He scanned the board quickly and decided on a Hellfire Ale. He would need all the courage he could drink for his upcoming date with Tiffany.

"Why ghouls?" Tim asked.

"They used to think we were the only ones who could investigate all the others," Jasper said. "That we were dispassionate and scholarly."

"Precisely," George said. "Jasper might go to the opera, but that doesn't make him any less of an insufferable know-it-all."

"Possibly more of one," Jasper admitted.

"It's not about how you get in the door, it's about what happens after," Lonnie said as Tim's drink arrived. Tim couldn't remember if he was supposed to blow out the orange fire on the top of the glass or not.

"Heard you closed your first case file," Xana said. "Pretty good for your first couple of days on the job. Cheers!"

They all raised their glasses. Tim tried to blow out the flames, but they didn't go out. Instead, he ended up blowing foam over Lonnie's crudités.

"Shit!" Tim said. "Sorry."

"Don't worry about it," Lonnie laughed. "To Tim!"

Tim took a sip of the ale, which was easily stronger than any other beer he had tried in his life. It burned all the way down his throat, although not unpleasantly.

"Thanks," he said. "Hey, you guys have never had a case file vanish pretty much right after you submitted it, have you?"

"No," George said. "Not that I recall."

"Me either," Xana said. "What? All your work just went poof?"

"It got processed, but then I couldn't find it," Tim said.

"Did you forget some pertinent detail?" Jasper asked. "Some material fact that you needed to insert into the narrative after the fact?"

"No," Tim said. "Meh. It's probably some stupid IT problem."

"Ugh," George said. "Don't get me started on IT. Bunch of useless trolls. Even the ones that aren't trolls are useless. Last week I had to call the service desk because my laptop wouldn't boot up. First thing he asked me was if I spilled blood on it."

"Well, in fairness, you have done that in the past," Lonnie said.

"Yes, but it wasn't my blood that time," George pointed out.

Tim stayed at the bar for an hour before heading out. He needed to get home, shower and psych himself up for his ordeal. His mother had made reservations at The Graveyard, which had been hip and trendy in her day but was now mostly a hangout for seniors looking to take advantage of the half-price buffet before 7pm. Tim would not be surprised if he were to look over and see his mother sitting at one of the other tables.

"How do I allow myself to get into these situations?" he wondered.

He crossed the street and realized that he was only a half a block from Madame Zoudini's parlour. For no particular reason, he turned left instead of right and headed in that direction. Less than 30 seconds later, he was standing in front of the window. The lights inside and over the

"House of Spiritual Awakening" sign were off, leaving the place dark and giving it a genuinely sinister aura.

How much longer would it last? That was hard to say. Madame Zoudini's place was threadbare and old school, catering to a clientele that was shrinking by the day. Even with the claim settlement, chances were good that she would be gone before the end of the year. There were rumours that developers were eyeing this block for a massive new construction project that would have retail on the ground and 20 storeys of condos above. As one of the few chunks of land that could be developed in the area, it was a surprise that the existing site had survived for as long as it had.

One day, Tim thought, I'll walk down this street and point at a demon gelateria or vampire blood bar and say: See that? That's where I worked my first case in the SIU.

He didn't know exactly to whom he would be saying that. Hopefully not Tiffany.

He was about to turn and walk back to the subway station when he saw a flash of light from inside the parlour. Somebody was moving around in there with a flashlight.

"What the hell?" Tim said, stepping quickly to the side so that whomever was in there wouldn't spot him loitering on the sidewalk.

Who could that be? Madame Zoudini was, as far as he knew, still at the Crowley Clinic. Even if she woke up out of her coma, they would hold her for at least another 24 hours before letting her go. Especially after her last outburst in the outpatient ward.

I should call the cops, he thought, reaching into his pocket to pull out his cell phone.

He paused. What if it was some friend or distant relative, though? What if they had heard about what happened and came back to help? Maybe they had let themselves in to the place to check out the extent of the damage or collect some of her things to bring to her in the clinic.

If he called the cops and it turned out to be some friend or relative of the client, then the client would most certainly not be happy. Which would mean that Volkerps would not be happy. Which would mean that Tim would eventually not be happy.

But if somebody was breaking into the place and he could have stopped it but didn't, then the same chain of events would apply.

Tim put his cell phone back in his pocket. He still had the key. He had intended to give it back to Madame Zoudini at the clinic, but the levitation and fire had put a crimp in that plan. Maybe if he just let himself in, he could scope the situation out and make sure nothing was wrong. If it was a robber, he'd call the cops. If it was a friend or relative, he could at least claim to be conducting an investigation on behalf of Crimson Seal and show them his SIU ID badge if they didn't believe him.

Tim pulled out the key and also took out his clip-on camera, which he attached to his glasses. No matter what happened, it was always better to have video evidence.

He decided that it was too loud and obvious to let himself in through the front, so he made his way quietly around the building through the laneway to the back door.

It was already open.

Okay, Tim thought. Not a good sign, I grant you.

He pulled the door open slightly and stepped inside. Based on memory, he knew he was standing in Madame Zoudini's tiny kitchen and bedroom area. He made his way forward slowly. He knew there were a lot of items crammed into the space, most of them evidently moved here when Madame Z consolidated rental spaces.

He heard a thump from the front room and what sounded like hissing. This was in turn followed by a much louder bang and even more hissing.

I changed my mind, Tim thought. This is a bad idea.

He turned around to head back to the rear entrance, but his foot caught on the edge of the fold-out bed and he tripped, landing on top of what sounded (and felt) like an entire box full of pots and pans.

Tim scrambled back to his feet just as the door to the parlour slammed open. A bright light hit him right in the eyes, momentarily blinding him. He was dimly aware that something that was not human was charging towards him. He tried to get out of the way but had nowhere to go in such a cramped space. He heard some kind of hissed expletive and felt something large and heavy crash into the side of his skull. He saw stars flash in front of his eyes and was dimly aware of the fact that he was falling again, and then wasn't aware of anything at all.

7

"What in the hell happened to you?" Keef asked as soon as Tim stepped in the door of the apartment.

Tim made his way to the bathroom and flicked on the light. There was a bruise on his left temple, but it wasn't as bad as he'd feared it would be. He wasn't bleeding and his skull appeared to be intact, at least. He popped an extra-strength ibuprofen and went to the kitchen to grab a bag of frozen peas to hold against the side of his face. It felt pleasantly numbing.

"Aren't you supposed to be out on your date with Tiffany right now?" Keef asked as Tim sat down on the couch.

"I was," Tim said. When he had awoken on the floor in the back of Madame Zoudini's shop, he checked his phone and found that he had missed his date. There were five messages from Tiffany. The first two were concerned, the next couple were less nice, and the final one was basically just a long string of nasty things that she hoped would happen to him for standing her up. He had tried calling her back, but it went straight to voicemail. Her message had been changed to refer to him specifically and in unflattering terms.

"Did things go badly?" Keef asked. "Did you say something nasty about her hair? You know, like, by accident? Did she clock you?"

"No," Tim said. He explained what had happened in Madame Zoudini's parlour.

"Man, that sucks," Keef said. "Are you okay? Do you have a concussion or anything?"

"I don't think so," Tim said, rearranging the peas.

"Hey, at least you got out of the date," Keef said.

"Yeah," Tim said. His phone buzzed. He looked at it and saw his mother's face on the call display. He let it go to voicemail.

"Did you get a look at whoever did it?" Keef asked.

"Me?" Tim said. "No. But that doesn't necessarily mean that I can't identify them."

Tim got out his laptop and plugged in his camera. Whomever had hit him had fortunately missed his glasses, where his tiny Bluetooth camera had been clipped. He cued up the footage and hit play. The camera wasn't really designed for extremely low-lighting situations, so all he could see was an area about two feet in front of him. He heard the thump and saw himself step back, then involuntarily cringed in anticipation as several dark shapes ran into the room. The one in front swung something at him and then the image pitched backwards and sideways, coming to rest on a closeup of a chair leg.

"Ouch," Keef said. "Can't tell much from that."

"No," Tim agreed. He imported the footage into his image editor. It wasn't as good as the one they used in the Risk Mapping department (it couldn't remove clouds or pedestrians), but it might be enough to get something. He zoomed in on the first dark and blurry thing that came through the door, upping the contrast and reducing the motion haze. Gradually, something more recognizable began to come into focus.

"That's a demon," Keef said, watching the whole thing over Tim's shoulder.

"It certainly looks like one," Tim said. He had gotten a hint of sulphur when the door opened, although the smell was partially masked by an even stronger blast of Axe Morningstar, a spray-on cologne that was popular with demons in particular for its ability to mask the stench of rotten eggs. Tim was quite familiar with the stuff. Volkerps used the anti-perspirant version, as demons were one of the few beings at work not subject to the scent-free workplace rule.

Tim zoomed in on the creature's face, which looked like it had three eyes. The first two eyes were in the usual locations on either side of the nose, but the third appeared to be on the lower half of the left cheek. As the image came into sharper focus, he could see that it wasn't an eye—it looked like some sort of tattoo.

"Uh oh," Keef said.

"What?" Tim asked.

"I know that guy," Keef said.

"You *know* this guy?" Tim said in disbelief.

"Well, not this particular guy," Keef said. "But I recognize that brand."

"Brand?" Tim said.

Keef pointed to the circular design on the creature's cheek. "See that? It's the Mark of Azazel. That means he's part of the Hellspawn Triad."

"Wait a minute," Tim said. "Are you telling me that the demons who raided Madame Zoudini's third-rate tarot house are part of an organized criminal syndicate?"

"Well, that guy is," Keef said, shrugging. "They all have the same brand."

Tim had heard of the Hellspawn. Name any paranormal criminal activity—identity theft, selling cursed artefacts, succubus trafficking—they were heavily involved or more likely running the show. They had branches in every major city in the world, but were mostly focused in Japan, where they had originated. Their methods of enforcement made the average Mexican drug cartel or mafia family look like a Rotary Club in comparison.

When the mayor of Chicago had started up a special commission to start cracking down on their activities, for example, they had stolen his identity in the middle of a key council vote and had him calmly cut off his own left hand and eat it. Not surprisingly, the commission was quietly shelved and the matter never revisited. A similar thing happened to Nobel Peace Prize-winning U.N. human rights crusader Fatima Bhokako when she started making noise about the rise in underage succubi being funnelled into the sex trade. In her case, however, her limousine was surreptitiously replaced with one that drove itself off the Williamsburg Bridge and into the East River and then folded itself into a toaster-sized box for good measure.

Like all wide-ranging criminal organizations, however, the Hellspawn were not immune to the occasional regime change as dozens of mid-level bosses jockeyed with each other for the top job. Different groups had their own territories and identifying marks and methods of working, mostly depending on whatever their operational specialty happened to be.

"Crap," Tim muttered. "How do you know this brand belongs to those guys?"

"They run most of their operations out of a night club in South Hades," Keef said. "Everybody knows about it. I've been there a few times. Circle 9. It's not bad. Really good apps, but the drinks are overpriced. At least on vampire nights. But the prices always get jacked up for those."

Tim's mind was roiling. He had heard of the Hellspawn Triad, but this was his first direct contact with them. It was well known within the company that the Hellspawn represented a massive chunk of Crimson Seal's loss margin, as insurance fraud was one of the Triad's most reliable revenue streams. The company paid out billions of dollars in claims every year. The SIU was small. They couldn't investigate all of them. They had to prioritize and only go after the ones they were confident they could get.

How on earth was the Hellspawn connected to Madame Zoudini? If he could figure out what it was and open an investigative line into the Triad, it would be a massive boost, career-wise.

"This club," Tim said. "You've been there before? You could get us in?"

"Ye-eah," Keef said. "It doesn't exactly cater to humans, though, dude. Unless they're, uh, how can I put this delicately? On the menu, if you know what I mean."

"What, cannibals?" Tim said.

"No," Keef said. "Vampire fetishists looking to get turned. Underage girls mostly. They've read way too many Twilight and Anne Rice books. Think undead life is just some never-ending dry hump at the prom. It's one of the reasons I don't really go there much."

Tim was familiar with the phenomenon. The hysteria peaked roughly once every ten years, usually in the wake of some popular YA novel or movie that portrayed vampires as glamorous, sexy and full of world-weary ennui, like some cross between existential philosophers and soap opera stars. These movies rarely depicted scenes of scruffy and ema-ciated vampires loitering on the sidewalk while they waited for the blood clinic to open, sucking on dead pigeons and licking used syringes.

"Understood," Tim said. "I don't need you to eat anyone. I just need you to help me get inside."

"I dunno, man." Keef said. "I wasn't really planning to go out tonight. I just downloaded this new character skin for *Moonlight* that I was all ex-cited to try out. You should see it, man! It has laser-guided battle axes that are actually built into the gauntlets! So, I can throw them and then they just come shooting right back into my hands? And the boots! Oh man, you won't believe-"

Tim estimated that his brother spent at least 75 per cent of his time playing video games. It was something that had not changed since Keefer had become a vampire. On more than one occasion, Keef had gotten so wrapped up in his online life that he had almost lost his actual one, having forgotten to close the blinds in anticipation of sunrise and getting third degree burns on his face and torso. Many times, the idiot had fallen asleep in the chair right next to the window with the controller still in his hand. Tim still remembered being jolted out of bed by the screams.

"Keef."

"Yeah," Keef said, snapping out of his digitally-induced reverie. "Sorry. What were you saying?"

"Let's go."

"Oh," Keef said. "Okay. But you can't go dressed like that, man. You look like my Grade 8 science teacher. You remember Mr. Kerlikher? All the kids used to call him Buttlicker 'cause he used to wear those tan pants? Yeah, you can't go looking like that guy. This place is still sort of pretending to be cool and hip and what have you. You show up looking like that and even my legendary mind control skills won't be enough to get you in the door."

Tim sighed. Despite being a vampire, Keef had not mastered many of the supernatural powers that were supposedly inherent to their species. This was mostly because they weren't powers so much as skills that required time and effort to develop. Whether it was the power of suggestion, flying, or even turning into other animals (which only a small number of vampires could actually do), Keef was far too lazy to put in the time required to be able to master any of them. The most that he had managed to do to date was turn himself into spectral sand. Unfortunately, he had done this in the hall on his way back from a club and had been vacuumed up by Mug. Keef's adventure in escaping the central vac collection tank in the basement was something they had both studiously avoided talking about since.

"All right," Tim groaned. "What did you have in mind?"

8

Circle 9 was, like many nightclubs in town, built on the site of an old church. The main difference was the fact that the church in question had never been torn down.

Climbing the stairs from the subway station, the first thing Tim saw was the massive black stone bell tower that rose ten stories into the air. The bell had been replaced with a gigantic disco ball, which sent a spiral of multicolored lights skimming across everything in range. Spotlights shone on four glass boxes that were suspended from the front of the building. A woman was dancing suggestively in each of the boxes. As Tim got closer, he could see that each of them had horns and a tail and was dressed in little more than elaborate body paint. It was hard to tell if they were real or holographic. Tim hoped that they weren't real—even for a demon, it was a chilly night.

"Wow," Tim said. "It's more understated than I was expecting."

"We'll use the VIP entrance," Keef said, pointing them to a small side door to the left of the main entrance, where a large line of humans was waiting to get in.

"Are we VIPs, though?" Tim asked, pulling uncomfortably at the white silk shirt he was wearing. He was also wearing his brother's leather pants and even a cape, both of which he had resisted vigorously.

"It's always bad on during solstice week," Keef said as they crossed the street. "They let virgins in for half price."

Tim eyed the long line of mostly female patrons, many of whom did not look to be of legal drinking age and were shivering in skimpy dresses to avoid the coat check fee. "I imagine they take their word for it on that."

"This place never gets busted," Keef said, shaking his head. "Probably because of who owns it."

The wind caught Tim's cape, blowing it around in his face. He swatted it away with an annoyed grunt. "I can't believe I let you talk me into wearing this ridiculous stuff. I feel like a pedophile children's entertainer at a Halloween party."

"Trust me," Keef said. "The women at this place go crazy for this stuff. You want to get mom off your back in a hurry? Just take a stroll down the sidewalk past that long line of women there. Problem solved. Of course, they're all going to want you to bite their necks and suck their blood."

"That might be a small price to pay," Tim muttered.

The two of them reached the VIP door, where a pair of enormous red demons in black suit jackets were guarding the entrance.

"Hey, Tommy!" Keef said, slapping palms with the demon on the left. "Nice pickings tonight, I see!"

"Hey Keef," the first demon said, nodding at Tim. "Who's this?"

"New familiar," Keef said. "Figured it was time to show him the ropes. Master's gotta eat, right?"

The demon glared at Tim, who smiled weakly. Familiars still existed but were a dying breed. Most modern vampires just used apps to handle organizational stuff, like transportation, blood delivery and other everyday things. For example, Coff-n-Out, which was a vampire moving service, had just had an initial public stock offering that had quadrupled the company's value in under an hour.

"Okay," the demon said, turning to his companion. "Spritz 'em, Spez."

The second demon turned and brought out a small stone basin into which it dipped a short metal rod with a ball on the end. It took the dripping rod out and sprayed some on Keef and then Tim, muttering something under its breath as it did so. The walls were vibrating too much from the music inside for Tim to catch any of the words. What was this? Holy water? Seemed kind of out of character, considering the surroundings.

"Welcome, gentlemen," the first demon said, motioning them inside. "Happy hunting."

Keef and Tim moved through the door and down a narrow stone corridor, which was lit by candles mounted in wall sconces.

"What was that?" Tim said, brushing the drops from his forehead. "Holy water?"

"In this place?" Keef scoffed. "As if. You'll see when we get inside."

They reached the end of the corridor and turned left, entering the main body of what had once been the church. It was a standard Gothic cruciform shape, except there was a tall DJ platform where the altar would normally be and the space for the pews had been converted into a lighted dance floor. Hundreds of bodies were gyrating on the glass as the DJ, whose neon backdrop identified her as Laydee Medusa, cranked out the beats.

The bar was at the back, in the raised space that would have been occupied by the choir and organ. Tim saw bottles full of red liquid stacked three stories high. The area around the dance floor was lined with confession booths, some of which were open and some of which had their curtains drawn.

Interesting, Tim thought. I wonder what the original architects would think of the place now?

He looked at Keef and noticed that his face was glowing with blue dots from where he had been sprinkled with the water on the way in. Tim looked down at himself and noticed the same thing.

"Separates the predators from the prey," Keef said, pointing to the dance floor.

Tim looked over and noticed that Keef was right: all the humans on the dance floor were speckled with glowing red dots.

"More interesting than a hand stamp, I guess," Tim said. He scanned the crowd for any sign of the demons with the face brand but saw none. "I thought you said these Hellspawn guys hung out here?"

"They do," Keef said. "But they do their thing in the private crypt downstairs. Not even VIP access will get us in there, so you'll need to figure another way. I can only get you so far."

The two of them made their way to the bar, where Keef ordered an O-Neg Highball and Tim got a Donner Party Cocktail, which was about the only thing he could find that did not appear to have synthetic blood in it. A pack of women dressed as nuns went by, giving Keef a barrage of meaningful looks. Keef winked and smiled.

"I thought you said you didn't like this place," Tim said.

"Oh, it's not so bad," Keef said. "Could you cover my drink? I didn't bring my wallet with me."

"Of course," Tim said, tapping his phone on the pay pad. It was a good thing they weren't planning to stay long. The drinks in this place cost more than a ticket on most regional airlines.

Tim took a sip of his drink, which tasted like cold chicken, and reflected that maybe he should have considered the historical context before he ordered it. He scanned the room and spotted a couple of large demons standing in front of a stone staircase in the back corner. Both of them had the brand on their cheek. A couple of nuns wandered over and the demons pointed them forcefully to the other side of the DJ booth.

I'm guessing that's not the bathroom, Tim thought. *But how do I get down there?*

He was in the midst of formulating a plan when a large figure in a black trench coat appeared out of the crowd and began walking towards him. The figure wasn't tall but was quite wide. Tim guessed that he was barely five feet tall, but probably weighed more than 200 pounds. His hair was styled in some sort of elaborate spiky pompadour that made his head look like the bow of an aircraft carrier. He had pasty white cheeks and was wearing the kind of blocky sunglasses generally favoured by senior citizens. He was also wearing a necklace of what at first looked like clam-shells. As he got closer, however, Tim could see that they were garlic bulbs strung together like popcorn on a Christmas tree line.

Tim was still pondering all of this when he saw the figure reach inside his coat and pull out what looked like a gun.

"Die, bloodsuckers!" the figure yelled.

Tim was suddenly blinded by a bright light that hit him full in the face. This was followed a moment later by a low-pressure spray of luke-warm water.

"Oh, for crying out loud," Tim heard his brother groan. "Not again."

"Vampire scum!" Tim heard the figure shout. His voice was on the squeaky side. "Feel the wrath of my sun gun! Scream at the blast of my holy water cannon!"

Tim blinked the lights out of his eyes in time to see his eccentric attacker run down the length of the bar. Anyone with the day-glo blue spritz on them was the target of a fierce barrage from the large orange squirt gun he was carrying in his left hand.

"What the hell?" Tim said. "Who is that?"

A security demon raced at the figure and tried to grab him around the midsection. Despite his girth, the figure was surprisingly nimble on his feet and managed to dodge out of the way.

"That is Stake," Keef said.

"Who? Tim asked.

"Stake," Keef said. "Don't know what his real name is. Considers himself some sort of vampire hunter. Every once in a while, he sneaks into one of the clubs and makes an ass of himself."

"He looks like he came in third in the dress-up competition at Comic Con," Tim observed.

"He thinks he's Blade," Keef said. "There are just a few minor differences. He doesn't know any martial arts, his weapons are a flashlight and a kid's water gun, and he's a complete moron."

Tim watched as Stake avoided a second bouncer and ran out onto the dance floor, where he accidentally knocked over a couple of nuns who had been dancing on one of the speakers.

"Go back to hell, devil turds!" Stake shouted. "My vengeance knows no mercy!"

"This isn't real holy water, is it?" Tim said, wiping his face.

"Nah," Keef said. "Somebody told me he got ordained online with that church that doubles as a casino. You know, the Church of the Divine Profit or whatever it is."

Two more security guards had charged out onto the dance floor to try to rein in the oversized vigilante. Tim looked over and saw that there was no one guarding the stairs into the basement. This, he figured, was probably going to be his best chance.

"I'll be right back," he said.

"Careful, man," Keef said. "You get jammed up down there and I can't help you."

"Relax," Tim said. "I'm just going to take a quick look around. Anyone asks, I'll say I got lost on my way to the bathroom."

Tim skirted around the bar and jogged across the floor to the stairs. Everyone else's attention was diverted by the scuffle with Stake, who had been captured by two of the large security demons. One had him around the chest while the other had his legs as they carried him to the door. He wasn't going easily or quietly, but he was going.

"You demon-dongs might get me this time, but I'll be back!" he yelled as the beam of his flashlight bounced around wildly. "Just wait! This is my city, you understand! Mine! It belongs to humans, not you filthy monsters!"

The crowd cheered as he was carried out. Tim wondered what would motivate a person to dress up like a comic book character and take on real, live vampires, especially when the vast majority of vampires were quiet, law-abiding citizens and he was so obviously unqualified for the task. There was a fringe minority of humans grumbling for tighter laws and even full segregation of supernatural minorities, but they were mostly relegated to online troll factories and the darker corners of social media. It was rare to see them proudly declare themselves in public.

Whatever the case, he didn't have time to ruminate on it at the moment. He reached the top of the stairs and took a quick look around. There was no security watching. He started down. It was incredible how quickly the air cooled and the cacophony of sound from above quieted—almost like dropping below the surface of a lake. He reached the lower platform, where the stairs took a 90-degree turn to the left. There was no security here, either. He continued down into the crypt, clipping his camera on to his glasses as he went.

The air was chilly. Tim found himself pulling the cape in tighter, which made him feel slightly ridiculous. The crypt had stone floors off-set by blood red walls covered with framed photographs. Tim leaned in to look at the closest one, which showed a two-headed demon standing next to Kanye West. Both of the demon's heads were smiling and all three arms were extended, with two hands flashing peace signs while the third pointed to the rapper, who had a glazed expression and looked vaguely catatonic. The demon was wearing what looked like a sharkskin jacket and at least six watches. One of his heads had sunglasses while the other was proudly displaying a double row of gold tooth implants.

I guess that's the big boss, Tim thought. Subtle dude.

Tim glanced at some of the other photos as he made his way down the hall. He saw the same demon standing next to famous vampire actress Lucy DeVange, comedian Patton Oswalt, and zombie TV actor Dud Grub, star of the recently cancelled prime time hit, *Dud's Brain*, which had been a staple of ZBC's Thursday night lineup until eight former female co-stars had come forward with accusations that the highly-paid reality star had forced his way into their trailers and attempted to eat more than just their brains.

Tim saw a door up ahead on the left. It was slightly ajar. He approached it slowly and peeked inside. He saw what looked like a large, circular office. There was a shiny cherrywood desk on one side and a raised stone crypt on the other. There didn't appear to be anyone inside. Looking closer, Tim could see a black stone statue sitting on the desk. It was, he was sure, the same one he had seen in the front parlour of Madame Zoudini's shop. He had checked there after he regained consciousness, but the statue had been missing. The demons had grabbed it and brought it here. It looked like Keef was right about the Hellspawn connection.

Tim pushed the door open and crept into the office. As he stepped inside, he could see that the crypt wasn't actually a burial place. Maybe it had been at one time, but the coffins had been removed and replaced with a hot tub that looked large enough to hold at least a dozen people. The walls closest to the hot tub was covered with a massive curved TV screen. On either side of the screen were two large oil paintings. The first one depicted the three-armed demon boss holding a pitchfork and looking rather ridiculously like the lord of an English country estate, standing next to some sort of sport car that was in turn parked in front of an enormous manor house. The other painting depicted what Tim assumed to be three naked female demons doing something that looked like it would require a lot of pre-stretching and enhanced anatomy, even by supernatural standards.

Classy, Tim thought.

Tim leaned down in front of the desk and looked more closely at the statue. Yep. It was definitely the same one that he had seen at the fortune teller's place. He didn't dare touch it again. How had the demons been able to grab it? Maybe the curse only applied to humans.

"It's nice, eh?"

Tim jumped and spun around. There were suddenly three demons standing behind him. The one in the middle he recognized from all the photos in the hall. The other two were smaller and had brands on their cheeks.

"Uh..." Tim stammered.

"Lemme guess," the main demon said. "You got lost on the way to the bathroom?"

"That's the guy from Zoudini's," one of the other demons said, pointing at Tim.

"Is it?" the central demon said, smiling. "I'm Azmoda. Why don't you sit down for a minute so we can get to know each other better?"

Tim swallowed. He would really rather not stay, but he had the distinct impression that he had little choice in the matter.

9

"So ... what were you doing at Zoudini's?" Azmoda said, pouring out two glasses of what Tim suspected was Red Fairy Absinthe, a drink that was known to be occasionally fatal to humans. He snapped his fingers to set fire to the tops of both and handed one to Tim, who was sitting on the opposite side of the desk flanked by the two guards.

"I'm an insurance investigator," Tim said, taking the glass. He figured there was no point in lying. "I was checking out her claim for identity theft to make sure it was legit."

"Insurance?" Azmoda said, taking a large gulp and refilling his glass. "Hey! You and me, we're in the same business."

Tim took a cautious sip. He felt his body temperature rise by what felt like 20 degrees. "Our companies probably employ different processes when it comes to underwriting."

Azmoda laughed. "Zoudini was behind on her payments to us. I figured she set the fire so you guys'd pay up, so I sent in my guys to see what was going on. But she wasn't there."

"She's still recovering," Tim said.

"What?" Azmoda said. "It was legit?"

"Looks that way," Tim said. He had to be careful about what he said here. If he was careful, he might be able to get some information out of these guys. Assuming they didn't kill him, of course.

"How about that?" Azmoda said. "I always pegged her as a fake. Gave the whole racket a bad name, you ask me. But, long as she kept it to humans, nobody really gave a shit, right boys?"

"Right boss," the demons on either side of Tim said in stereophonic unison.

"Humans are so damn easy to steal from," Azmoda said. "I mean, you actually line up to give your money to something you know is bull-shit. And then they hand you this nice big pile of bullshit, and you take it and say 'Thank you! May I have another?' and hand over even more money! Your type is so incredibly fucking stupid that I can't believe it! But hey, no offense."

"None taken," Tim said.

"I mean, if it wasn't for human stupidity, we'd probably be outta busi-ness. Right boys?"

"Right boss," the demons said.

"How d'ya like my club, incidentally?" Azmoda asked. "Pretty nice, huh?"

"It certainly seems very popular with a certain, uh, demographic," Tim said.

"Vampires?" Azmoda said. "Between you and me, I can take or leave 'em. Frankly, they're a pain in the ass. Drink sales always drop by half on vampire nights 'cause they're always sucking on each other. And don't get me started on the number of times one of 'em's asked me to install blood sprinklers over the dance floor. I hate to break this to you idiots, but blood coagulates, okay? You can use those things once. Twice, tops. You for-get to clean the lines? You're screwed. Now you gotta pay some jackass a week's receipts just to come in and run heated drain cleaner through your whole fire suppression system. Otherwise the city's all over your ass for some stupid code violation. Not that I don't have friends at city hall, you understand. I just don't like to waste their time or mine over some blocked pipes."

"I understand," Tim said.

"But listen to me," Azmoda said, laughing. "You don't need to hear about the trials and tribulations of the small business owner. How's your drink?"

"It's got some kick," Tim said.

"No shit it does," Azmoda said. "My cousin Uzguur brings that stuff in special. Sold a whole case of it to D-Mnz just last week. He's a close personal friend, so I gave him a little discount."

Tim was aware that D-Mnz was a demon hip hop artist who owned a private penthouse in the Venkman Building in the Upper Styx. His song, *Succubitchas,* had been streamed more than 12 million times in a single day when it was released the month before. Tim didn't really care for it himself, as he thought it used too much autotune.

"Nice," Tim said. Was this guy just toying with him before they killed him? He honestly didn't know. Demons had strange customs. They would eat any kind of meat except goats, which they considered sacred.

"You work in insurance," Azmoda said. "I imagine that means you know a fair bit about cursed artefacts."

"A bit," Tim said.

"So what can you tell me about this one?" Azmoda said, pointing at the statue. "The boys found it at Zoudini's. They removed it purely out of concern for her welfare of course."

"Of course," Tim said. If Madame Zoudini had been paying protection money to the Hellspawn, that certainly explained why she was so desperate to keep her business running as customers began to dry up.

"Thing is," Azmoda said. "I've dealt with a lot of what you might call *enchanted tchotchkes* over the years. Monkey paws. Magic lamps. Cursed clocks. Even a dildo possessed by a Sumerian priest! You believe that?"

"I do," Tim said. In his time as a claims adjuster, he had seen weirder things.

"You won't believe who I sold it to!" Azmoda said. "You wanna know?"

"That's okay," Tim said.

"Okay," Azmoda said. "I won't say his name! All I'll say is that the Patriots have sucked since he retired. Anyway, like I said, I've seen a lot of weird shit in my time. But nothing like this."

"Like what?" Tim asked.

"You see that?" Azmoda said, pointing to a symbol carved into the base of the statue. Tim leaned forward for a better look. The carving was so faint that he had completely missed it the first time he saw the thing. It looked like an uppercase "B" except the straight line extended below the rest. The upper half was also oversized and square. The overall effect was to make it look like a hammer laid overtop of the letter.

"Interesting," Tim said. He didn't recognize the symbol immediately, but there was something strangely familiar about it.

"Think so?" Azmoda said. "Wait till you see this. Guul?"

Azmoda waved to one of his goons, who walked around the desk to stand next to his boss. Azmoda nodded to the goon, who leaned forward and put one of his ten clawed fingers on the symbol as casually as someone pushing an elevator call button.

As soon as he touched it, the goon was engulfed in a circle of bright red flame. His head fell back and his jaw dropped open so dramatically that Tim thought it had fallen off. There was no heat from the flame, which went all the way up to the stone ceiling. A horrible sound began to emanate from the demon. It sounded like a mix of roars and barks. Black bolts of lightning shot out in all directions. Tim jumped out of his chair and hit the floor as one blasted through the space where he had been sitting. The chair, however, appeared to be unaffected. Tim saw multiple bolts pass through Azmoda, who looked nonplussed. When another bolt passed right through his head, Tim realized that it wasn't real lightning. It looked like some elaborate special effect.

The barking noises stopped. Azmoda nodded to the goon, who removed his finger from the seal. The flames and lightning disappeared immediately.

"See what I mean?" Azmoda said. "You ever see anything like that before?"

Tim got slowly back into his chair. "Never."

What was that? Tim's first guess was that it was some sort of leftover from the initial event. It wasn't unusual in cases of identity theft and poltergeist occupation for there to be traces left behind of the departed entity, but that was usually in the form of less attractive things like ectoplasm, maggots and bugs. This was something altogether different. It was almost more like some sort of recording of the event—a voice message for anyone who had missed the initial one.

"And that voice," Azmoda said. "I have to confess, I'm not multilingual. I don't speak most of the old languages, although, Azag knows, my mother tried. Sent me to demon school every Sabbat without fail. Boring as a human baseball game. How do you people watch that? Three hours of mostly fat guys just standing around scratching their bags. Every once in a while, something happens and they sort of have to move. What is that? School? We used to sneak out all the time. Bunch of young demons. What the hell did they expect? There was a pet store in the mall. We used to break in through the back and eat the hamsters. Until they exorcised us, anyway. I never got caught, though. That was Beuleth. He used to stuff 13 of them in his mouths at the same time. Of course they're gonna notice if their entire inventory disappears, you dipshit."

"Uh huh," Tim said, unsure what any of this might have to do with him.

"Anyway," Azmoda continued. "I know this is trying to say something. I just don't have any idea what it is. Could be a curse. Could be a pronouncement. Could be a molten lava dip recipe for all I know.

Whatever it is, though, I've got a feeling that it's important. Which probably means it's worth a lot of money to someone. You can tell me what that is, maybe I can cut you in on a piece of the resulting action, you see what I mean. It's always helpful to have a person in a job such as yours work with us instead of against us. Mutually beneficial."

"Ri-ight," Tim said. "Unfortunately, I have no idea what it's saying, either."

"Bummer," Azmoda said. "Okay then, boys. Throw him in the pit."

"What?" Tim said, sitting up straight in his chair as the two goons came around either side of the desk towards him.

"Nothing personal," Azmoda said. "But if you work in this business, you either work for me or you don't. As in, breathe."

Tim felt four sets of powerful claws lock around his arms and lift him up out of the chair. "But-"

"Don't worry about it, kid," Azmoda said. "I'm sure it ends eventually. You probably won't be falling forever."

The demons lifted Tim up into the air and carried him towards the hot tub. One of them leaned over and turned one of the adjuster knobs on the corner. Instead of activating the jets, it caused the water to drain away and the bottom of the tub to drop open, revealing a red swirling hole in the ground that appeared to go on indefinitely.

"You don't want to turn that knob when you're in there with a couple of demonesses, believe me!" Azmoda said, cackling.

Tim tried to shake himself loose from the demon's grip, but their hands were like steel clamps. "Wait!" he shouted. "You don't need to do this! Help!"

"Relax!" Azmoda said. "No one up there can hear you. Besides, you're not the first or most distinguished person to end up in there. You bump into Bannon on the way down, you tell him I said hi, okay?"

The demons stepped up onto the platform and braced themselves to toss Tim into the swirling hot tub void. Tim weighed his options. As far as he could tell, he didn't have any.

There was a loud crack. Tim felt the grip on his right arm loosen as the demon who was holding him let out a shriek and fell sideways off the platform. The demon on Tim's left lost his balance and the two of them fell forward. Tim fell on the edge of the hole while the demon went right in. Tim felt his left arm almost wrenched out of its socket as the demon held on for dear life.

Tim grabbed desperately with his right, looking for something—anything—to hold on to so that he didn't go sailing over the edge. He felt his fingers grab the edge of the top step, but his hands were sweaty and he could feel them sliding on the smooth stone. The demon lost its grip on Tim's arm and grabbed wildly, seizing hold of his flapping cape.

Tim grunted, feeling the material dig painfully into the back of his neck.

If I ever get out of this, he thought, I'm going to kill Keef for making me wear this stupid thing.

Tim reached up with his now free left hand and tried to grab the clasp holding the cape in place. He could reach the metal, but he couldn't get his fingers in underneath to undo the snap. Below him, the demon swung around, trying to get a grip with one of its other claws. There was a tearing sound and suddenly the demon was dropping into empty space. The cape had been made of such cheap material that it had simply given way under the thing's weight.

Tim felt the pressure suddenly disappear on the back of his neck, but his relief was short lived. The demon had pulled him far enough forward that he was tilting into the hole. He tried to get a better grip with his right hand and missed. His legs flailed wildly as he felt gravity tilting not in his favour.

"Yaaaah!" Tim yelled.

He was tipping head-first into the hole when he felt someone or something grab him by the ankle and pull him backwards. He rolled over and looked up at a surprising face.

"Carmilla!" Tim shouted.

Carmilla was crouched at the bottom of the stairs holding what looked like a telescoping club in her right hand. The demon was lying on the floor behind her, screeching in pain and clawing at its right leg, which was quite obviously broken.

"What the hell are you doing here?" Carmilla said. "Run!"

Azmoda roared, pulling open one of his desk drawers to grab what looked like an ordinary gun. Carmilla spun around, reached into her jacket pocket, and pulled out what looked like a cell phone. She pointed it at Azmoda and pushed a button. Two darts shots out of the end and embedded themselves in the demon's chest. As soon as they made contact, there was a jolt of blue electricity between the two of them that lifted the crime boss shuddering to his feet and dropped him to the ground with a thud.

"Whoa!" Tim said. "What are you doing here?"

"Never mind that!" Carmilla said. "Are you trying to get yourself killed? You've been on the job for what? Three days?"

"Uhhh…" Tim said. He actually had no memory of anything beyond the last 30 seconds.

"Let's go!" Carmilla said, pushing him towards the door. "Before the rest of his goons show up!"

"Right," Tim said, staggering forward and almost tripping over the prone demon. He saw the statue sitting on Azmoda's desk and stopped. "Wait!"

"Wait what?" Carmilla said. "Are you nuts?"

Tim ran over to the statue and was about to grab it when he stopped himself, remembering the shock he'd gotten the first time he touched it. Maybe that wasn't the case anymore?

He reached out carefully and touched a fingertip to the statue. It gave off a jolt.

Nope. That was still the case.

Thinking fast, Tim reached up and unfastened the clasp holding his cape. It was torn, but there was probably enough of it left to do the job. He dropped the cape over the statue and lifted it off the desk. No jolt. Good.

"Come on!" Carmilla said, pushing him towards the door.

The two of them ran out into the hall. The statue didn't seem to weigh that much, although Tim thought that might be down to the large volume of adrenaline coursing through his veins as it might to the fact that it was a cursed object of unknown origin.

"Thanks!" Tim said as they ran. "How did you know I was here?"

"Shut up and keep running!" Carmilla said.

A door opened in front of them and two demons stumbled out. One was holding a metal rod with a red-hot tip while the other was holding his face. Evidently, Tim thought, they had interrupted some sort of initiation ceremony.

Before the demon could say or do anything, Carmilla tasered the first one and hit the second in the face with her baton. Both went down immediately, although the second made more noise in the process.

"We need to split up!" Carmilla said.

"We do?" Tim said. He felt a whole lot safer now than he had five minutes ago.

"Security upstairs will be waiting for us!" she said. "Take the side exit!"

She reached down and grabbed a white key card off the jacket of the recently tasered demon and handed it to Tim. She then pointed him to a door at the end of the hall, about 20 yards past the stairs leading up. Tim didn't know where it went, but hopefully, it was out of here.

"Okay," Tim said. "What about you?"

"I'll find my own way out," she said. "Now go!"

Carmilla turned and ran up the stairs, taking them three at a time. Tim watched her go with a vague sense of anxiety. It was hard to resist the urge to follow in the same direction, but she was probably right. They would have a better chance of evading security if they went their separate ways.

Tim ran to the end of the hall and pushed on the door. It didn't budge. For a moment, he thought he was done for, then remembered the card. He saw a magnetic reader located on the wall next to the door. Leaning over carefully so as not to drop the statue, he waved the card in front of the reader. There was a beep and a click. Tim pushed the door open and suddenly found himself back outside in a narrow stairwell.

He jogged up the stairs and found himself in the alley next to the club. There were garbage cans lined up in ragged rows next to the shipping entrance of the uniform supply company next door. All the lights were out and the alley appeared deserted.

Tim took a moment to orient himself and then turned right and began jogging. If he was correct, this direction would take him a block over onto Milton Street, which was far from the entrance to the club and any security cameras that Azmoda and his gang might have set up there.

His mind was racing. What had just happened back there? Why did Azmoda want the statue? What had Carmilla been doing in the place? And what the hell was he supposed to do now?

He was pondering all of those questions when a figure in a black robe and hood stepped out in front of him. Tim barely had time to register the figure's presence before there was a bright flash.

The next thing he knew, he was lying on the ground in a puddle staring up at a crow perched on a broken streetlight. He sat up and looked around. The figure was gone.

And so was the statue.

Damn, Tim thought.

He reached up and unclipped the camera from his glasses. It appeared to be undamaged.

Good. If he got the evening's events on film, then maybe the whole thing wasn't a total loss.

10

Tim booted up his laptop and plugged in his phone. The footage appeared to be all there. He started at the end and worked his way backwards.

The figure who had surprised him in the alley looked to be around five foot eight, but the hood covered his entire face, which made identification impossible. He or she hadn't said anything, either, so there was no way to match the voice up with anyone who might already be in their database. Crimson Seal kept elaborate files on all known fraudsters. Voice recognition was a handy thing to have, especially when dealing with shapeshifters.

Tim zoomed in on the source of the flash that had rendered him unconscious for long enough for his assailant to grab the statue and run. As he suspected, the object in the hooded figure's hand was an ordinary cell phone.

There were a large number of curse apps on the market. They were almost all illegal, of course, but that didn't stop unscrupulous hackers from creating them. Most of them were designed to induce specified types of mind control. Date rape apps were depressingly popular. So much so, in fact, that some clubs made all male customers surrender their phones at the door. Other apps were designed to have the victim empty their bank account or hand over the keys to their car. No fewer than eight recent candidates for office had been disqualified after it was discovered that they had deployed volunteers to polling stations who had used an app designed to hypnotize people into voting for them.

The few curse apps that were legal were mostly of the self-defence variety. One emitted a frequency that only werewolves could hear that was supposed to drive them away. The Council for Werewolf Rights was trying to have that one banned, but every time they started to get enough traction to put it on a ballot, somebody got attacked and they went right back to square one. Another app was supposed to use the phone's flashlight function to simulate daylight to drive away vampires, but that one only worked with certain models. A company called Pentacle produced a whole series of apps that were supposed to keep the user safe from identity theft, but they went bankrupt when it was discovered that they had been hacked by Russian demons who had reverse-engineered the app to have users unwittingly transfer millions of dollars to the account of a numbered corporation in Ukraine.

Tim couldn't see exactly which app had been used on him. Based on the fact that the footage showed he had only been unconscious for about a minute, however, he was pretty sure that it was only designed to briefly incapacitate him and didn't have any more long-lasting effects. The amount of time a victim could be affected by an app was usually in direct proportion to their exposure to it. That was one of the key reasons that celebrities never posed for selfies with fans anymore. Helen Mirren's career had never really recovered after she stripped naked in the middle of Times Square and sang "What Does the Fox Say?" to a gaggle of bemused German tourists.

Tim saw himself fall down and the image roll to the left, where it pointed at a sewer grate. He had been hoping that maybe he would have seen who was under the hood when they leaned over to grab the statue, but the camera was pointing in the wrong direction, so no such luck.

He backed up past his escape and his time dangling over the pit to the moment when Azmoda's goon had touched the statue. He replayed the moment a dozen times, doing his best to tweak the audio so that the sounds emerging from the goon's mouth were more decipherable. He had managed to tune out most of the rumbling and screeching, but still the words themselves made absolutely no sense. He tried running them through language recognition, but the search returned nothing. He was on the verge of giving up when he rewound the video one last time. He was so tired that he didn't bother to kill the speaker, so the audio played in reverse. What he heard next made him almost fall out of his chair.

"*I am Belial! Master of demons!*"

Tim was so surprised that he hit stop.

"Holy shit!" he gasped.

The message was in English—*backwards* English.

Tim wanted to kick himself. Why hadn't he thought of that? It wasn't unusual in cases of identity theft for demons to force possessed individuals to talk that way (or reverse French or Spanish depending on the victim's linguistic preference). A human possessed by a demon was not all that different from a puppet in that a demon couldn't really make them do something the vessel was not designed to do. Levitation, stigmata and projectile vomiting could all be handled with basic curses, but language was a different matter. Language had to go through the human brain, which was not accustomed to demonic language or pronunciation. It could be done over an extended period, but demons were generally lazy and identity thefts were hit and run operations, for the most part. When a demon tried to talk through a human, it often resulted in a short circuit in the cerebral cortex, causing the person to say everything in reverse.

If the message encoded in the statue was basically just a spectral recording of the original event, then it followed that this was how it might sound.

Tim excitedly cued up the message again, this time so that it ran backwards.

"*I am Belial!*" the voice said. "*Master of demons! Hear me, Sons of Darkness! The time of my return is nigh! Find the lost sixth key! It is buried in the middle of the net! Free me from my prison and those who cast me down shall burn forever!*"

Tim hit stop.

The name Belial he recognized from his demonology studies at university. He didn't remember too much detail other than the fact that Belial was one of the major demon kings, but none of them had been active for thousands of years and some scholars even disputed their existence. If such a character really existed, then what had he been doing for all this time? Demons were everywhere. Why would one of the most supposedly powerful demons of all time decide to just vanish, even to his own kind?

The rest of the message was a bit more of a mystery. Tim had no idea who the Sons of Darkness were. The name did not correspond to any gang, cult, church or organization with which he was familiar. Maybe they had existed millennia ago but had long since disbanded. The same went for the sixth key. He was going to need to go back and do some research to see if any of it made any sense.

He was jarred out of his thoughts by the sound of the door opening and his brother stumbling inside with two women.

"Hey, there you are!" Keef said. "They throw you out?"

Tim thought of the pit under the hot tub and shuddered. "Something like that."

"Told you, man!" Keef said, shaking his head. "This is Chendra and Nakita. Did I say that right?"

"Chandra," said one of the women, giggling. They were both dressed in floor-length black dresses and were wearing a large amount of pasty white retro-goth makeup.

"Right, sorry!" Keef said, laughing. "They just stopped in for a bite on the way home. Right, girls?"

The three of them giggled like they had electrodes attached to their sphincters. Tim shook his head. His brother was, once again, smashed out of his mind on mulled blood. As much as Keef pretended to have principles about matters of vampire etiquette, they went out the window in these types of situations. Would he still be doing this in 200 years? Probably.

"Ladies, how rude of me," Keef said. "This is my brother, Tim."

"Are you a vampire, too?" asked one of the women. By process of elimination, Tim assumed her name was Nakita.

"No," Tim said.

"Tim works for an insurance company," Keef said.

"Oh," the women said, clearly underwhelmed. Tim had seen the reaction before. That was the reaction most people gave when he told them that he worked in insurance.

"Hey, where's my cape?" Keef said, frowning.

"Sorry," Tim said. "It, uh, got stolen."

"Shit!" Keef said. "It was vintage! Guy I bought it from told me Dracula himself had used it. Just to wear around the castle. He had a different one when he was out … seducing local village women."

"Ooooh!" the women said, clearly more impressed with this piece of information.

"You owe me a cape, man!" Keef said.

"Right," Tim said. *And you owe me a years' worth of rent.* There was no point in arguing with his brother when he was in this state, though.

"Where were we, ladies?" Keef said. "Which one of you would like to be the first to try out my coffin?"

The women both got into a screaming competition to see who could be first.

"Calm down, everyone!" Keef shouted. "There's plenty of room in there for all of us. Now who wants a drink? I know I do."

The three of them marched into Keef's room and closed the door. Tim found his noise cancelling headphones and put them on. Since it didn't seem like he was going to get any sleep, he figured he might as well do some research. He still had his alumni account, which gave him access to the university archives. He logged in and looked up Belial.

The earliest references were in the Dead Sea Scrolls, particularly the section entitled "The War of the Sons of Light Against the Sons of Darkness."

Tim felt a shiver run down his back. The voice in the statue had specifically referenced the Sons of Darkness. He read one of the excerpts:

> *You made Belial for the pit*
> *Angel of enmity*
> *In darkness is his domain*
> *His counsel is to bring about wickedness and guilt*
> *All the spirits of his lot*
> *Are angels of destruction*
> *They walk in the laws of darkness*
> *Toward it goes their only desire*

"Sounds like a hoot," Tim muttered to himself.

The next reference to Belial was in the *Clavicula Salomnis Regis* or *Lemegeton*, a 13th century grimoire of unknown authorship, also referred to as the *Lesser Key of Solomon*. It was made up of five books. The first was the *Ars Goetia*, a supernatural who's who that identified the 72 leading demons of the time. Book two was the *Ars Theurgia Goetia*, which included a whole raft of rituals, many of which were tied to compass points on a celestial calendar. Third was the *Ars Paulina*, a collection supposedly compiled by the apostle Paul that acted as an addendum to book one. The *Ars Almadel* was a how-to guide for communicating with demons and other entities and included handy instructions on creating wax tablets and other devices used for supernatural communication. Finally, there was the *Ars Notoria*, which contained a series of incantations designed to grant the reader special powers ranging from eidetic memory and levitation to invisibility.

There was also believed to be a lost sixth book, the *Ars Azazel*, the content of which was unknown.

Tim paused. The five books made up the *Lesser Key of Solomon*. If the *Ars Azazel* existed, then an argument could be made for referring to it as the lost sixth key. Which was exactly what the voice had said in the recording.

The voice had said that the lost key could be found in the middle of the net. What on earth did that mean? It sounded terribly vague.

Tim kept reading. A few pages later, he found a clue. The three nets Belial used to entrap humanity were fornication, wealth, and pollution of the sanctuary.

"Okay," Tim said. "But how do you hide a book in the middle of all that?"

Tim looked up the Sons of Darkness, but there was precious little information on them. They were believed to be followers of Belial who would fight on his side when the demon king rose up to assume domain over the earth. Their leader called himself Paimon the Blood God.

Probably uses a different name in his online dating profile, Tim thought.

Tim sat back and tried to make sense of things, which was difficult because it was late and he had experienced a longer day than average, what with almost being dropped into a bottomless pit by demons and all.

Okay, he thought. *What we've got here is a short-term identity theft used to deliver what appeared to be some sort of prophecy about a demon who had been off the scene for an unusually long time. Said prophecy had taken physical manifestation in a cursed object, in this case, a statue. That was rare. Only the most powerful entities could do it. Most identity thefts were so subtle that even the victim's families didn't notice. This one had been, based on the evidence, something of an event.*

The statue had then been stolen by the Hellspawn Triad, who had grabbed it in lieu of payment for lost extortion revenue. They didn't know what to do with it and it had then been briefly stolen by Tim before finally being stolen again by an unknown third party.

Who had that been in the alley? A member of the Sons of Darkness? Had Tim come face to face with Paimon the Blood God himself? Or was it just some random ghoul trolling the back streets for an easy mark to roll?

Tim doubted the latter. Ghouls often used curse apps to incapacitate their victims, but they usually worked in pairs. Their accomplice (often a zombie) would distract the victim by asking for directions or trying to eat their brain and while the person was looking the other way, the ghoul would move in swiftly and relieve them of their consciousness and valuables. They usually targeted seniors, as it was easier to make it look like the victim had fainted due to some medical issue, like low blood pressure or a heart attack. And what use would a street ghoul have for a prophecy-spewing statue?

Tim yawned. The only thing he knew for sure was that he needed to be at work in five hours and that four and a half hours of sleep was definitely not going to cut it.

He took off the headphones and was immediately assaulted by the squealing and sucking noises coming from his brother's room. He decided to leave them on. An uncomfortable sleep was better than trying to sleep through that.

11

Tim got out of the car and looked up at the house at 111 Dunwich Street. It was an ordinary-looking brown-brick 2-storey Cape Cod-style, which had been popular at the time of its construction 40 years ago. It was set so far back from the road that it looked like it was trying to hide behind the dying elm tree in the yard, which was mostly weeds. There were city waste collection bins in a loose semi-circle in front of the garage: blue for recyclables, green for organics, and black for everything else. The green had been knocked over and raided by rioting racoons, who had ripped open all the bags and eaten most of what was inside.

According to the claim file, the house was supposed to be owner-occupied, but a quick search of online rentals revealed that the place was really occupied by as many as 40 students at a time. The real owners hardly ever set foot in the place. West Purgatory was a popular neighbourhood for absentee landlords. The university was only three blocks away and did not have much residence space, so demand was high and space was at a premium. Less scrupulous owners charged more than a thousand dollars a month for little more than a spot on a bunk, which were often stacked three high and four to a room. Students with no other option often found themselves sharing a bathroom and kitchen with a small army of others. Most prisoners had more space and better access to amenities than that.

Packing people in like sardines led to a predictable series of consequences: fights, assaults, property damage, wild parties, theft, arson … you name it. The residents who actually lived in the neighbourhood got so fed up with it that the city started clamping down, conducting surprise fire safety inspections and issuing hefty fines. They even set up a snitch line for the civically minded to report violators. Things had gotten slightly better, but where there was demand, there would always be supply.

Having been caught up in this dragnet and hit with a municipal cease-and-desist letter and sizable fine, the owners of 111 Dunwich had apparently decided to cut their losses and get out of the rental game. But since the house would require substantial repairs and renovation to be rendered habitable enough for sale, they had decided that the fastest way to get their money back was to file a claim for Possession of Personal Property. They had even doubled down on everything by claiming that the entity in question was a djinn.

The reason this was significant was because djinn were extremely difficult and in some cases even impossible to exorcise. Once a djinn took possession of a house, a car or even a toaster oven, the item was an automatic write off at full replacement cost. That meant the payout was considerably higher—often double—what an insured would get for a lesser entity.

The policy in this case did not have a Djinn Exclusion because it wasn't in one of the excluded territories. Djinn had a long record of popping up more often in some locations than others, and Dunwich was not one of their preferred hangouts. In fact, the claims database showed that no djinn had surfaced within a kilometre of this spot in more than 126 years. It was one of the reasons so many people had flocked to the suburbs over the years. Djinn loved action and mayhem, and there was precious little of that out here.

Although the occupancy issue could technically constitute misrepresentation and automatic cancellation of all coverage, the municipal citation was not sufficient legal proof that the owners were not actually living in the house themselves from the perspective of the policy wording statutory terms and conditions. Crimson Seal would probably have to sue in order to invalidate on those grounds, and a protracted legal fight would most likely end up costing far more than the settlement value.

The fastest and easiest way to deny the claim was to prove that the house had never been possessed, or at least that the entity involved wasn't a djinn. That was how the SIU had gotten involved and was the reason that Tim was standing in front of the place now.

He took a sip from his water bottle, then screwed the lid back on tightly and tossed it back on the seat. Although he was 99 per cent confident that there was no djinn in the place, he didn't want to have any water on him when he stepped inside. Certain djinn had particular power over water and could do extremely unpleasant things with it. As an elemental demon, they could control water, earth, air and fire. The electrical supply to the house had been disconnected as a matter of procedure. The water supply had also been shut off at street level. There wasn't a lot he could do about the air. A couple of companies had come out with portable respirators that were supposed to be djinn-proof, but it hadn't taken long for those claims to be proven violently wrong.

Tim clipped on his camera and double-checked his evidence kit. An adjuster had already been through the place with the Hazardous Entity and Materials Team and found nothing. The place was empty and this was just a matter of procedure. In all likelihood, he would be in and out of the place in under 30 minutes. The chances of dying in an unpleasantly painful way were so small they were practically insignificant.

Right, he thought, closing the car door and locking it. Just keep telling yourself that.

He started with a slow circuit of the exterior of the house. The garage was off its track and wouldn't open. Based on the cobwebs and the rust, it looked like it had been that way for quite some time. The agent who had bound coverage hadn't inspected the place since the policy was issued 12 years before. That wasn't unusual. Agents hated doing grunt work like that and only got around to it when underwriting forced them to. Most agents avoided property and auto and stuck to life insurance, where the commissions were higher and the loss ratios were a lot lower. They left stuff like this to their staff, most of whom were extremely overworked and underpaid.

He let himself in through the rusty chain link gate and stepped into the backyard. There was a bare dirt patch near the house where a make-shift patio had been set up with a yellowed plastic table and chairs. One of the table legs had snapped and been propped up with a couple of beer cases, both of which appeared to be empty, the cardboard so faded and warped that it looked like dead skin. Somebody had stuck an old golf umbrella in the centre hole to act as a sun shade, but the fabric was long gone. Lying on the ground next to the table was a plastic clock that promoted Infernal Ale. It showed a smiling demon holding a bottle of said beer aloft under the words: "It's Always Infernal Time!" Tim leaned in and saw that all the numbers had been replaced with the words: 'Infernal Time!"

"Yep," he said to himself. "I guess it is always Infernal Time."

There was a rusty metal shed in the back corner of the lot, which was overgrown with weeds that were almost as tall as the tree out front. The houses on either side had erected tall, solid-board wooden fences that ran side-by-side with 111's decrepit chain link one. It appeared that the neighbours were keen to block out as much of this place as they legally could.

The ground was also littered with broken bottles, old cups, discarded clothing and who knew what else. He decided to limit his reconnoiter. There was nothing to gain wandering around back here except the need for a tetanus booster.

Tim walked back around and pressed his thumb to the lockbox on the door. It beeped and popped open. He reached inside and removed the key, inserting it in the lock next to the large red and yellow sticker advising that no one should enter the house and that all questions should be directed to Crimson Seal's toll-free claims number.

Before he opened the door, he reached into his kit and removed the goggles, sliding them on overtop of his glasses. These could be adjusted to filter through various spectral light phases, which he would need to be able to do for confirmation. Once they were comfortably in place, he attached the wireless camera, pushed open the door and stepped inside.

The first thing to hit him was the smell. It was a dank mixture of rotten food, wet earth and mould. He reached into his kit and put on a filter mask. The food smell was probably coming from the kitchen. The power had been off for more than a week, so anything that was in the refrigerator or left on the counter would be well decomposed by now. The earthy smell was probably due to the fact that the place hadn't been cleaned possibly ever. The air was probably full of spores, but he couldn't risk bringing a respirator in with him. The mask would have to do.

The entry hall was only about five by five and so crammed with junk that Tim had to step over a box full of metal coat hangers just to be able to close the door behind him. He flicked on his flashlight and panned it around. To the left was what he assumed to be the living room. On the far wall was a flat screen TV hanging at a 45-degree angle. He could see a hole in the wall where one of the mounting brackets had given way swallowing a snakelike trail of cords. In the middle of the floor was a futon frame with a bare mattress hanging off one side. It was folded down and appeared to have functioned as a bed for one of the four people who lived in this room. On the left side in front of the window was a bunk bed. The window had been covered with what looked like a table cloth held up with tacks. On the right was a plastic patio lounger partially covered with a sheet.

Straight out of Better Squats and Hovels, Tim thought.

He adjusted the filter on his goggles to ultrainfernal and panned the flashlight around, paying particular attention to the areas around vents, electrical sockets and window frames. He saw none of the telltale glowing red traces he would expect to see had any of the surfaces come into contact with a Level 6 demonic entity.

Tim flicked the filter back to visible and moved on into the kitchen. It was slow going as he had to step over and around all kinds of boxes, furniture and assorted junk. He heard a skittering sound and panned the light around but saw nothing. It was probably just rats. He tried to remember the last time he'd gotten a rabies shot. Probably back when he had still been working for his father. He decided that he'd upgrade all of his shots after he left this place, whether he was bitten or not.

The rotten food smell was considerably more powerful in the kitchen. The counter was covered with stacked plates and pots. He shone the light over them and saw dozens of cockroaches flee back into the dark. He really should check the fridge, but it had been unplugged for a long time and was quite clearly the epicentre of the stench. Whatever was in there was probably worse than any supernatural entity would be able to stand. If he had been wearing a respirator, then maybe he would venture a look, otherwise, he was happy to leave it shut. He was probably going to need to throw most of the clothes he was wearing in the garbage, anyway. No need to add multiple decontamination showers to the bill.

He scanned the sink and stove with the U/I filter and saw nothing. It was looking increasingly like there was nothing to find. This claim was headed for the rejection pile.

Tim heard a bang and a brief flash of light as the front door opened and closed.

"Hello?" said a male voice. Tim heard a series of clicks that he recognized as the sound of a light switch being flicked back and forth. "Hell's with the lights?"

Tim made his way back into the hall. A kid in his early 20s was standing inside the door. He was wearing a jersey for the Los Angeles Undertakers basketball team and a pair of ragged cargo pants that were decorated with a neon blue camouflage pattern that would not render him invisible in any biosphere on planet Earth.

"Who the hell are you?" the kid barked.

"I'm an investigator with Crimson Seal Insurance," Tim said through the mask. "Who are you?"

"Dwayne," the kid said irritably. "This is where I live. Or it used to be. I come back from my uncle's funeral and the damn place is sealed up. All my shit is here, man!"

"You need to stay out of the house," Tim said. "The owner has reported the presence of a Level 6 demonic entity. No one can access it until we complete our investigation. I need you to step back outside. Any possessions you may have will be returned following-"

"Fuck that," Dwayne said, stepping inside. Tim could see that he had brown hair buzzed so short that he was essentially bald. His nose appeared to have a zig zag in the middle just below the bridge, evidently where it had been broken. Based on the guy's height and size, Tim pegged him as either a football player or wrestler. Based on the nose, he guessed that the guy probably wasn't very good at it. "What's with the lights?"

"The power and water have both been shut off," Tim said. "As a precaution."

"What are you?" Dwayne asked. "A cop?"

Tim shook his head.

"Then you can't tell me shit," Dwayne said. "These assholes charged me six months' rent in advance and the next thing I know they're gone? As if. I tried to get in yesterday, but the place was all locked up and no one was answering the door. I came by again and saw a car out front, I figured they were finally back."

Dwayne reached into his pocket and pulled out his cellphone, activating the flashlight feature. He pushed past Tim and pulled open the door leading to the basement.

"Sir," Tim said. It galled him to address a kid who was probably only about six years younger than he was as "sir," but he didn't know the guy's name. And he needed to maintain a certain level of professional decorum. "For your own safety, I need you to exit the premises-"

"Fuck you!" Dwayne barked. He said it in such a casual and non-malicious way that Tim got the impression that, for Dwayne at least, this was something of a default response to all kinds of queries. Tim could hear the sound of heavy feet descending the creaky wooden stairs. "I live here, man! Why don't *you* exit the premises? Fuckin' stinks in here."

Tim followed Dwayne downstairs. Like the upper floor, most of the basement space had been converted into makeshift bedrooms. There were two bunk beds crammed into what was essentially the utility room. If the person on the bunk on the lower left rolled one way instead of the other, they would bump right into the furnace.

Dwayne stomped over to the bunk on the far right and began fishing around under the bed, which was right next to the water heater.

"Least my laptop is still here," he muttered, pulling out a small black carrying case and unzipping it.

Tim checked the space between the bunks closest to him. A bulky grey furnace sat against the wall next to the electrical panel. Tim shone his flashlight on the panel and saw to his surprise that the master switch was not in the off position. Some of the circuit breakers had flipped, but the rest of them appeared to be live. That explained why the switch upstairs hadn't worked, but if he flipped the one down here, there was a good chance the lights would come on.

What the hell? Tim wondered. Shutting off the power was one of the first things that the HEMT teams were supposed to do during a sweep. Had they just missed it?

Tim glanced down at the bunk. A bright green and purple book on the lower bunk on the left-hand side caught Tim's eye. He went over and picked it up. *The Complete Moron's Guide to Spells and Incantations.* It was part of a popular series of titles dealing with all things supernatural. There were books on zombies, vampires, werewolves ... you name it. Most of them presented little depth and even less research, choosing instead to re-enforce popular misconceptions and prejudices.

Somebody had folded down a corner of one of the pages about one third of the way through the book. Tim flipped it open to the dog-eared page and felt himself go suddenly cold. It was the start of a chapter, with one word in big bold letters at the top of the page:

DJINN

Tim swallowed. He put the book down and noticed that the circular rug on the floor next to the bed was uneven, like it had been lifted and put down in a hurry. There was something underneath it. Tim put the book on the bed and crouched down to move the rug aside.

Underneath, somebody had drawn a circle with a pentagram inside. There were words running around the inside of the circle. The words were not written in English and some of them were smudged, but Tim knew enough to know what they were supposed to be saying to recognize it for what it was.

A circle of protection.

Tim flipped the filter on his goggles back to untrainfernal and passed his flashlight slowly around the room. There were red streaks and smudges everywhere. Big ones.

"We need to get out of here," Tim said. "Now."

Dwayne, who was on the other side of the room appeared not to have heard him.

"Dammit, my battery's dead," he said, shaking the laptop before dropping it down in the case. "If I lost my entire humanities assignment because of this, I'm going to sue these assholes, man. You're insurance, right? How much money do I get if I have to do my first semester all over again?"

"Listen to me," Tim said, standing up. "We need to leave this place. It's-"

"Excuse me," said a voice.

Both Tim and Dwayne turned and shone their flashlights towards the far wall, where a young woman was standing in the doorway leading to the second bedroom. To Dwayne, she appeared to be about 20 years old, with blonde hair and an hourglass figure barely covered by a skimpy negligee. To Tim, who still had the untrainfernal filter activated on his goggles, the figure looked radically different.

"Hey!" Dwayne said. He smiled and stood up, puffing out his chest and swinging his arms in a way designed to flex his shoulder muscles. "Who are you? Are you Natasha's cousin?"

"Dwayne!" Tim hissed. How stupid was this guy? Did he really think that a beautiful woman was just standing around in the basement of an abandoned house in lingerie just waiting for them to show up? Tim realized that this was a rhetorical matter that had already more or less been decided, but that didn't alter their current predicament.

Dwayne waved a hand at Tim, indicating for him to be quiet.

"Why yes!" the woman said, smiling.

"I thought so!" Dwayne said, nodding. "You kinda look like her! She's super hot, too!"

Dwayne winked in a way that he seemed to think was incredibly charming.

"You wouldn't happen to have a drink, would you?" the woman said, playing with her shoulder strap. "I'm really thirsty."

"Totally," Dwayne said, pulling a water bottle off his hip. "I've had a few sips, but you can have the rest."

"No!" Tim said. He tried to step forward to stop Dwayne handing over the bottle, but Dwayne shoved him aside.

"Fuck's wrong with you man?" Dwayne said. "Lady says she's thirsty."

Dwayne tossed her the bottle, which she caught easily.

"That isn't a woman, you idiot!" Tim said.

"Fuck you talking about?" Dwayne said. "You ever seen a woman before? I'm guessing not. I'm not with this guy. Don't even know him. He just showed up here."

"How sweet," the woman said, ripping the metal cap off like it was made of tissue and tossing it aside.

"Uh, hey," Dwayne said, looking slightly concerned for the first time. "That was kind of expensive, you know?"

The woman tilted her head back and poured the entire contents of the one-litre bottle down her throat in a rush.

"Wow!" Dwayne said. "You weren't kidding!"

The woman looked back at Dwayne, smiled, and crushed the bottle in her hand.

"What the fuck?" Dwayne said. "Jerome Muglin signed that! It cost me 500 bucks online!"

The woman opened her mouth and spat the water back in Dwayne's face in a high-powered jet. He screamed in pain as all of the flesh on the front half of his skull melted off like ice cream under a welding torch. The same thing happened to his hands as he threw them up to defend himself. He slipped on the floor and fell on his back, a screaming skull with skeleton claws.

Tim closed his eyes but couldn't ignore the screams.

I tried to tell you, he thought. You dumbass.

Tim opened his eyes. Dwayne continued to writhe on the floor as the flesh melted away into a red puddle around him. There was a blue flash as the woman transformed back into her natural form. Tim had only ever seen pictures of djinn in textbooks, but this one was every bit as hideous as all of the scholarly examples.

It had six arms, which gave it a distinct, spider-like appearance. It's four heads consisted mostly of eyes. The mouth was a gaping wound in the middle of its chest that opened vertically, giving it the appearance of a cracked rib cage. Tim watched it open and close as multiple black tentacle-like tongues rolled in and out over its jagged rows of teeth.

"Why am I melting?" Dwayne yelled from the floor. The top half of him was now just bone. "This is so fucked up!"

The djinn opened its mouth and charged. Tim tried to get out of the way but tripped over his own feet and landed on the floor next to the bed. He looked up and saw the monster racing towards him.

Maybe, he thought, applying for this job was not one of my better ideas.

The creature got to within a couple of feet of him before it stopped abruptly. There was a crackle of purple lightning and then a sharp bang as the creature was lifted up off its feet and thrown back across the room. It landed next to the partially disintegrated Dwayne, who was still coming to terms with his situation.

"Somebody get me to a hospital!" Dwayne shouted. "This better be reversible or I'm gonna be so pissed, man!"

Tim jumped to his feet in surprise. What the hell had happened? He should, by all rights, be in an even worse situation than Dwayne right now, but somehow the demon hadn't been able to touch him. How?

Tim looked down and saw that he was standing roughly in the middle of the circle that had been drawn on the floor.

Well I'll be damned, he thought. Or rather, not. The *Moron* guides might be full of superstition and nonsense, but in this respect, it looked like they were right on the money. The circle of protection had actually held. He made a mental note not to slag off the series quite so much in the future. Assuming, of course, that he found a way to step out of this circle without being killed. And he was going to need to step out of the circle if he was going to leave this house.

He pulled out his cell phone and was not at all surprised to see the signal connectivity fluctuating wildly between full strength and zero. Powerful entities had a tendency to cause serious service interruptions. The chances were low that he would keep a signal for long enough to call for help. And even if he did, it would take the Hazardous Entity Response Unit at least 20 minutes to get out here, by which time the demon would no doubt have figured out another way to get to him. Whatever he was going to do, he was going to need to do it quickly.

On the other side of the room, Dwayne was getting back to his feet. He was quite a sight. The top half of his body was just skeleton while below the waist his muscular legs filled out his green track pants. Tim saw him pull the waistband of his pants forward to check that another key anatomical element was still there.

"This is so weird!" Dwayne gasped. His bones made constant clicking noises as they moved.

"Dwayne, listen to me!" Tim said. "We can fix you! But I need your help to get us out of here!"

In reality, Tim was not remotely certain that Dwayne could be successfully uncursed, but that was what you were supposed to say to injured people, wasn't it? To keep them calm. To keep their heart rates down so they didn't bleed out or go into shock. Granted, Dwayne did not have a heart inside his empty rib cage, but the principle was probably the same.

"Fuck that, man!" Dwayne said. "I'm outta here! Good luck, buddy!"

Dwayne turned and ran up the stairs. Tim heard him trip about halfway up. There was a thump and a lot of rattling sounds, which were followed by prodigious cursing.

The djinn also picked itself up off the ground. Its mouth opened and a jet of steam shot out, but it too was unable to penetrate the edge of the protective circle. Tim watched the purple smoke encircle him and tried to take his own advice about remaining calm. He needed to think. Djinn were nasty, but not impossible to defeat. The HEMT techs used a spectral phase inhibitor device to incapacitate the demon for long enough to capture and contain it in a special zero-point para-ball, which looked like a softball made of black volcanic glass. Tim had seen many of them during his days as an adjuster. One of the techs kept one on her desk, which she used as a paperweight.

"Almost took my leg off, that one," she said. "I call him Binky."

Unfortunately, Tim did not have either of those devices at his disposal. What he did remember from his time studying djinn in university and during his Supernatural Chartered Insurance Professional certification courses was that they tended to be focused on the one or sometimes two elements over which they had power and avoid the others. Generally, the more powerful a djinn was in one area, the weaker it was in the others.

This one had attacked with water twice. That meant that it was probably weak on—and even possibly vulnerable to—fire.

Tim had a small butane lighter in his SIU kit, but it was barely large enough to light a cigarette. It was designed for small forensic tests, not for repelling aggressive Level 6 demons. He could try using it to set fire to a blanket or pillow from one of the bunks and throwing it at the thing, but that would probably be less effective. He'd probably just end up setting his clothes on fire.

"I know how to get you out of there!" the demon said. It had transformed into an old man with bright red eyes, pale white skin and long fingers. All demons had a default alternate appearance and Tim guessed that this was the one this particular demon probably used. It had only appeared as the sexy coed to lure Dwayne. Demons were quite good at sizing up human weakness at a glance.

The djinn moved over to the large and rusty water heater in the back corner of the room. Part of the requirement for a HEMT sweep was to turn off the water and electricity and drain the water heater, but Tim had a sinking feeling that most of the things on that list had not been done.

The djinn leaned over and ripped off the spout for the emergency drain. Water began to gush out onto the floor next to its feet. As it pooled on the concrete, the water began to boil and spouted writhing purple and black flames. The floor was on a slope leading to a central drain. A drain which, Tim couldn't help but notice, was right in the middle of his circle of protection.

The flaming puddle grew rapidly, rolling across the floor in Tim's direction. As it hit the circle, the flames stopped, but the water trickled in, slowly dissolving the chalk that had been used to do the illustration. As the chalk dissolved, the flame moved closer.

Uh oh, Tim thought. This is not good.

Tim turned back to the electrical panel. The switch for the furnace was in the on position. The furnace, on paper at least, still had power.

He grabbed the trunk at the end of the bunk closest to him and pulled it closer, lifting the lid. Inside was a tangle of old sweatshirts, textbooks and two cans of beer. He tossed them all out onto the floor. The trunk was just large enough to fit him. He hoped.

Tim leaned forward and pulled off the service cover on the furnace, tossing it sideways onto the lower bunk. He pulled off his goggles and stuffed them in his SIU kit. He wasn't going to need those for this.

Working with his father's supernatural pest control service when he was in high school, Tim had become very familiar with a wide variety of household mechanical devices and appliances, as they were often a preferred hiding spot for particular types of poltergeists. Furnaces were one of their favourite places. They presented one of the easiest ways to cause a lot of trouble for residents with a minimum of effort and also provided a convenient way to get around the house via the duct network. Sometimes people didn't even realize they had an entity and just assumed the appliance was on the fritz, often paying a small fortune to repair companies for new motors, igniters and other components.

He shone his flashlight into the furnace and checked the pilot was on, which it was. He turned the valve to shut off the gas supply and watched the pilot flicker out. He then reached over and yanked out the wires leading to the blower. That would prevent the pilot from re-igniting when the supply was turned back on. Modern furnaces had a safety bypass designed to automatically shut off the supply if the blower failed to ignite after three tries, but Tim could see that this was not a modern unit. And from the level of dust on the components, it had not been serviced in a very long time.

Tim turned the valve to restart the gas. A red warning light began flashing as the blower failed to ignite. Tim smelled the gas as it seeped out into the room. He wasn't sure how long it was going to take before there would be enough to serve his purposes. Thirty seconds or maybe a minute. He looked down at the circle. Almost half of it had washed away now. The flames were coming right up to the tips of his shoes.

No time to speculate, he thought.

Tim opened his SIU kit and pulled out the lighter, then lifted the lid of the trunk and climbed inside. The djinn laughed so hard that it transformed back into its non-human version.

"You think you can hide from me in there?" it said. "That's hilarious! Wait till I tell everybody back at the Pit! They'll never believe me. Unless I bring them your face. That might do it."

Tim squeezed himself into the trunk and tried to pull the lid down, but it wouldn't close. His SIU kit was sticking up. Tim pulled it off and tossed it out. If he survived this, he would requisition another one and pay for it out of his own pocket if necessary. He could see smoke rising up from the floor next to the trunk. Demon fire wouldn't set off the gas, but he knew something that would.

Tim pulled the lid down and reached up to stick the tip of the lighter out through the narrow opening. Had it been long enough?

"Or maybe I'll just eat your face and bring them your balls!" the djinn hissed.

Tim heard splashes as the demon crossed the floor towards the trunk.

Oh well, he thought. It's now or never.

He clicked the lighter. There was a boom and a flash. Tim felt the trunk upended as it was knocked sideways by the blast. The lid opened and he dropped sideways onto the floor, rolling into the cold water.

Everything in the basement that could burn was burning. This included the djinn, which was screeching and rolling around on the floor trying to put itself out. The water didn't appear to be quite deep enough, however, and so it was having only limited success. The furnace was a blackened hunk of twisted metal and the bunk closest to it had collapsed, sending the flaming mattress flying across the room.

Tim ran for the stairs. He had decided that it would be prudent to complete his investigation at a future date.

12

Tim got back to his apartment to find Mug dangling from the lobby ceiling, swinging back and forth in an orange safety harness about ten feet off the floor. As with most things, his situation had no discernable effect on Mug's expression or apparent mood.

"Mug?" Tim said, stopping next to the mail slots. "Are you okay?"

Mug grunted, swinging slowly around like the world's ugliest chandelier.

Tim had never learned to speak Zombie (or Unghurr, as the Society For the Advancement of Undead Rights preferred to call their language) as it wasn't part of the core curriculum in high school and only starting to appear in course catalogues at a select few universities. There wasn't even a translation app for smartphones. Although they were slowly starting to make a few small steps in the direction of inclusion, zombies were still considered the bottom of the societal barrel. They still worked the worst jobs, whether it was playing the most bruising and physically damaging sports, picking the most dangerously inaccessible crops, or cleaning the toilets at werewolf bars.

"Oh, hello Tim," Dede said, gliding through the office wall. She noticed his slightly charred appearance. "Long day?"

Tim nodded. "What happened to Mug?"

"No one's sure," Dede said. "We think he might have gone up there to replace a bulb or something and his harness jammed."

"How long has he been up there?" Tim asked.

"Most of the afternoon," Dede said. "I was trying to get a hold of him because the garbage disposal in the party room was blocked again. I don't know how many times I've told them not to put bones in it. I even posted a sign! Anyway, I came down and here he was."

"Shouldn't we try to get him back down?" Tim suggested.

"Oh yes," Dede said. "It would be dreadful if he fell on anyone from up there. We've got some painters coming in to re-do the gymnasium and they have a ladder. Should be tall enough to get him down."

"When are they coming?" Tim asked.

"They were supposed to be here already," Dede said, looking at her watch, which had actually stopped working at roughly the same time as her physical body.

"Maybe you should call them," Tim said.

"Mmm, good idea," Dede said, wandering back through the wall.

Tim took one last look up at the swinging handyman and then headed for the elevators. There were only so many problems a person could solve in a single day and he was well over his limit.

He reached his apartment and let himself in, where he was greeted by another unexpected sight. A woman in her 20s was scuttling across the floor like a beetle. She was wearing a black Bauhaus concert T shirt and green leather pants. When she reached the wall, she paused for a moment, looked up with wild, red-rimmed eyes and then climbed that, too.

"What the hell?" Tim muttered.

"Oh, hey, bro!" Keef said, materializing from the kitchen. "This is, uh … oh crap. I can't remember if her name is Arya or Nadine."

"Why is she climbing my walls?" Tim asked with the sinking curiosity of a person who not only knows the answer to the question he has just asked, but also the answers to the several inevitable follow-up questions. He looked over at the kitchen table and saw several empty blood bags, some of which had fallen on the floor in puddles.

"Uh, yeah," Keef said. "Um, would you mind if she hung out here for a while? Her parents are pretty closed-minded about the whole transitioning thing."

"You told me you weren't going to do this anymore," Tim said, closing the door. He looked up to see Arya or Nadine was now making her way across the ceiling.

"That was totally my plan," Keef said. "That's why I avoided the clubs, man! You know I don't want the hassle any more than you do."

"There isn't another one scuttling around in here someplace, is there?" Tim asked, looking around anxiously. Freshly turned vampires could be unpredictable and ravenously hungry until they stabilized.

"No," Keef said. "She passed out at the first sight of blood. Kind of funny when you think about it. You wanna be a vampire, but you zonk at the sight of an open vein? Good luck not starving to death, chickie!"

"She can't stay here," Tim said.

"I can't kick her out!" Keef said. "She's got nowhere to go! At least, not that I know of. What do you want me to do? Just toss her out in the street? You know what'll happen to her if I do that!"

Tim did know. Chances were good that she would be picked up trying to eat somebody's dog and taken to a detox clinic, where she would be locked in a cell and given Hemetol, a chemical compound that would interrupt her biological conversion to vampirism by making her permanently allergic to actual blood. Those who were subjected to this treatment were limited to synthetic blood compounds for the rest of their lives. In theory, this made them less of a threat to the human population, but also made them second-class citizens in the vampire world, which regarded them as little more than junkie slaves.

"You said you were done with this!" Tim said. "No more turning coeds into vampires! The last one stole my laptop and sold it for a 24-pack of AB Negative!"

"I know!" Keef said. "But you know what happens to me when I go to the clubs! I can't help myself, man!"

"So this is my fault for taking you there?" Tim said. "Is that what you're saying?"

"No," Keef said. "Well, maybe. I dunno. Look, let's not get into all that right now, okay? Just let her stay for the 48 hours. By then, she'll be stable and I'll figure something else out. It's already been almost 24. She's, like, halfway there already!"

Tim watched as the woman crawled down off the ceiling onto the floor. She approached the couch slowly, like a lion sneaking up on a wildebeest, and then pounced, sinking her stubby fangs into one of the cushions.

"Fine," Tim groaned. "Just keep her out of my room. And the kitchen. In fact, just don't let her out of your room. I wake up with her sinking her teeth into any part of my anatomy and I'll stake her myself. Got it?"

"Totally," Keef said. "You won't hear word one. Guaranteed."

Tim trudged into the apartment as Keef enticed the fledgling vampire back into his room with a bag of Scabs. Tim deposited his laptop bag on the counter and pulled on gloves to clean up the blood bags and their spilled contents.

Maybe this was a good time to look for another apartment, he thought. A smaller one. One that would not have enough room for his brother and his ever-growing army of vampire groupies. There were some nice condo towers going up in Lower Purgatory. Maybe he would check out the floor plans after dinner. Some place with really big windows that let in a lot of natural light would be a nice change. He saw so little of the sun that he and his brother were starting to develop the same complexion.

He had just finished sanitizing the table and mopping the floor when he heard a knock at the door. Tim pulled his gloves off and went to answer it. Hopefully it wasn't his brother's other female guest from the previous night, back after having changed her mind about the squeamishness. The other, even less attractive alternative was that it was his mother, back with another one of the girls from her salon. If it was either of those, he decided that he would definitely move and not tell any member of his family where he was going. They would just show up one day and he would be gone. Let Keef try and get a place on his own, the freeloading bloodsucker.

He opened the door to see Carmilla standing in the hallway.

"Carmilla?" he said, surprised. "How did you know where I live?"

"Please," she said, walking past him and into the apartment. "I'm an investigator. Your address is right in your file, dude."

Tim closed the door. "Yeah, I guess that's true."

"Cool building," she said. She inclined her head at the sound of scuttling from Keef's bedroom. "What's that?"

"My brother," Tim said. He thought about elaborating but couldn't think of a way to do it that wouldn't sound ridiculous. "Listen, I never got to say thanks for getting me out of that jam the other night."

"No problem," she said. "You got anything to drink?"

Tim went into the kitchen and opened the fridge, where he pulled out a couple of Hellfire beers. The only good thing about having Keef as a roommate was that he didn't have to worry about him stealing food from the fridge. He popped the caps and returned to the dining room. Carmilla was sitting at one of the chairs, looking around.

"Your brother's a vampire," she said, taking the bottle.

"Yes," Tim said, sitting down. He thought about asking her how she knew that, but the zero-sun curtains and empty bags of Scabs were pretty obvious clues. "It makes for an occasionally strained living arrangement."

"I bet," she said. "Heard you had an interesting day today."

"Yeah," Tim said. "If you call being nearly melted by a djinn interesting, sure."

Carmilla put her bottle on the table and looked him in the eye. "You were set up."

Tim almost choked on his beer. "Say what?"

"I checked with HEMT," Carmilla said. "Nobody in their unit swept the place before you got there. You were the first one into the hot zone."

"But..." Tim could barely believe her. "The file said they went through the place two days ago and found nothing."

"It did," she said. "They didn't."

"But how in the hell could that happen?" Tim asked.

"Simple," Carmilla said. "Somebody put a false entry in the claim file."

Tim was stunned. "But who would do that?"

"Somebody who doesn't want you around," Carmilla said. "Somebody looking for a plausible and non-suspicious way to get rid of you."

Tim's mind was racing. "Okay, the claims file is assigned to SIU, which means it's locked..."

"Right," Carmilla said. "So theoretically, the only person who could edit it would be somebody from within the department."

"But I just went out for a drink with all of them!" Tim said. "They told me the department's like a big family! They told me that everyone in SIU looks out for each other!"

Carmilla nodded. "They told me the same thing when I started. It's bullshit."

"They seemed sincere at the time," Tim muttered, his voice trailing off. He felt foolish for having believed any of it.

"Look," Carmilla said. "SIU investigates all of the big money stuff. We have almost no oversight. We report directly to the board, not to anyone internally. You want to get away with a truly massive fraud, it helps to have somebody in our department willing to look the other way."

"You're suggesting that somebody in SIU is on the take," Tim said. "But who?"

He thought of Xana and her 22 kids. The occasional bribe would buy a lot of school lunches or swimming lessons. Or Jasper, who didn't like the fact that he no longer got his anniversary bonus because he had been there so long. That was the kind of petty thing that might make someone decide there was nothing wrong with making some extra money on the side. Lonnie had said at one point that he liked to take a lot of vacations to werewolf resorts, which were expensive. And George had mentioned something about blood spa treatments, which weren't cheap, either.

"Don't know," Carmilla said. "Could be any of them. Or all of them."

"I don't believe this," Tim said. "I only just started at this job!"

"Why do you think there aren't a whole lot of openings?" Carmilla said.

"So that's why you prefer to stick to yourself," Tim said.

"Right," she said. "I'm the only one I trust."

"So why are you telling me this?" Tim asked.

"Dunno, really," Carmilla said. "You're new. I was new not so long ago."

"Is that why you were at Circle 9 that night?" Tim asked. "You were watching out for me?"

Carmilla laughed. "No. I'm working on a big auto case. Azmoda owns a bunch of chop shops all over the city. They traffic in cursed parts. Insert them into high-end cars they use in staged accidents. Bodily injury claims through the roof. I've been tracking them for months. But lately, the Triad's been getting pushed off its corner by some new gang. Call themselves the Sons of Darkness."

Tim sat up a little straighter in his chair.

"You've heard of these guys?" Carmilla said, noticing his reaction.

"After a fashion," Tim said. "They might have a connection to an identity theft that I was working."

Was the person in the hood who had stolen the statue outside the club one of the Sons of Darkness or just some random weirdo? Cursed artefacts were one of the most commonly stolen items, as the black market for them was enormous. The vast majority of them were fake, but that didn't stop people from paying through the nose for a cell phone case they believed would make a work rival type a series of obscene texts to the boss. Or a water bottle that made their breath smell like urine. Or a Fitwatch that caused heart attacks.

"So, what's your story, anyway?" Carmilla said. "Nobody with any ambition wants to work in the SIU. It's a dead end. You're out of sight, out of mind. The ones who do know about you are either suspicious you'll investigate them or afraid that you already have. Never met a human who actually wanted to be there."

"What are you doing there if it's so bad?" Tim asked reflexively.

"Short-term detour," Carmilla said.

"Short term?" Tim said. "Haven't you been there for, what? Twenty years or something?"

"Twenty-one," Carmilla said. "Originally applied to be a cop. They turned me down because of my ... background. It takes forever for me to even get legal standing to file an appeal, but I'm not giving up. The claims investigator job seemed like a good stopgap. At least I get to keep some of the skills sharp."

Tim nodded. The police department was, predictably, one of the public bodies most resistant to integration. In a city where many human residents lived in the suburbs and still considered supernatural individuals to be a threat, the idea of a vampire or werewolf answering the call for a late-night break-in was still taking its time to become an easily-accepted cultural norm. Only three of the 44 city council members were non-human, and they all represented inner city wards. This was exacerbated by the fact that many non-humans were ineligible for the necessary ID required to vote in the first place.

"Right," Tim said. "I could see you doing that."

"You didn't answer my question," Carmilla said.

"I was the first one in my family to go to university," Tim said. "That was a big deal for my parents. My dad has spent his whole life running the supernatural pest control business he inherited from his father 30 years ago. My mother runs a salon. My brother got into college, but he dropped out almost immediately. Then he became a vampire, which made it even harder for him to hold down a job than before. Even one that catered specifically to his abilities. I did an internship at Crimson Seal shortly after I graduated. Then I got offered a contract. Then a full-time gig. It was always really important to my parents that I had a job they could brag about to their friends."

"My mother's the same way," Carmilla said.

"I never really had any intention of moving up the corporate ladder," Tim said. "Still don't. When I started, I thought that insurance was the most boring thing in the world. But then when I worked as an adjuster, I started to see the flipside of it all. The seamy underbelly. I did some work on some claims that turned into pretty big fraud investigations. One of them, they were even talking about bringing in a forensic accounting team from outside to look into the finances. But the most interesting cases always got taken away and handed over to SIU. The more it happened, the more I started to think that was where I wanted to go, too."

Carmilla's phone beeped. She pulled it out of her jacket and glanced at the screen.

"I have to go," she said, getting up.

"Okay," Tim said, standing up. Half of her beer was left in the bottle. "Any suggestions on what I should do?"

"Yeah," Carmilla said. "Try not to die. And let me know if you hear anything."

13

Tim emailed to say that he was sick and wouldn't be coming in the next morning. He wasn't really sick, but he thought almost being killed by a djinn was as good a reason as any to take a day off. Plus, he kind of wanted to find out which one of his coworkers might have tried to get him killed before he went out for another drink with them.

He also had no intention of hanging around the apartment with the curtains drawn while his brother tried to pry his new girlfriend down off the ceiling, either. He needed to get out of the apartment and start hunting down answers to his many questions.

He had only worked one case since starting in the SIU before the apparent bureaucratic mix-up with the djinn. Volkerps had seemed genuinely shocked that the wrong date had been entered for the HEMT sweep, but he was a demon and it was hard to get a read on whether or not his concern was genuine. In reality, anyone in the department could have done it.

It followed, therefore, that the Zoudini case was the reason somebody might have tried to bump him off. But why? It wasn't like he really knew anything. He was sure that the possession was real and had spawned a cursed artefact that had recorded what appeared to be a resurrection prophecy, but he didn't know what the prophecy meant, even after he had managed to translate it.

The prophecy had mentioned the Sons of Darkness, which also happened to be the name of a new criminal gang making inroads in the city, but Tim had never heard of them before. He did know somebody who might be able to point him in the right direction, but there were a couple of other things he wanted to check out first.

Number one was the source of the prophecy. Resurrection prophecies weren't unusual. Lots of demons who had been in one way or another cast out or exorcised tended to indulge in them. It was basically the metaphysical equivalent of flipping your victim off from behind bars. Most of them were harmless and temporary. In his line of work, Tim's father had seen quite a few of them. It was kind of a job hazard for exorcists, which was one of the reasons that they had formed a union and were one of the most expensive remediation specialists you could hire. Most ordinary demons could barely manage a few backwards profanities or at most a threat to return and eat somebody's reproductive organs before they snapped out again.

Belial, however, did not sound like one of your average, appliance-squatting entities. He was a former king, one of the legendary demon overlords of a time when they and not humans had been in charge of things. His exploits were a matter of record in some of the oldest grimoires in history. He was the master of an army that had ruled—according to legend—for thousands of years. Based on the accounts, he was not an entity of the friendly, demon-next-door variety that many companies used to sell their time share condos, sports cars and breakfast cereals. He was a murderous, torture- and genocide-loving monster of immense power and fearsome temper.

So why, exactly, had his resurrection prophecy come out of the mouth of a second-rate registered non-seer on the verge of financial ruin?

A prophecy like that was supposed to have an audience. The bigger, the better. It was supposed to cajole supporters and terrify enemies. But the only person who had heard it first hand was a 61-year-old widow with six cats and an unnatural interest in penguin mating habits. It made no sense.

Tim's first stop was the Crowley Clinic. His hope was that Madame Zoudini had regained consciousness and might possibly be able to shed more light on what had happened. It wasn't unusual for victims of possession to gradually recover more memories of their experiences over time. When he inquired at the front desk, however, he got something of a surprise.

"Sorry," the clerk said. "No record of a patient with that name."

"Are you sure?" Tim said. "Maybe she recently checked out."

"Nope," the clerk said, leaning in to look more closely at his computer. "I have no record that a patient with that name was ever admitted."

"That doesn't make any sense," Tim said. He double-checked the spelling of both the psychic's real and professional names without success. The clerk even spun the monitor around to confirm both.

"Sorry," he said. "You must have us confused with another clinic. Maybe it was the Sanctum Centre."

"No," Tim said. "It was definitely here. She only checked in a few days ago. Are you positive?"

"Sorry," the clerk said, shrugging.

This is crazy, Tim thought. Patients didn't just disappear without a trace.

"Okay," Tim said. "Would I be able to speak to Dr. Blatty? She was the one I was talking to originally."

"Sorry," the clerk said. "Doctor Blatty no longer works here. I believe she transferred to another facility."

"What?" Tim said. "That also doesn't make any sense. She told me she still had a full month to go on her residency."

"Sorry," the clerk repeated. "I'm afraid I don't know all the details. Is there anything else I can help you with?"

Tim stood at the counter in disbelief. "This woman was admitted in a coma," he pressed. "When she woke up, she levitated three feet off the bed on a huge ring of spectral flame!"

"Yes," the clerk said with a slightly patronizing smile. "We do see quite a lot of that sort of behaviour, I'm afraid. The unusual is a matter of routine around here."

"Do you know where Dr. Blatty went?" Tim asked.

"I'm afraid I can't discuss personnel matters," the clerk said.

"Surely there must be somebody in here who remembers this woman!" Tim said, unable to hide his exasperation.

"Sir, I'm going to have to ask you to lower your voice," the clerk said. "This is a wellness facility."

"Sorry," Tim said. "I'm just having a hard time trying to understand how one of your patients could just disappear!"

"Sir," the clerk said, adopting a more officious tone. "Our patients do not just disappear, as you put it. We are a fully licenced and registered facility rated as one of the top five spectral-"

"Apologies," Tim said, cutting off the promotional spiel. "I didn't mean to disparage your top five facility."

The clerk cleared his throat and settled himself at the keyboard. "Is there anything else I might assist you with?"

"It appears not," Tim said. "Thanks."

Tim turned and headed back out through the double doors. What in the hell was going on here? The last time he had seen Madame Zoudini, she had been levitating off her bed spouting flames, all because he had shown her a picture of the statue that had suddenly appeared in her front parlour—the same statue that had been stolen by gangsters and then stolen by person or persons unknown. He briefly thought about trying to sneak up to peek into her room, but there was little chance that he would be able to do that unseen by security. If he was caught, they could ban him from the place, which would make doing his job exceedingly difficult.

So what had happened? Had her admitting record been wiped out by a computer glitch? The same kind of computer glitch that had caused Tim to walk into a house occupied by a djinn? The chance of such a co-incidence was, for someone with years of risk analysis experience, zippo.

But if she wasn't here, then where in the hell was she? Had she woken up in the middle of the night and wandered off, unnoticed? Patients did it all the time, especially if they had a bit of supernatural help, although facilities like the Crowley Clinic were anxious to downplay such incidents for obvious reasons. You didn't get to be ranked fifth in the country if you kept losing track of your patients, after all.

Tim drove to Madame Zoudini's psychic shop, but the windows were dark and there was no answer at either the front or back doors. He no longer had the key, so he couldn't just let himself in, even if he wanted to.

Okay, he thought. On to option two.

Tim drove across town to the lower Purgatorio District. He was about to turn on to Anita Browdley's street, but the road was blocked by orange cones strung with yellow caution tape.

Oh crap, Tim thought. This doesn't look good.

Tim found a parking spot on the next block and walked back to Browdley's street. He stepped between the cones and made his way down to where Madame Zoudini's last customer lived in a 2-storey blackstone walkup next to a gourmet charcuterie.

The deli was still there, but Anita Browdley's apartment was mostly gone.

Tim stared at it in disbelief. Browdley's apartment was a charred ruin. The entire second floor was gone and the first floor was melted rubble. The buildings on either side were totally untouched, a dead giveaway that the blaze was not of the regular, non-spectral variety. There was a fire station only three blocks away. That meant that they would have arrived within five to ten minutes of the call. It looked like they had managed to save some of the lower foundation, but none of the main structure or contents. The fire had been swift and merciless. Anyone who was inside at the time it started would have been a goner. Fire departments did have special gear to deal with demon fires, but they burned so hot and so fast that the only realistic chance of survival was not to be anywhere near one when it started. Tim knew, based on his experience as an adjuster, that this place was a total write off. They would need to knock the remains down and rebuild totally from scratch.

Tim entered the charcuterie and found a satyr working behind the counter. He had curly horns, a long beard and a nametag that identified him as Dalag. His hooves were covered up with trendy white moon boots and he had a spangly yellow belt over a green hospital robe. Tim didn't know why such an unusually high percentage of satyrs were hipsters, but there was a lot he didn't know about satyrs.

"Hi," Tim said.

"Oy, man," Dalag said. "Wanna try a sample of hellhound groin? It's infused with werewolf gland and some distilled vampire regurge. Just put it out five minutes ago!"

"Uh, no thanks," Tim said. He didn't like the sound of any of those things individually and doubted that combining them together somehow made them more appetizing. "Were you around when the fire happened next door?"

"No, man," Dalag said. "Happened just the other night. Street's been blocked off for like, the whole day. Kinda sucks for business."

Tim reminded himself that satyrs were not renowned for the empathy. "Did you hear what happened?"

Dalag scratched his chin, pulling on his beard. "I think they said it was some electrical thing. That's what I heard, anyway."

Tim nodded. He knew that it definitely was not some sort of electrical thing. "Did you know the woman who lived there?"

"Yeah!" Dalag nodded. "She used to come in here all the time! Loved the Chupacabra meatballs! Real sad."

"She was in there when it happened?" Tim asked.

"That's what they said," Dalag said. "There was a medical examiner's van out there for a while, but I guess it was so hot that, you know, there wasn't really anything for them to haul away?"

"Right," Tim said. "Thanks."

"You sure I can't interest you in some troll hearts?" Dalag said, brightening again. "Or maybe some seasoned unicorn hoof? All locally sourced!"

"Maybe another time," Tim said. "Thanks."

Tim opened the door and made his way back out onto the street to take another look at the ruins. It looked like the fire had started on the main floor, blocking both the front and rear exits at the same time. Anyone who had been upstairs when it started would have had a matter of seconds. If she had been asleep at the time, Anita Browdley would probably not even been aware of what was happening. Unpleasant as it was, it was probably better that way than if she had woken up and tried to get out. It looked like she would not be getting married and taking that honeymoon to Antarctica after all. Tim wondered if her fiancé had also been in the building at the time.

Okay, he thought. I've got two witnesses. One of them has disappeared and the other one just died in a fire that was quite obviously deliberately set. And somebody might have tried to kill me, too.

Although he wasn't an actuary, Tim was willing to bet that the chances that all three of those occurrences may have been coincidental was what a loss prevention manager might call statistically irrelevant.

The big question was what to do next. If somebody at work was trying to kill him, he needed to figure out who that was, because there was nothing to stop them giving it another try.

His phone buzzed. He pulled it out of his pocket and saw a reminder for a lunch appointment in 15 minutes. Tim smiled, allowing himself to relax a little.

He had a date. Sort of. And it was the first one in ages that had not been orchestrated by his mother.

14

Tim had dated Tabitha Graves in their last year of university.

They met at the movies. They were the only two people who had showed up for a screening of the old zombie cult classic *Life of the Living Dead*, a documentary-style slice-of-life drama about a day in the life of an undead window cleaner. The movie had come out in the mid-60s and had been intended as a socially-conscious call-to-arms to promote the plight of the undead community and boost their call for more human-like rights. Unfortunately, it had been shot, edited and produced so incompetently that it had probably set undead rights back by a decade. The main actor wasn't even a zombie himself, and his tics, mannerisms and makeup varied wildly from one scene to the next. One minute he would be speaking English (with a noticeable Australian accent) and unable to use his left hand, and in the next shot he would be near comatose and missing the top half of his skull. Some scenes were narrated in a series of groans that was, it seemed, supposed to approximate Unghurr, but bore as much relation to it as dog barks did to whale song.

The movie was released to general confusion and mockery and then promptly disappeared before being resurrected on the rep film circuit as a low-grade cult film. People would dress up in overalls, carry buckets and toss squeegees at the screen during key scenes. Tim hadn't dressed up, but he hadn't been able to talk any of his friends into going either. Tabitha, it seemed, had met similar resistance. The two of them had sat rather awkwardly in the otherwise empty theatre. She had made a crack about brains, he had laughed, and it had gone from there. They had chatted briefly after the movie. She gave him her number, and they had dated for the next eight months.

Nothing had really gone wrong. They had never had any big fight or anything like that. When school was done, she had left town to go to law school. Tim had stayed, having landed the internship at Crimson Seal. They had kept in touch. She had graduated and, instead of taking the bar exam had enrolled in police college. She had risen quickly through the department and was currently working as a sergeant in charge of the paranormal crimes division, where she had run several task forces on organized crime. Her name had been in the news most recently after her team took down a Triad-affiliated gang running a succubus trafficking operation out of an old monastery.

Tim still thought about her all the time. It bugged him that the timing on their relationship just never seemed to have lined up. She was dating some lawyer in the prosecutor's office named Jared, who, based on the photos on the city website, was regrettably handsome. Meanwhile, Tim's mother kept ambushing him with unregistered seers. Not that there was anything wrong with seers, per se. The ones that his mother tended to hire didn't seem to have a lot to talk about beyond reality TV or the dating habits of the celebrities who appeared thereon.

It had been a year since they had last seen each other. Tabitha had been promoted to sergeant and some of her friends had thrown a party. Tim had stopped in to pass on his congratulations and had gotten to meet Jared, who was even more regrettably handsome in person than he was online. Tim had not stayed long. The party was mostly cops, none of whom he knew. When he went to leave, she had kissed him on the cheek and then squeezed his hand a little more tightly than usual.

"I miss you, Gurg," she said, smiling. Gurg was the name of the zombie window cleaner in *Life of the Living Dead*. "Call me sometime."

Tim had smiled and said *you bet* but hadn't actually done it. Tabitha was happy about her promotion and slightly buzzed after a few too many glasses of Chablis. Simple as that.

And then last week she had emailed him and asked if he wanted to go to lunch. Tim had just started his new job and so they had gone back and forth a couple of times before settling on a date and time. She had suggested the Cursed Bride, which happened to be the same place they had gone for their very first drink after the movie all those years ago. Tim didn't think there was anything to the choice beyond nostalgia, or at least, that's what he kept telling himself.

She was waiting in a booth near the entrance when he arrived. Her black overcoat was folded neatly on the seat next to her. She never liked to hang up her jacket at restaurants. It went back to the time her jacket had been stolen by a werewolf who was high on wolfsbane. Her cell phone and keys had been in the inside pocket. She had gotten both back, but they had been covered in so much fur that no amount of dry cleaning would get the musk off.

She was neatly dressed in a dark blue suit jacket with narrow lapels. She had cut her strawberry blonde hair. Where it had previously been halfway down her back, now it was styled into a pixie cut. Tim assumed that was because she was tired of having to tie and band it up to meet the police department's uniform code for female officers. Still, it looked good.

"Tim-boy!" she said, getting out of the booth to give him a hug.

"Hey Tabby," Tim said. She smelled good, too. "You look terrific. How's things?"

"Busy," Tabitha said. "I've got two task forces running concurrently and they just decided to do a major software upgrade on the incident reporting system that almost deleted our entire known offenders database."

"Ugh," Tim said as they sat down. "Your IT department sounds suspiciously like ours."

"The place is so full of trolls right now that we might as well relocate to under a bridge," Tabitha said.

Tim laughed. "Yeah, they're not the most outgoing bunch. I had to return my old laptop when I left the claims department. They were in the sub-sub-basement. I had to use the flashlight on my cell phone to see where I was going. They like light even less than the average vampire."

The waiter came over to take their drink orders. Tabitha got a water. Tim was off the clock and decided on a beer.

"Ooh," Tabitha said after he had ordered. "You insurance types like to hit it hard, I see."

"It's my day off," Tim said.

"Didn't you just start?" Tabitha said. "How's the new job?"

Tim hesitated for a moment.

"Uh oh," Tabitha said, noticing his delay. "What's wrong? Demon boss?"

"Actually, my boss *is* a demon," Tim said. "But an extremely competent one. Has his Paranormal Risk Management certification and his Employee Resource Management diploma and everything."

"Well then," Tabitha said. "So what's the problem?"

Tim debated whether or not to tell her about his suspicions about what had happened with the djinn. His initial reaction was no, obviously not. He didn't have any proof of anything. He would probably sound like he was losing his mind. On the other hand, he had never lied to Tabitha or felt the need to do so. If he started into it now, however, it would probably consume their whole lunch. He decided he would wait until he had something more concrete to go on.

"It's just a very isolated department that hasn't had anyone new step into it for a very long time," Tim said. "They have their own way of doing things. I think it'll just take a little bit of getting used to, that's all."

"You're doing investigations now, though, right?" Tabitha said. "That's cool! You've always wanted to do that."

"That's true," Tim nodded. "In some repects, I guess our jobs are kind of similar."

"What have you worked on so far?" she asked. "Or are you not allowed to say?"

"No, I can talk generally," Tim said. "First one was an identity theft. Business was in trouble, so they thought she might be faking it."

"And was she?" Tabitha asked.

The waiter arrived with their drinks. Tabitha glanced at the menu and ordered a chicken salad. Tim had skipped breakfast and was starving, so he got a burger.

"No, she wasn't," Tim said.

"That sucks in a way, I guess," Tabitha said. "If she was, then you get credit for catching the fraud and your company doesn't have to pay out."

"Well we would," Tim said. "Except she disappeared."

"What?" Tabitha said. "As in left the country?"

"Don't know," Tim said. "She was checked into the Crowley Clinic. I went back to do a follow-up interview and she wasn't there."

"That doesn't make sense," Tabitha said. "Why leave just before you get the payout?"

"It gets better," Tim said. "When I asked, they told me no patient by her name had ever been there."

"They what?" Tabitha said.

"I asked to talk to the resident who had been on call when she was admitted," Tim continued. "She wasn't there, either. They told me she had transferred to another facility, but they wouldn't say which one."

"Okay," Tabitha said. "That is some extremely dodgy-sounding behaviour, Timmy."

"It gets weirder," Tim said. He explained what happened with the fire, his adventure with the djinn and Carmilla's warning. It actually took less time than he thought. Their food arrived just as he was finishing, but Tabitha didn't touch hers.

"Okay, not to get all official and everything," Tabitha said. "But I think it might be a good idea for you to come in and give a statement. Just so we've got some of this on the record."

"I can't!" Tim said. "I shouldn't even be telling you this stuff now."

"We both know that corporate NDAs and confidentiality agreements don't legally extend to criminal activity," Tabitha said. "I don't care about that side of it. I am legitimately worried about you. A case could be made that your life is in danger."

"It's not just that," Tim said. "I don't know what any of this stuff might mean. You work in the organized crime unit. Have you heard of a group calling itself the Sons of Darkness?"

"No," Tabitha said. "Who are they supposed to be?"

"When the identity theft happened, a statue appeared," Tim said. "Looks like a record of the prophecy. It got stolen by some gangsters."

"Which gangsters?" Tabitha asked.

"The ones that own Circle 9," Tim said.

"Azmoda?" Tabitha said, her eyebrows rising.

"That's him," Tim said. "I went down there to check it out."

"Tim," Tabitha said, lowering her voice. "The Hellspawn Triad are not terribly fond of people popping by to check them out."

"I know," Tim said. "They dangled me over a pit and almost dropped me in, but I got away."

Tabitha rubbed her temples and then giggled in disbelief. "Oh, Gurg."

"Anyway, the rumor is that the Triad is being pushed out of its operations by this new group," Tim said. "Call themselves the Sons of Darkness. It's possible one of them knocked me out and grabbed the statue when I ran out into the alley. I don't know, though. Whoever it was, they didn't have any identifying marks or brands. The Triad are at least easy to recognize on that front."

"And here I was thinking that this might be a fun little lunch," Tabitha said. "You know, get together, sit down. Have a few laughs. Now I'm fairly sure I'm going to have to transfer you into witness protection."

"Sorry, Tabby," Tim smiled.

"Was this all on your first day on the job?" she asked.

"More or less," Tim said.

"Well, that makes a big difference," Tabitha said sarcastically. "At least you didn't manage to stick your head in every hornet's nest in the city on your first day. It took two. Maybe even as many as three."

"But enough about me," Tim said, taking a bite of his burger. "How are things with you? You commissioner yet?"

Tabitha sighed and shook her head. "Don't try to change the subject."

"I'm serious!" Tim said. "How's Jared? You guys been to Italy yet? I know you were talking about it."

"Jared and I broke up," Tabitha said.

Tim stopped chewing. "Really?"

"I found out he was cheating on me with one of the assistant prosecutors," Tabitha said. "For, like, the last six months."

"Oh Tab," Tim said. "I'm sorry. That's terrible."

"And all of his friends knew about it, which makes it even worse," Tabitha said. "I would meet these people at parties! They would come over to the apartment for dinner. And they would just stand there eating my chevre crostini and drinking my wine and pretending that my so-called boyfriend was not sneaking out every lunchtime to fuck his assistant in the parking garage. It's so galling!"

"Just tell me where they are and I'll beat them up," Tim said.

"Save it, He-man," she said. "I'd rather not have to arrest you for assault. Besides, Jared used to compete in amateur MMA events. He'd probably kill you. And then I'd have to arrest him. As satisfying as that would be, I'd rather throw him behind bars for something that doesn't require your gruesome death as a pretext for his incarceration."

"I could arrange to have all his blood drained," Tim offered. "I know people. Well, they're not people, strictly speaking. But you know what I mean."

"A sweet offer," Tabitha smiled. "But I'd rather stick to legal means."

"Suit yourself," Tim said. "Just putting it out there."

"How about you?" Tabitha asked, stabbing at her salad. "You seeing anybody?"

"No," Tim said. "But it's not for my mother's lack of trying. She keeps setting me up with psychics from her salon."

"And it's not working?" Tabitha smiled.

"No," Tim said. "But she doesn't quit. It would be admirable if it didn't make my life a rotating hell of excuses to get out of these dates. I straight up told one of them that I couldn't go to dinner once because I had just been rear-ended by a truck carrying liquid nitrogen and I was literally fused to the road."

Tabitha laughed.

"Now she's taken me out of the equation," Tim said. "She doesn't tell me in advance. She just has them show up unexpectedly at scheduled events. I feel like I'm on a hidden camera reality show that never ends. Why don't we all go to the water park? Oh, look! And there's Kourtney getting off the Wet Willie! Why don't you go ask her if she'd like a snow cone?"

"How's Keef?"

"That bloodsucker is bleeding me dry," Tim said. "He's been living at my apartment since his last familiar gave him the boot."

"I kind of miss Keef," Tabitha said. "Most vampires are so stuffy and uptight. He's way more laid back."

"A little too laid back," Tim said. "A few weeks ago, he passed out in an alley on the way home from a club and almost broiled himself when the sun came out the next morning. He spent the day hiding in a dumpster."

"In other words, he hasn't changed," Tabitha said.

"Nope," Tim said. "Although he did scare the crap out of an employee for the Thai restaurant next door. Poor guy was just taking out the trash and wasn't expecting anybody to be hanging out in there. How's Tina?"

Tina was Tabitha's older sister. She worked as a pharmaceutical researcher. The last Tim had heard, she was working on an experimental treatment to make werewolves less hairy, but it had been pulled in the initial trials after producing the opposite effect. Some of the volunteers had even grown hair on their tongues. The media coverage had been predictably mocking.

"Good," Tabitha said. "She just had a little girl, so I'm an aunt now! Her name's Ariadne. She is, of course, totally adorable. Empirically. I'm not just saying that because I have aunt bias. I have about a hundred thousand photos on my phone, but I won't force you to look at them all now."

"Congratulations!" Tim said.

"Thanks," Tabitha said. "It's great, but it does kind of make me feel old."

Tabitha's phone chirped. She picked it up and had a short conversation that involved a lot of cursing under her breath. She hung up and grabbed her jacket.

"Sorry," she said, getting up. "I have to run. One of my C.I.s just got arrested selling stolen blood out of the trunk of his car during an undercover operation."

"No problem," Tim said. "I got this."

"Thanks for lunch," she said, throwing her coat on. "I'll get the next one. Do I have anything on my face?"

"You're good," Tim said, giving a thumbs up.

"Anything stuck in my teeth?" she asked, baring them.

"Jut the remnants of scumbags you have chewed up and spit out in the cause of justice," Tim said.

"You're cute," she said, kissing him on the cheek. "Look, about that other stuff we were talking about. Don't do anything stupid, okay? No more chasing after demon gangsters! Try not to get yourself killed in the next 24 hours or so. I'll do some discreet poking around from my side and see if I can find anything out. Sound good?"

"You got it, sarge," Tim said.

"I'll call you," she said, running out the door.

Tim sat back down and finished off the last of his fries. Although his work situation had not technically changed, he felt a whole lot better about his prospects than he had before lunch.

The waiter came by and he ordered another beer.

What the hell, he thought. It's my day off. And the only thing waiting for me back at my apartment is a stoner vampire and his wall-climbing new girlfriend. No reason to rush.

15

Tim went back to the office the next day, where he spent most of the morning and much of the afternoon dealing with the fallout from the Dunwich case file.

The main issue was the fact that he, an employee of Crimson Seal Insurance, LLC, had voluntarily triggered an explosion that had resulted in a fire that had destroyed most of the house, upping the reserve on the original damage claim by several hundred thousand dollars. In addition, he had been present at the scene when a third party, identified as Dwayne T. Uffelman, had sustained serious upper-body injuries that had melted much of the flesh from his head, torso and arms, leaving him as a half-skeleton, a condition that doctors believed could not be cured and that would be with him for the rest of his life. Attorneys for Mr. Uffelman had already been in contact with the company and advised that their client planned to bring a hefty lawsuit, the damage limit for which would be, in the words of their letter, "commensurate with Mr. Uffelman's great personal suffering and loss of earning potential as he was no longer able to pursue his second audition for the hit television series *Ultimate Ninja Warrior.*"

Volkerps had told Tim not to worry about any of it. Tim had the entire event on video, which corroborated his version of events. He had spent most of his morning being interviewed by two ghouls from the legal department, neither of whom had been the least bit interested in anything other than establishing a microscopically precise sequence of events. Tim was forced to re-watch every millisecond of the footage several times and provide them with his explanation for every movement and decision. He knew that it was part of their job, but it didn't make for a terribly enjoyable part of his.

"Why did you feel you needed to detonate the gas line?" one of them asked in his low, droning monotone voice. "Why not simply attempt to flee the premises without causing additional structural damage?"

Tim knew that ghouls made especially good lawyers because of their attention to detail and refusal to become emotionally engaged under any circumstances, but their questions quickly became irritating.

"Did you see what happened to the first guy?" Tim snapped. "He just tried to exit the premises. Now the only night of the year he can walk around with being stared at is Halloween."

Although Tim appeared to be in the clear, the legal department had still recommended that he be suspended from active investigations pending the findings of their internal review. Volkerps had not cared for this suggestion.

"Like Asag I will!" he had thundered, sending lightning bolts as far as the water cooler. "If I suspended an investigator every time a case file went a little sideways there'd be nobody left in the department to do the damned investigations!"

Tim appreciated the vote of confidence. After the ghouls had left, however, Volkerps had suggested that Tim might want to just hang around the office for a few days until the worst of it blew over. There were a large number of reports from the audit department that required review. Maybe it was better if Tim handled that.

The audit department ran reports on a weekly basis that reviewed transactions in the policy system. The reports were looking for a particular set of patterns that might point to suspicious behaviour on the part of advisors who might be doing the kinds of things they should not be doing. They were designed to look for internal fraud, but the transactional patterns they picked up were so broad that most of the time they were just simple mistakes and there was nothing shady about them. The reports hadn't been reviewed in almost a year, so there was a sizable backlog.

After going through the first 200 records, Tim had only found one case that looked like it might be more than a simple screw up. Most of the agents were well aware that their every move in the system was tracked by multiple programs. If they really wanted to rip off the company, there were many less transparent ways to do so.

"How are you doing?" Lonnie said, stopping by Tim's desk. "You look pretty good for a guy who went toe-to-hoof with a djinn."

"Yeah," Tim said, rubbing his eyes. "You should see the other guy."

"If you want somebody to go with you on the next call, just let me know," Lonnie said. "You know, once they let you back off reports."

"Thanks," Tim said. In the back of his mind, he couldn't help but wonder if it had been Lonnie who had set him up. The problem was, it could have been practically any of his coworkers. It wasn't a pleasant feeling.

He was halfway through his second day of reviewing the reports when his phone rang. He glanced down at the screen and saw Tabitha's caller ID. He immediately abandoned the file he had been looking at, which involved a backdated transaction to add a car to a policy the day after it had been totalled in an accident, and ran out into the hall to answer. She said she had been doing some digging and had some interesting information to share. She wanted to know when they could meet up. He impulsively invited her over for dinner, which she accepted.

Tim told Volkerps that he would work from home for the rest of the afternoon, packed his laptop up and headed for the door. On the way home, he stopped at the market and got some boneless chicken breasts, peanut oil, eggs, panko, parmigiana cheese, fresh pasta and crushed tomatoes. Tabitha had always liked his chicken parm recipe, which was one of the few things he knew how to make. Being a single man who lived with a person who ingested only blood, he rarely got the chance to cook something that was genuinely worth eating. He stopped at the enoteca next door and debated for five minutes about which bottle of wine to get. Brunello went well with this dish, but it was expensive and might make it look like he was trying too hard. Chianti was cheaper, but maybe too much so. In the end, he split the difference and went with an Amarone.

He got home and turned on his laptop, unmuting the speaker so that it would ping him if he got an email or somebody tried to contact him by messenger. Technically, this was a violation of the company's work from home policy, but he wasn't terribly concerned about that. If the company's lawyers had gotten their way, he'd be suspended right now, which would have meant he was getting paid to sit around and do nothing anyway.

The first thing he did was vacuum, sweep and scrub the apartment from floorboard to ceiling. Luckily, Keef was staying at his new girlfriend's place, lending his expertise to her project to modify everything to her new vampire lifestyle. Tim had no idea how long this new relationship would last. If history was any guide, it would probably explode fantastically sometime in the next 72 hours, but at least that meant his layabout brother was sponging off somebody else for a while. He filled almost two whole vacuum bags with dried Scabs crumbs and other junk.

Ugh, he thought, tossing the bags in the disposal chute. And that's probably not even half of what's in here. He reminded himself to take another look at those new condo plans the next time he got a chance. At this stage of dirt, moving really was pretty much the only option. He didn't have time to patch and paint the claw marks that Keef's new flame had left in the walls and ceiling, but they were only visible if you got right up close to them, so they could wait.

Once he had cleaned the place to the extent that it was cleanable, he started to work on prepping dinner. It would have been nice to have been able to soak the chicken in seasoned buttermilk for 24 hours prior to cooking, but he didn't have quite enough notice. He carefully trimmed off any excess fat and tendon and cut the breasts into medallions, which he coated in flour, soaked in egg and then transferred to the panko, which he had seasoned with his own mix of spices and ground parm. From there he transferred them into the pan, where the peanut oil was heated up to the point where they crackled as soon as he put them in. The chicken was ready to go in the oven and the pasta water was starting to bubble when his buzzer went 30 minutes later.

Tabitha looked like she had come straight from work. Her eyes were tired and her shoulders were drooped, but she brightened noticeably when she caught the whiff of fried chicken in the air.

"Ooh!" she said. "Is that chicken parm I detect?"

"It is," Tim said, taking her jacket.

"Nice!" she said. "I haven't had that in ages. Yours is the best."

"Thanks," Tim said. "Do you want to eat first?"

"Absolutely," Tabitha said. "I haven't had anything since a bagel this morning that looked like it had been run over by a tractor. And tasted like it."

Tim poured each of them a glass of wine. He would have decanted it, but his only decanter was somehow full of—surprise!—Scabs crumbs.

"I always loved this old building," Tabitha said. "It's so much nicer than those bland glass towers they're putting up next to the river."

"I was actually thinking about moving to one of those bland glass towers next to the river," Tim said.

"Why?" Tabitha said. "This place has so much personality!"

"Personalities," Tim said. "Some of them enjoy popping their heads up out of the sink in the middle of the night when you get up to pee. It's not really something that you ever get used to."

The two of them sat at Tim's small dining room table and ate, continuing their conversation from the previous lunch. Once they had finished, Tim loaded the dishes into the sink and Tabitha opened her briefcase, pulling out a map of the city that she unfolded on the table.

"Okay," she said. "I asked around with some of the other gang units. Nobody's heard the name 'Sons of Darkness' yet, but there is a new group on the street that's been pushing the Hellspawn out of some of their traditional territories." She pointed to areas that were circled in red and blue. "Okay, the red circles are strip clubs and massage parlours, which are really just fronts for brothels. Most of the women are succubi trafficked in from Russia and Eastern Europe, but it's a mix. The blue are casinos and underground gambling halls. The Hellspawn use all of them as drop points for drugs. The dealers pick them up and sell them on their individual corners. The Triad like to use dybbuk for that because they can disappear for short periods if they spot a cop."

Tim looked at the circles, which formed a rough circle around Central Hades. His eye was drawn to the centre of the circle, where it spotted something familiar.

"Here," he said, pointing. "This block."

"What about it?" Tabitha said.

"Right in the middle," Tim said. "That's pretty much exactly where Madame Zoudini's shop is."

"Okay," Tabitha said. "Do you think that's significant in some way?"

Tim grabbed his laptop and played Tabitha the recording of the prophecy that he had reversed so that it was in English instead of gibberish.

"The prophecy says that the lost key is in the middle of the net," Tim said. "According to the Lesser Key of Solomon from the Dead Sea Scrolls, the three nets of Belial are fornication, wealth, and the pollution of the sanctuary."

"Fornication and wealth," Tabitha said. "I think that brothels and casinos would certainly qualify in those two categories."

"Exactly!" Tim said.

"That just leaves pollution of the sanctuary," Tabitha said. "Any idea what that means?"

"Not sure," Tim said. "But almost everything in this city was built on top of something much older. Especially in that part of town. Maybe it refers to an old temple that was knocked down or destroyed to make room for a coffee shop or something like that."

"Demons can be real NIMBYs in that way I guess," Tabitha said, smiling.

"Especially if it's your temple," Tim said. "Imagine you're an ancient demon king like our buddy Belial, here. You're banished, your followers are all killed, and somebody knocks down your house and builds a craft beer distiller on the ruins. Chances are that you wouldn't take it so well."

"But the demon kings are just myth," Tabitha said. "I don't even know any demons who believe in that stuff."

"Until a few days ago, I would have agreed with you," Tim said. "Now, I'm not so sure."

"So you think these Sons of Darkness are working to bring their old boss back?" Tabitha said.

"That's my working hypothesis," Tim said. "If they're the ones who grabbed the statue, then they've got to be looking for this lost key, whatever it is."

"I also did some checking into your missing patient," Tabitha said. "Nobody's reported her missing. Beyond that, there's not a lot that I can do to look for her without being seen to be looking for her, if you know what I mean."

"That's okay," Tim said. "Unfortunately, it's probably too late, anyway. Based on the way she vanished and the thoroughness of the subsequent cover up, my guess is that she's no longer findable. Not in any recognizable form, anyway."

"I don't like this," Tabitha said. "And I especially don't like that you seem to be right in the middle of it."

"Me either," Tim said. "What do you suggest?"

"Well, I would tell you to drop it, but I know you better than that," Tabitha said, smiling. "You are a stubborn bastard, Timothy Lovecraft."

"You are the only person who gets to call me Timothy," Tim said.

"And you are the only one I will permit to call me Tabby," she said. "To everyone else, I am Sergeant Graves. Even my mother calls me that."

"I must confess something," Tim said.

"Oh yes, Timothy?" she said. "And what is that?"

"I always regretted not following you out there when you went to law school," he said. "Dumbest thing I ever did."

"Only as dumb as my leaving in the first place," she said, leaning forward.

Their lips had barely made contact when the door burst open and Keef walked in carrying a duffel bag over one shoulder and dragging a suitcase with only one rolling wheel behind him.

"You believe that?" he barked. "She kicked me out! There's gratitude for you!"

Tim and Tabitha separated with a start.

"I help fulfil her lifelong dream of immortality and what does she do?" Keef said, tossing the duffel bag on the table with a clank. "Tosses me out for the first Robert Pattinson-looking dirtbag to come down the pike! Says she thinks we should be free to bite other people! I said, that's fine with me, baby! See you down at the blood bank! Hope you don't get a bag of tainted O Neg just because you don't know what the hell you're looking for!"

"Hi Keef," Tabitha said, clearing her throat.

Keef looked up. As soon as he saw Tabitha, his eyes lit up. He ran across the room and scooped her up into a hug.

"Tabitha!" he shouted. "Holy crap it's so good to see you again!"

Tabitha laughed. "Thanks, Keef! It's good to see you too."

"You have no idea how miserable this hump has been since you left," Keef said, putting her down and pointing at Tim. "I know actual zombies who had more life in them."

Tabitha blushed. "How's life, Keef?"

"Oh, you know me," he said. "Easy come, easy go. Long as I got my blood, I'm just another bat hanging from the old cave roof. Hey, you guys hungry? I got a deal on Scabs down at the 24K. Eight bags for ten bucks!"

He unzipped his duffel bag and pulled out a six pack of Blood Blast and a large bag of Scabs, some of which spilled out of a rip in the bottom.

"Ah shit!" he said, trying to plug the hole and only enlarging it. Tim watched helplessly as chips flew all over his freshly swept and mopped floor. "That's why they were on sale! Those sons of bitches!"

"Oh man," Tim muttered under his breath.

Keef scooped some chips up off the floor and stuffed them in his mouth. "They're a little stale, but not too bad. You want some?"

"Thanks, Keef," Tabitha said. "But I should probably get going. Us humans have to be up early tomorrow."

"No sweat," Keef said, settling into his usual place on the sofa. "Rain check."

Tabitha turned and looked at Tim.

"Yes," she said, kissing him on the cheek. "Rain check. Definitely."

Tim watched disconsolately as she packed up her laptop, threw on her coat and headed out the door. Keef popped open one of the Blood Blasts and took a long gulp, letting out a burp.

"Oh man, that hits the spot," he said, grabbing the remote and turning on the TV. "I'm happy for you, bro. Always liked that chick. Hey, they're doing a softcore zombie marathon on Deadflix. You wanna watch some undead gettin' it on?"

"Thanks," Tim muttered. "But I think I've got some dishes to wash."

"Your loss!" Keef said. "You're missing some classics, though! *The Dead Shoes* is on at midnight! A young zombie's erotic journey from life to death to Las Vegas showgirl! It's got it all, it really does!"

"Thanks," Tim said. "But I'll pass."

Tim turned and headed back into the kitchen. Maybe he would shower tonight instead of in the morning. Sometimes it wasn't such a bad thing that the hot water wasn't always working.

"Suit yourself!" Keef called after him as he went. "You know where I'll be if you change your mind."

All too well, Tim thought. He decided the shower could wait until morning. Now was as good a time to look at those new condo floorplans as any.

16

Tim spent most of the next day going through the audit reports with a golem from the accounting department. The golem's name was Ted. He was eight feet tall and made of solid red clay that had originally come from the land excavated for the foundations of the old city hall. His first job after he was animated, in fact, had been to guard the construction site and make sure there were no thefts.

"Not that different from what I do today," Ted said, smiling to the extent that his face could do that. Most golems had been sculpted to look fearsome or blank and Ted, despite his best efforts, was definitely the former.

They were reviewing the transactions of an agency where reports had identified a long series of irregularities over a three-year period. Not surprisingly, this three-year period coincided with a time where the agent had gotten divorced and been charged (but not convicted) with several minor criminal offences ranging from misdemeanor assault to driving while impaired. Despite hefty legal bills and a growing fondness for betting (and losing) on Chupacabra fights, said agent had also recently purchased a 40-foot sailboat and two Mercedes roadsters for his twin daughters.

"They key is to look below the numbers," Ted said as they went through the extracted worksheets one at a time. "We golem have a saying: If the ground is too flat, then that's where the worms are. The real story is always what's going on beneath the surface."

Tim emerged several hours later feeling like he never needed to look at another spreadsheet for as long as he lived. Instead of heading for the subway station to get the train home, he made his way south down Paradise Avenue to the point where it crossed Purgatory Avenue at Milton Square. This was the geographic centre of the Hades district; the point that he and Tabitha had been looking at on her map the night before.

He could see Madame Zoudini's dark storefront a half a block up on his left. The rest of the places were equally bereft of customers. There were pawn shops and tattoo places, liquor stores and massage parlours, run-down theatres with blank marquees and hotels offering hourly rates. Looking at it now, it was hard to imagine that Hades had at one time been the thriving centre of the city. People used to flock to this place to go to shows, eat at restaurants and listen to live music.

The crowds had become a magnet for crime and years of bad management had let the area rot. Numerous ill-conceived rejuvenation plans had been proposed and half-heartedly implemented, but they had all failed. A get-tough-on-crime style mayor had managed to sweep most of the worst of it out of sight, but the majority of the criminal activity had simply relocated itself in the surrounding area. They weren't quite as visible out there on the street, but they were still there, humming away just below the surface.

The only things visible on the surface now were a couple of skateboarding demons grinding away on the metal rails surrounding the stairs in the square. They looked to be no more than 12 or 15 years old. One of them had a bandanna tied around his horns that hung down over his eyes in the way that had been made trendy by demon hip hop artist Li'l Horny Bastard, who had recently been jailed for elder abuse. His friend was a dybbuk. Tim wondered if they were lookouts for the Triad or just bored kids looking for something more interesting to do on a Friday night.

This is the centre of the net, Tim thought. At least, geographically. A three-block walk north on Purgatory Avenue would bring him to the casinos and gambling dens, many of which were located in the basement of the old industrial block near Harris Street. A similar distance in the opposite direction would bring him to the strip clubs and massage parlours of the old Tenderloin District. Circle 9 was three blocks away on Paradise and the labs that made many of the drugs sold on the corners were hidden on the upper floors of the old industrial buildings to the north.

Tabitha had not said as much, but it was common knowledge that the reason most of the crime survived in those areas was not because of bribes paid to bent police officers and city officials–although that certainly happened–but was more due to a philosophy of ruthless practicality. The reasoning was that these things were going to happen, so instead of chasing them all over the city, it was easier to confine it to one central area. Here, in theory, it was easier to keep an eye on it. Tourists didn't come to this part of town any more and residents knew well enough to avoid it, too, preferring to stick to the tonier environs further to the east and west.

Tim looked around the square. There had never been a cathedral or temple here that he knew of, and a check of the planning archive at city hall had confirmed it. That meant that two of the nets—namely fornication and wealth—intersected here, but the third, pollution of the sanctuary, did not.

Maybe I'm misreading the whole thing, Tim thought. Maybe I'm just getting overexcited about my first case and thinking that there's more to all of this than there really is.

Maybe, he thought. But that didn't explain why Madame Zoudini had gone missing. Or who had grabbed the statue. Or the fact that somebody at work might have tried to kill him.

His mind drifted back to what Ted had said earlier that day: *The real story is what's going on beneath the surface.*

But there's nothing beneath the surface here, Tim thought. It's all just-

He stopped.

Except there was something beneath the surface.

The Crypt Network.

Tim couldn't remember exactly how old it was. It had to go back at least 30 years and maybe as many as 50. It had been one of many ambitious plans designed to turn the neighbourhood around and, in retrospect, one of the dumbest.

The argument in favour of the idea had gone something like this: People don't go to central Hades because there's so much crime. People don't like walking the streets surrounded by blood junkies looking to score and succubi trying to turn tricks. But what if they could go there without walking the streets? What if we took all the businesses and moved them underground?

As dumb as it sounded, the idea had gotten enough traction that a portion of the Network had been built. The plan was to build almost 40 kilometres of tunnels in five phases, but the project never made it to the end of Phase 1. The idea that people would want to do their shopping and eating in a dank concrete tunnel out of sight of the sun, trees, easy exits and working elevators was not, much to the city planner's apparent amazement, an immediate hit. Instead of moving people away from crime, they gave crime a whole new arena in which to thrive. Although a few retailers moved in at the beginning, lured by generous city incentives on their leases, fewer than one third of the available spaces were occupied by the time of the grand opening.

Although the development commission was confident that "If we dig it, they will come!" and said as much into every microphone and recorder they could find, the Crypt Network did not go on to become the grand cornerstone of civic rejuvenation that they had been hoping for. Instead, it became a prime example of exactly what not to do, even being included in several master's level university case studies.

People stayed away, the businesses quickly moved out, and everyone more or less forgot about the thing. That included the police, who pretty much gave up on patrolling the area. The Network was a maze. Many tunnels were unfinished and led to dead ends. There were no signs telling you where you were relative to any known landmarks. It wasn't just easy to get lost down there, it was almost impossible to avoid it. Everyone knew that the Crypt Network was one of the biggest no-go areas in the city. Things wandered those tunnels. Things that made even vampires and werewolves nervous. It was rumoured that not even the Triads went down there.

Tim drummed his fingers on the wall as he tried to decide what to do next. He had only ever been down in the Crypt Network once before. That had been in his last year of high school, when he was working for his father's supernatural pest removal service during the summer in order to save up some money for university. A pet store on lower Purgatory had found someone or something had been breaking in to their store at night and draining all the blood out of their tropical birds. A quick investigation had revealed an unfinished ventilation tunnel from the Crypt Network ran along the wall right next to their basement, which had allowed a group of homeless vampires to sneak in and snack on the cockatiels. Tim and his father had done a quick inspection to determine the cause. Officially, they were supposed to be accompanied by a city engineer, but the civil servant in question, a large-bellied man named Royson, had refused to even get out of his van.

"Sorry guys," he said, slurping his coffee from a large silver thermos and clutching a vampire-repelling sun gun nervously in his other hand. "City doesn't pay me enough in a year to spend more than 30 seconds in that place."

When questioned—Tim and his father weren't legally allowed to alter or even touch city infrastructure without a certified municipal engineer present—Royson had elaborated on the point. The city employee's union had recently declared the Crypt Network to be a hazardous workplace, so no worker could be forced to enter it if they didn't want to go.

The principle was well taken, Tim thought, but it did create something of a Catch-22 for anyone else looking to do anything down there. You couldn't make changes involving the Crypt Network without a city employee present and no city employee would go into the Crypt Network. It was one more example of how the city was turning its back on the place.

Although it would have been preferable to block up the shaft, Tim's father had decided that the potential liability exposure was too great and settled for spiking the entrance with a couple of vampire-repelling devices, in this case a Sun Alarm (which used a proximity sensor to trigger a blast of artificial daylight, which would give any vampire within a six-metre radius a nasty burn) and a Garlic Blaster (which would send a spray of concentrated synthetic garlic gas at anyone who got too close).

"It's like any other potential B&E," Tim's father had said at the time. "If they're determined to get in, they will. But in these situations, you make it just a little bit harder and they'll move on to a softer target. Vampires are lazy."

Tim knew that the last bit was more than just a dig at his brother. Vampires did have a reputation for extreme laziness, especially right after they had fed. It was one of those cultural stereotypes that tended to hold up. No less so than in Keef's case.

At that time, the Network had already lost almost all its old retail sheen and looked more like a cave. Wiring hung like vines from the ceiling. Stagnant water pooled on the floor. In some places it was knee deep. The air was musty and cool, smelling like an unpleasant mix of subway exhaust and dead things.

Chances were good that it had not improved in the years since.

Screw it, Tim thought. I'll take a quick look. There's nothing down there that I don't deal with at work on a daily basis, anyway.

Tim made his way around the park to the subway entrance on the opposite corner. It was the closest access point for the Network, which in most places had been built below the existing transit tunnels. He jogged down the first flight of stairs and then, instead of continuing down to the bright lights and ticket kiosks, turned left into the darkness.

The section under Milton Square had been one of the first parts of the Crypt Network to be built and its proximity to what was at the time one of the city's busiest spaces had meant that it was one of the most densely populated in terms of stores and restaurants. This stretch had been like the root of the tree and, as such, had been the last to die. Some of the stores had even held out to the bitter end of their lease agreements, apparently unwilling or unable to give up as easily as everybody else.

Tim stepped over the warped plastic barricade advising DO NOT ENTER—AREA UNDER CONSTRUCTION and kept walking. He didn't know if the sign was somebody's idea of a joke or just the cheapest way to warn people off, as no actual construction had happened here in a very long time. Tim got out his cell phone and turned on the flashlight. There were a few overhead fluorescent bulbs that were still working, but they were few and far between. He also checked to make sure that he had enough charge to use his SunBlast vampire repelling app. Not that he was expecting to, but in light of his experience of the last few days, he knew that there was nothing wrong with being prepared.

The first few storefronts that he passed were boarded up, although in every case the boards had been pulled aside to fashion crude entrances. Many of the facades were decorated with spray-painted words and logos. Some of them had towels, flags and sheets hanging over them in order to preserve some measure of privacy for the squatters huddled inside.

Tim couldn't see anyone in the main corridor, but there were signs of habitation everywhere. Shopping carts were parked in front of some of the stores, some of them still loaded with plastic bags full of cans and other junk. The ground was littered with empty blood bags, almost all of them stamped with the name and address of one of the local synthetic blood clinics. Every few yards there were piles of small corpses, mostly squirrels and pigeons, all of them desiccated and bent wildly out of shape.

Wow, Tim thought. It's worse than I thought.

Tim passed the front of what had once been The Black Lagoon, a seafood restaurant that had been briefly famous as the spot where the celebrated merman chef Renaud Gillman (not his actual name, just the one he was given around the same time as his second Michelin star) had set up shop. Headline writers had not been subtle with the water metaphors when the whole culinary empire went bankrupt three years later. It had probably been the most famous of the eating establishments to land in the Crypt, but supply chain interruptions and a nasty poltergeist had doomed the place almost before the first Lobster Thermidor hit the plate. Some had speculated that Gillman's refusal to pay "enhanced insurance premiums" to the local Triads had not helped.

Out front was an elaborate fountain of Neptune, meant to be a smaller scale copy of the one in the Piazza Navona in Rome. Patrons had once made their entry by walking over a glass floor that led neatly between the jets of water and into the dining room. Now, the king of the sea was missing his trident and somebody had built a makeshift shelter using a tarp tied to two of his horses. These were not the kind of features that tended to get a restaurant a feature spot on a TV show like *Chef's Planet*.

"Hello there."

Tim jumped and turned to his left. He had been so busy gawping at the ruins of the former restaurant that he had completely failed to see the woman who was now walking along right next to him. She looked to be in her 50s, but he could tell based on her eyes that she was a succubus, which probably meant that she was a lot older than that. She was wearing a short black dress and worn running shoes with a hole in the right where the big toe would be. She had bruises on her chin and upper arms.

Junkie, Tim realized. Watch it.

"Hi," Tim said stiffly. Her ability to enchant was sorely depleted, but not entirely gone. He needed to be careful.

"What brings you down here?" she asked. Her voice sounded like gravel being fed through a pipe organ. At one time, she had probably been a great beauty. But that time was not this time.

"No real reason," Tim said.

"Oh, you don't have to be ashamed down here, baby," she said, pulling at the strap on her dress. "You looking for a friend?"

"Not at the moment," Tim said, walking a little faster.

"I'm a friend," she said, pulling at the strap to reveal a shriveled breast. Tim couldn't help but notice that it showed the dark webs of black veins just below the surface; a classic side effect of injecting oneself with tainted synthetic blood in large quantities. "You and me, we can be best friends."

"I'm sure that would be great," Tim said. "But at the moment, I really need to get going."

Tim smiled and made a sharp left turn at the next junction. This would take him to the stretch of the network directly underneath Madame Zoudini's and, hopefully, away from his new friend.

"Suit yourself," she shrugged.

Tim glanced over his shoulder to make sure she wasn't following along behind him. That was a big part of the reason why he didn't see the hulking figure step out of the shadows on his left, although he did feel the stinging blast of the Taser when it caught him in the ribs.

17

The next thing Tim knew, he was being dragged by his feet. He saw a sulphur-yellow bulb sputter overhead as a pair of powerful hands dragged him to the side of the corridor and behind a cracked sheet of plywood. His head lolled to the side, where he saw an image of six vampire heads with different haircuts. The faded text underneath encouraged the reader to: "Choose from the latest in bloodhunter style at Vlad's House of a Thousand Cuts!"

Great, Tim thought. I'm being mugged in front of a vampire hair salon.

He heard a voice that he recognized as belonging to his succubus best friend, although her tone had become much more raspy and urgent.

"Hurry up and stick him, Gerry!" she said. "He's good for at least eight bags!"

Tim raised his head slightly. He could see the one who had dragged him by the legs was a zombie with a rusty metal plate covering most of the right-hand side of his skull. He was wearing a ripped black leather jacket and a pair of green cargo shorts that were several sizes too small for his enormous frame. The succubus was crouched next to the zombie going through what Tim recognized as his wallet.

"Can't find a card," she said, tossing the wallet aside. "We'll tell Pedro it's AB. He hardly ever checks!"

The zombie was gathering together a pile of clear plastic blood bags. He carefully plugged an IV line into one of them and then went about the process of trying to attach a needle to the other end.

Crap, Tim thought. Baggers.

Baggers incapacitated their victims and, with varying degrees of skill, drained their blood. Often, they didn't use the blood themselves, but sold it to downmarket blood banks in exchange for drugs, money or both. Some of them operated out of clinics and brothels, but most of them were seat-of-the-pants operations. Some only took a pint or two, but most drained their victims down to the last squeezable drop.

Tim felt his pockets for his cell phone, but it wasn't there. The Taser had failed to completely knock him out and hadn't really even stung all that much. Chances were, it was low on charge. That wasn't surprising. There weren't exactly loads of places to recharge a conducting energy device in a place like this. Tim flexed the muscles in his arms and legs. Both appeared to be working fine.

"Hurry up, Gerry!" the succubus hissed. "Mama's feelin' the burn, here! Let's drain this little bastard! Move it!"

The zombie finally got the needle attached. Tim wondered why the succubus didn't do the dirty work herself but could see that her hands were shaking too much. If she tried to do the extraction, she'd probably just end up sticking herself. Another side effect of long-term synthetic abuse.

The zombie groaned and turned towards Tim, holding the needle up carefully in front of him. Zombies were obedient, hard to kill and immune to most curses and demonic possession. Those were some of the key reasons that they were so popular as athletes, general labourers and even butlers. They weren't renowned for their intelligence and didn't tend to talk back, two traits that team owners and other rich types prized above all.

Sometimes, however, those traits could be exploited.

Tim waited until the zombie leaned forward and then brought his right foot up with as much force as he could manage. He connected with the zombie's elbow and sent his arm shooting up in a violent arc that drove the all six inches of the needle straight into Gerry's left eye socket.

"Gerry!" the succubus screeched as her companion staggered sideways and nearly fell over. Although Tim knew that zombies could be incapacitated by blows to the brain, you had to pretty much pull the whole thing out of their head and squash it to take them down. The needle would buy him time. Not a lot, but hopefully enough.

Tim sat up. The succubus screamed and launched herself at him, but she was weak from withdrawal and he was able to push her aside. He grabbed his wallet and cellphone from where she had dropped them and got to his feet. He was still a little dizzy and tripped over the plywood on his way out of their hovel.

Tim took a deep breath. Was it his imagination, or could he hear a faint droning noise that seemed to be getting steadily louder? Like a small, single-engine plane coming in for a landing. He shrugged it off. He needed to get out of this place, preferably with the same amount of blood he'd had when he came in.

There was a crash as the zombie stumbled through the rough wooden door and staggered in Tim's direction. Tim managed to get out of the way as the zombie lost its balance and tripped over a bench that had been attached to the floor. The IV line was still attached to the needle protruding from its eye, giving the zombie the appearance of a rhythmic gymnast twirling a long white ribbon in his wake.

"Die you bastard!" yelled the succubus. She was holding a knife, although Tim had no idea where she might have been hiding it. He thought about his phone, but she was too fast. Before he could move, she had vaulted the door and was flying at him like an angry Valkyrie. Tim tried to jump out of the way, tripped over the zombie, and ended up hitting the ground. He clenched his teeth and prepared to fend her off as she launched herself at him.

She was at the midpoint of her jump when a figure on an electric scooter came zooming out of nowhere and knocked her to the floor. The scooter swerved to a halt and a figure in a long black leather trench coat got off. The figure was about five and half feet tall and on the chubby side.

Tim had seen him before.

"Stake?" Tim gasped.

"You okay, man?" Stake asked.

"Uh, I think so," Tim said.

The succubus screamed and got back to her feet. One of her arms was hanging at an unnatural angle and appeared to be broken, but the one holding the knife seemed to be working just fine.

"Look out!" Tim called.

Stake reached up and, with only moderate difficulty, pulled a silver baseball bat out of some sort of holster on his back.

"Don't worry, man!" Stake said, swinging the bat with practiced efficiency. "I'll take care of these scum baggers!"

The succubus charged at Stake, who stepped aside with a speed and nimbleness that was surprising for a man of his size and swung the bat, catching the succubus under the chin. Her head snapped back with a crack and she crumpled to the floor in a heap.

Gerry the zombie had managed to get back to his feet and was groaning angrily at the sight of his partner down on the ground. Stake clipped the bat to his back and went over to his scooter, where he lifted an object out of a customized luggage container on the back. Tim didn't recognize it as a chainsaw until Stake started it up and hit the trigger. It wasn't one of the larger, gas-powered models, but one of the smaller electric types. It made a whining sound when it started that sounded about as fearsome as a small blender.

The zombie charged at Stake, who ducked easily under his grasping arms and brought the chainsaw around in a smooth arc that would have taken the top of Gerry's head off had it not been for the metal plate. There was a grinding sound and a flash of sparks as Stake dodged another swinging arm.

"This one's armoured!" he said, grinning.

Tim could only look on in disbelief. His brother wasn't kidding, he thought. This Stake guy was genuinely nuts.

Gerry did a stumbling turn and came charging at Stake again. This time, Stake jumped the other way and brought the chainsaw around in a lethal arc that saw the blade saw through the other side of the zombie's head just below the eye. Stake pulled the blade out with a snap, causing the top half of the zombie's skull to pop off and land on the floor. Tim tried not to look as the zombie's brain followed a couple of seconds later.

"Whew!" Stake said, turning off the chainsaw. "You okay, buddy? He didn't bite you, did he?"

"No," Tim said, still trying to process what he had just seen. "Thanks!"

Stake wandered over and took a quick look at the succubus, who was still not getting up.

"Is she dead?" Tim said.

"No, but her amateur Red Cross act is over for a while," Stake said, cackling. "I've been tracking these two for a while, now. My name's Stake."

He held out a hand, which Tim shook.

"Tim."

"Pleased to meet you, Tim!" Stake said. "Not a good idea for normies like yourself to wander around down here. This is my domain. I do what I can to hold back the forces of darkness."

"You certainly do," Tim said. His gratitude was precariously balanced. This Stake guy talked like he was narrating his own comic book.

"It's a dark, lonely crusade," Stake said. "But somebody's gotta do it."

"You do it very well," Tim said.

"Come on, man," Stake said, waving Tim towards his scooter. "We better get out of here. There are always more where they came from."

Tim looked at the scooter uncertainly. "Uh, are you sure we'll both fit?"

"No problem," Stake said, dropping the chainsaw back into place and patting Tim on the shoulder. "The Banshee here may not look like much, but it's got it where it counts."

Tim looked more closely at the scooter. Aside from a fire-breathing dragon airbrushed on the gas tank, it looked about as fearsome as a golf cart. "Right."

"Now let's get you back above ground," Stake said. "This place isn't a good hangout spot for ordinary civilians."

Civilians? Tim thought. *I'm talking to a wannabe superhero whose jacket is held together with electrical tape. The concept of ordinary was not in this guy's wheelhouse.*

Stake got on the scooter and started the engine, which did not exactly roar to life like an angry dragon. Tim climbed cautiously on to the back, wedging himself between the chainsaw and Stake's not inconsiderable girth.

"Better hold on tight," Stake said. "Don't wanna lose you when we peel outta here."

"I think I'm good," Tim said, bracing his hands against the chainsaw box.

Stake turned the wheel and the two of them putted from the scene at jogging speed. It occurred to Tim that he could hop off and run faster than this, but he didn't want to seem rude to the man who had, he was forced to admit, just saved his life, or at least some of his blood.

"So, what do you do, Tim?" Stake asked as they weaved around an overturned plant pot.

"Uh, I'm an insurance investigator," Tim said.

"Cool," Stake said. "So somebody torches their car and you figure out if they did it themselves?"

"Something like that," Tim said. "My company handles mostly supernatural stuff."

"Ever deal with any demons?" Stake asked.

"Well," Tim said. "My last case involved a djinn."

Stake hit the brakes, causing the tires to squeal slightly and skid on the tile floor.

"No way!" Stake said, turning in his seat. "Tell me about it! What kind of elemental was it? Did you see it in the flesh?"

"I did," Tim said. "It was a water."

"Those are supposed to be the worst!" Skate said. "Well, except maybe for air. What did you do? Do you carry a flame unit?"

"Not really," Tim said. "I can't really get into specifics because of confidentiality rules and all that."

"Well, you're still here, so I'm guessing you torched it," Stake said. "Am I right?"

"Used the furnace," Tim said.

"Awesome!" Stake said. "Take out the house?"

"Pretty much," Tim admitted.

"Man, we're like one and the same, dude," Stake said. "How do I get into your line of work? Do I need a degree or would my long history of kicking undead ass be enough? I think it should count for something at least."

"Well," Tim shrugged. "They would probably, you know, take it into consideration."

Stake released the brake and they quietly coasted off again.

"What brings you down here?" Stake asked. "Working a case?"

"Uh, sort of," Tim said.

"I see a lot of weird shit down here," Stake said. "One time, I was just sitting at a table in the old food court having my lunch when-"

"Stop!" Tim shouted.

"What?" Stake said, slamming on the brakes.

Tim was looking at the store next to them. It stood out for a couple of reasons. One, it was open. The folding metal security gates had not been pulled across in front of the entrance and the lights were on, although only about half of them seemed to work. It appeared to be a bookstore. There were actual books on the shelves, too. All of them were old and faded, covered in dust and mildew in many cases, but still there.

The other thing that had grabbed Tim's attention was the name. At one time, the place had been called the Word Sanctuary, but the sign holding up the first part had fallen down, leaving only the second half of the name.

The three nets, Tim thought. Wealth, fornication, and the pollution of . . . the sanctuary. Could it be?

He looked up at the ceiling. They were about two hundred meters down the hall from the junction. If his estimates were correct, Madame Zoudini's shop was situated pretty much directly over their heads.

Tim got off the bike and approached the storefront. He couldn't see anyone inside.

"That place?" Stake said. "Why are you looking at that?"

"It's open," Tim said.

"Yeah," Stake said. "But it's cursed. Or at least, that's what I heard. Come on, can you imagine a business that would operate out of a place like this that wasn't cursed?"

"I just need to take a quick look around," Tim said.

"Why?" Stake said. "Is it for a case? That's cool! I'll help!" Stake shut off the engine and got off the bike. "What are we looking for?"

"I'm not sure," Tim said. "Maybe nothing. Just be careful."

"Don't worry, man," Stake said. "I'm always careful. Especially when it's time to pull out the Hammer of Helsing."

"Hammer of Helsing?" Tim said.

"I sometimes call it the Blood Reaver," Stake said, pulling the bat off his back. "But I'm kind of saving that one for when I get an actual sword. You know, to avoid confusion."

"Okay," Tim said. "Then I guess we'll stick with Hammer of Helsing for now."

"I'm actually one of Van Helsing's direct descendants," Stake said. "Got the online DNA test and everything. Totally confirmed. Well, 99.999% or something."

"Is that why you, er, do what you do?" Tim asked.

"It's in my blood," Stake said. "I'm humanity's last line of defence. I'm actually saving up for a sword. The ones with the silver filigree are expensive, but that's what I've got to have if it's going to work as a real vampire killer. There is a family sword. You know, the one old Abraham himself used. But the foundation won't release it to me. Even with the DNA test! Can you believe that?"

"Hmmm," Tim said. He could totally believe that.

The two of them entered the store. The shelves were about six feet tall and made of dark wood. Stake pointed to himself and then to the left, then made a series of elaborate hand gestures that Tim imagined had something to do with a complex plan to reconnoiter the place.

"Uh, you go that way and I'll go this way," Tim whispered. "We'll meet up somewhere inside." He didn't imagine that it would take them long. It wasn't a large store.

Tim turned right and began making his way down the aisles. He could understand why the place hadn't been plundered by thieves. The shelves weren't exactly stocked with the latest bestsellers. The average age of the books on the shelves had to be at least 300 years old and the vast majority of them were in Latin.

"Aisle one clear!" he heard Stake shout from the other side of the store. "Proceeding to aisle two!"

"Great," Tim said.

Tim scanned the titles as he went. Was it possible that the *Ars Azazel*, the so-called lost sixth key of the *Clavicula Salomonis Regis*, was just sitting on one of these shelves? The idea seemed ridiculous. His Latin was rusty. The last time he had used it was in university. Despite promises that reading and speaking it was a key skill to have and the fact that a Latin test was part of the application process at Crimson Seal, he had never used it once during work. Some of the senior underwriters did, but mostly just to complain about the food in the cafeteria without the kitchen staff knowing exactly what they were saying. Many of the longer-serving staff had not been as enthusiastic about the introduction of vegan and gluten-free options at the expense of some of the more traditional, blood-based dishes.

He did recognize some of the titles as belonging to long-out-of-print grimoires, such as Uvan's *Canticus Sexus*, which had been the source of much scandal in its day and was claimed to be the first book ever officially banned by a regional authority, an assertion that was hotly disputed in scholarly circles. Nowadays, of course, this collection of sex spells was about as shocking as an actuarial segmentation report and only slightly more titillating.

Tim made his way around the shelves until he came to one that was closed off by a large and dusty pane of thick glass. This, he assumed, was the location of the valuable and rare volumes. The only problem was, it seemed to be empty. A small sign on the corner advised: "Please ask Staff for assistance!"

"Rest of the place is clear," Stake said, sidling up next to Tim. "Find anything?"

Tim looked more closely at the cabinet. The light overhead was flickering and it was hard to see anything with the thick film of grime on the glass, but he could see that there was something sitting on the shelf in the middle. He used his sleeve to wipe the surface and leaned forward. It wasn't a book. It was a file of some sort. The lettering on the front was faded, but if he squinted, he could just make it out:

SIGILLUM VERMICULO
SF DCLXVI
AZAZEL, ARS

"What the hell?" Tim gasped.

"What?" Stake said.

"That file," Tim said, pointing. "It's from my company."

"Huh?" Stake said. "What are you talking about?"

"*Sigillum Vermiculo*," Tim said. "That was Crimson Seal's original name. Back before it rebranded itself following the collapse of the Roman Empire."

"Whoa!" Stake whistled appreciatively. "What does the rest of it mean?"

"The second line is a number," Tim said. "The last line is what I thought was the name of a book."

"What does the number mean?" Stake asked.

"I'm not sure," Tim said. "But if I'm reading it right, the number is 666."

"Yeesh," Stake said. "That can't be good."

"No," Tim agreed. "Historically, it does have unpleasant associations."

"How do we get it out of there?" Stake said, rapping on the glass. He tried to slide the panel to the side but was blocked by the lock at the bottom left corner.

"It says please see staff for assistance," Tim said. "So ... "

Tim walked to the end of the shelf and turned right, walking to the back of the store. There he found a small desk on the back wall. Standing behind the desk was a figure with long black hair and pale arms. The figure was leaning forward with its face on the desk and the hair spilling over across the surface. Tim could see blue veins under the near-translucent skin on the arms, which were bone thin. The hands were more like claws, with ragged black fingernails, some of which were so badly torn that it looked like their owner had tried to claw his or her way out of a haunted well and failed.

"Uhhhh … hi?" Tim said tremulously.

The figure did not stir and gave no indication of having heard him.

"Hello!" Stake shouted, knocking on the desk right next to the figure's head. "We need some help with the cabinet back there!"

Tim took a step closer to the desk and saw a small bell on the corner. A handwritten sign had been taped to it that read: Please Ring.

"Ah! There we go!" said Stake, tapping the bell before Tim could stop him.

The figure twitched. Tim took a step back.

"I think we should leave," Tim said.

Stake rang the bell again. "Hello?"

The figure raised her head slowly. Like her arms, her face was white as bone and covered with black sores that seeped some sort of bluish liquid or pus. She opened her eyes, which were large and black.

"Can I help you?" she said in a surprisingly cheery voice.

"Yes," said Stake, as if he encountered sales people like this all the time. "We'd like to take a look at something in your rarities cabinet, please."

The figure reached under the counter and grabbed a key. "Certainly, sir. Follow me, please."

She stepped out from behind the counter and walked into the stacks. Tim and Stake followed, one more reluctantly than the other. They followed her back to the cabinet, which she unlocked and slid open.

"Which item?" she asked.

Tim pointed at the file. "Uh, that one right there."

She reached in and took out the file, handing it to Tim. He examined it carefully. The file was easily one of the oldest documents he had ever seen. It looked to be made of some sort of vellum or parchment and was sealed with a thick wax stamp that bore the Crimson Seal logo, although it was one that the company hadn't used in centuries.

"What is this?" Tim asked. "How did you get it?"

"I'm afraid I don't know," she said. "But I've only been with the company for the last 202 years. I would ask my boss, Sariya, but she's been trapped in that puzzle box there for the last 160 years."

She pointed at what looked like a child's jack-in-the-box sitting on the bottom shelf. There was an image of a grinning clown on the side with a rusty crank handle coming out of his mouth.

"Couldn't you just turn that and let her out?" Stake said, pointing at the handle.

"Oh, you wouldn't want to do that," she said. "Now, if you'll excuse me, another customer has entered the store. If I don't greet them in the first two minutes, I'll be cited on my next performance appraisal."

"But she didn't greet us in the first two minutes," Stake said as she walked away.

"That's okay," Tim said. "I'm guessing that she probably hasn't had a review in a while."

Tim crept after the figure as she rounded the shelf and walked to the front of the store. He watched her make her way down the central aisle and stop. Who else would be coming in to a place like this?

"Good evening and welcome to the Word Sanc-" she started. There was a flash and then she stopped abruptly and crumpled to the ground. Tim felt a shiver as a figure in a familiar black robe stepped out from behind the shelf and looked around.

"Shit!" whispered Stake. "It's the Sons of Darkness!"

Tim whirled around in surprise. "Wait," he hissed. "You *know* these guys?"

"Yeah," Stake whispered. "They're bad news."

A hundred questions flooded into Tim's head at once, but he pushed them aside. Their immediate priority was to get out of here.

"Relax," Stake said. "I know a secret way out of here. Lots of secret ways."

"Okay," Tim said. "How?"

"First, we need to create a diversion," Stake said, grabbing something off his belt. "When I say run, you follow me out. Okay?"

Tim nodded.

Stake tossed the thing he was holding across the floor, where it rolled between the shelves and clacked up against the far wall. It sat there for a couple of seconds.

"Don't look straight at it!" Stake hissed, shielding his eyes.

Tim closed his eyes just as a bright flash went off. He opened them again just in time to see the hooded figure run towards the source of the blast.

"Come on!" Stake said, grabbing Tim by the shirt.

Tim followed Stake as he ran down the aisle and turned left, moving quickly towards the front of the store. He stopped at each row to check that the coast was clear before proceeding. The two of them just reached the front of the store when a second hooded figure appeared out of nowhere and held up a hand. Tim was prepared this time, however. He closed his eyes as the cell phone curse went off and then knocked the device out of the figure's hand. Stake grabbed his bat off his back and clocked the figure in the back of the head, sending them sprawling to the floor.

"Come on!" Stake said. "Let's go!"

Two more hooded figures came running at them out of the store. Stake was already on his bike and had fired up the engine. Tim jumped on the back and the two of them motored away. Tim looked over his shoulder and saw, not surprisingly, that their pursuers were not terribly far behind.

"They're catching up!" Tim said.

"Relax," Stake said. "I've got some surprises loaded on this baby."

He pushed a button on the console. Tim heard a clank and then a pop. Moments later, his face and nostrils were full of sulphurous smoke.

"Sorry about that!" Stake said, choking. "Smoke bomb malfunctioned!"

"You think?" Tim gagged.

"Hold on!" Stake said. "I'll get us out of here!"

Stake swerved sharply and blasted through a couple of metal doors marked No Entry. As soon as they were through, he took another quick left turn followed by a right. It was dark, but Tim could tell from the dank smell that they must have entered some sort of maintenance corridor. Stake pulled over and shut off the bike, wheeling it into a closet marked "Network Access".

"I'll come back for it," he said. "Follow me."

Tim followed Stake down the hall to another door. They pulled it open to reveal a ladder leading down.

"This way!" Stake said, climbing on and beginning his descent.

"Wait," Tim said. "Shouldn't we be going up?"

"Just come on!" Stake hissed. "Unless you want them to catch you!"

Tim climbed on the ladder and followed Stake down. They climbed down what seemed like three or four stories before emerging on a dark platform. Tim gave his eyes a moment to adjust, but that was interrupted when a subway train blasted by within inches of his nose.

"Shit!" he yelped.

Stake grabbed Tim to keep him from falling over.

"There's usually five minutes between trains," Stake said once the train had passed. "That should give us enough time to reach the main platform."

"Should?" Tim said. He wasn't sure that he liked the sound of that.

"Yeah," Stake said, jumping down onto the tracks. "So move fast. And don't touch the third rail. Unless you like barbecue."

Tim jumped own and followed Stake. The two of them reached the platform and climbed up. Fortunately, the station wasn't busy and there was only a ghoul waiting, although he did give them a curious look.

"Thanks," Tim said as the two of them made their way out of the station.

"No problem," Stake said. "It's what I do."

"We should talk," Tim said. "I'd like to know whatever you can tell me about the Sons of Darkness."

"Sure," Stake said. "You got food?"

"Yes," Tim said. "What do you like?"

"I feast on fear," Stake said, then laughed at Tim's bemused expression. "Just kidding. Pizza would be great."

18

As they approached the front of the Decameron, Tim stopped.

"Before we go any further," he said. "I should let you know that my brother lives with me. And he's a vampire."

Stake nodded. "Is he a feeder?"

"Strictly consensual," Tim said. *Or so he tells me, at least.* "Other than that, he uses synthetics and edibles."

"Hmmm," Stake said, stroking his chin. "Okay. As long as he keeps the peace, I give you my word that I won't bust out any of my moves."

"Great," Tim said.

"But if things turn hostile, then all bets are off," Stake said.

"Noted," Tim said. He very much doubted that things would go in that direction. To Tim's knowledge, Keef had only ever been involved in one fight in his entire life. It had happened before he was turned, when his college roommate had filled his bong with cat urine. Even that wasn't really a fight in the traditional sense, as both of them had been too stoned to do much more than point fingers and mumble. How the cat urine was collected was a mystery that had not been solved. Tim figured that it was probably better that way.

Tim opened the door to find Keef standing in front of the TV wearing a VR headset and playing an online videogame called *Doom of the Damned*. The game allowed the player to assume the identity of a variety of supernatural entities and interact with other players in a futuristic cityscape. Keef appeared to be playing a vampire. As they entered, he was in the process of sucking the blood out of the leg of what appeared to be a large green demon with a body made of faces.

"Hey man!" Keef said over his shoulder at the sound of the door. Having vampire senses raised his level of awareness up from his usual stupor to that of a drowsy cat. "Just ordered this today. Isn't it awesome? Used your credit card. Hope you don't mind."

Tim sighed. Keef liked to play the physically disadvantaged card when it came to not being able to go out during the day. Vampires were overly represented amongst the unemployed and homeless population simply because it was harder for many of them to get jobs that didn't involve going out in daylight.

"Actually, I do mind, Keef," Tim said. "I'm tired of getting calls from their internal fraud departments asking me if I'm the one buying synthetic blood in bulk. Amongst other things."

They had spoken about this kind of thing before. Unfortunately for Tim, it was hard to hide his wallet and banking information from a roommate with supernatural abilities who was up all night and frequently bored.

"You gotta try it, man!" Keef said, taking off the helmet. He saw Stake and his eyes narrowed menacingly. "What the hell is he doing here?"

"He got me out of a jam with some baggers," Tim said. "And he might be able to help me with this work thing that I've been looking into. Stake, this is my brother, Keef. Keef, Stake."

Stake nodded and rested his hands on his belt. Keef bared his teeth.

"This guy?" Keef said. "He's a joke! He lives in his aunt's place! He's a mall cop, for crying out loud!"

"Oh yeah?" Stake said. "We'll see how funny it is when I feed you a light grenade and make you swallow it, you bloodsucker."

"Just try it, little man!" Keef said, pointing his controller. "I'll hang you upside down and drain you like a kosher brisket!"

"Can it, Keef," Tim said. "He's a guest. We don't eat guests. Just go back to your game and stay out of my way for a while."

Keef muttered something under his breath and put the headset back on as Tim and Stake moved into the dining area.

"Don't mind him," Tim said. "He just had a bad breakup. He's still processing it."

Tim opened the fridge and pulled out a leftover pizza from the previous day. It had been a 2-for-1 deal and he hadn't been able to eat even half of it. He put the pizza in the oven to warm up and motioned Stake to one of the chairs.

"Drink?" Tim asked.

"Thanks, no," Stake said. "I don't drink when I'm on duty. Can't afford to dull my edge."

"So how long have you been doing this?" Tim asked, getting himself a beer. "I mean, if you don't mind me asking."

"About the last eight years or so," Stake said. "Ever since I finished high school."

"You said 'on duty,'" Tim said. "Is that how you see it? Like a job?"

"Somebody's gotta do it," Stake said. "Cops won't. Government won't. That just leaves me."

"I see," Tim said. "But the vast majority of vampires are just ordinary, law-abiding citizens."

"Nothing ordinary about them," Stake said. "They have powers and abilities that we don't. It's just a matter of time before they realize that and decide that they'd rather be in charge of everything. On that day, everyone will wish they'd listened to me all along. Instead of making jokes."

"Sorry about my brother," Tim said. "If it's any consolation, he was a dick before he became a vampire."

"Yeah, I live with my aunt," Stake said. "She was the only one who would take me in after my parents were killed."

"Sorry," Tim said. "How did that happen?"

"Vampire," Stake said.

"Right," Tim said, nodding. He decided not to press for further details on that point.

"And yes, my day job is security guard," Stake said. "Actually, I'm the supervisor for all of Division One. Well, backup supervisor. But that's only temporary. I like the sound of the investigator job you have. That could be right up my street. I would still do it on the side, though. I have a bigger mission than that. A greater … responsibility."

The oven timer beeped. Tim served out the pizza for the two of them.

"Hope you like blood sausage," he said.

"What?" Stake said, startled.

"Kidding," Tim said, feeling awkward. He was starting to realize that there were certain things that Stake did not joke about.

"So this thing you found in the bookstore," Stake said. "Is it what you went down there looking for?"

"I don't know," Tim said, lifting the file out of his jacket pocket. "I don't know what it is."

"Only one way to find out," Stake said.

"Yeah," Tim said. He put the empty plates on the counter and cleared everything else off the table. He hesitated for a moment before cracking the wax seal. How old was this thing? Crimson Seal hadn't gone by its Latin name for nearly 2,000 years.

"Come on!" Stake said. "Do it!"

Tim cracked the seal and unfolded the file carefully. Inside was a key that looked like it was made out of black volcanic glass.

"Cool!" Stake said. "I wonder what that opens?"

"No idea," Tim said, picking up the key and turning it around in his hand. The writing on the file had to provide some sort of clue, he figured. After all, his own company's name was right there on the top. If he didn't know, then maybe there was somebody else at work who would. But whom could he trust enough to ask?

"You said you knew about these guys," Tim said. "The Sons of Darkness. You've seen them before."

"Totally," Stake said.

"Where?" Tim asked.

"Well," Stake said, putting down his pizza crust. "I have a pretty well-established patrol pattern across the city, but I have to shake it up so they can't predict where I might be and when. You dig?"

"I dig," Tim said.

"One of the places I used to keep an eye on was an old blood clinic down on Paradise," Stake said. "Baggers used to do a lot of selling to the clientele in the back alley. You know, when they were waiting around for the place to open at midnight so they could get their fix. A couple of years ago, the building, which is like this really old church that's been renovated about 100 times, was taken over by somebody else. The clinic got turfed out. I was expecting that it might get turned into condos or what have you. You know, the usual gentrification shit. I kept tabs on it because you'd still get the occasional feeder hanging around. Even saw some Triads sniffing around the place. Then, next thing you know, poof! They were all gone."

"Gone?" Tim said.

"Gone," Stake said. "Suddenly, I start seeing these suspicious characters in black hooded robes going in and out of this new secret entrance in the back. Plus, all this new security goes up. They've got cameras on every corner. Keypad and retinal scan door access. Reinforced polycarb windows. The works. Expensive systems and upgrades, too. Dexxer scanners. The good stuff. Real tech. Not the cheapo consumer-grade junk."

"Interesting," Tim said.

"No name on the door," Stake said. "Or anywhere else. The only ones coming and going are these black robers. Every Saturday night without fail. Almost like it's some club meeting."

"Or ritual," Tim said.

"Exactly!" Tim said. "I'm curious, so I keep watching. Pretty soon, the black robes start popping up in other parts of the city. Wherever they start showing up, my usual creatures of interest start vanishing. Not just the street level garbage either. I'm talking, like, the big boys."

"Like the Hellspawn Triad?" Tim asked.

"Yes!" Stake said. He had literally moved to the edge of his seat. His eyes were so wide that they looked like they were about to pop out onto his cheeks and roll across the floor. "I figure, whoever these guys are, they're seriously badass. I start talking to some of my contacts and informants. Most have no idea who they are. One guy, he tells me they tried to recruit him. That's how I found out their name."

"Recruit him to do what?" Tim asked.

"They said they were looking for something," Stake said. "But they wouldn't say what it was unless he joined."

"I have a feeling I know what they're looking for," Tim said, looking at the key sitting on the table. "It would be nice to know why they want it."

"Only one way to find out," Stake said, smiling.

"Huh?" Tim said.

"We sneak in there and find out," Stake said.

"Are you kidding?" Tim laughed. "You just told me that the place is guarded by more security than the Pentagon! How exactly would we just sneak in there?"

"I said it was good," Stake said. "I didn't say it was better than me."

Stake pulled off his backpack and unzipped it. He rooted around inside and pulled out what looked like a chunky cell phone.

"What's that?" Tim asked.

"Little device of my own invention," Stake said with an unmistakable note of pride in his voice. He turned the screen around so that Tim could see it and flicked a button. The screen filled with a CGI image of two eyeballs. "This can trick any retinal scanner in the world. Should be good enough to get us in the door."

"You made this?" Tim said, taking the device and turning it over in his hands. He forced himself not to sound too surprised or doubtful, which was tricky.

"Bet your ass!" Stake said. "All the steps I found online. And I scrounged most of the tech."

"Does it actually, uh, work?" Tim asked.

"Absolutely!" Stake said. "I mean, granted, I haven't had the opportunity to fully field test it, but it'll work. I guarantee it."

Tim handed it back. "You say they're meeting tomorrow?"

"That's right," stake nodded.

"Okay, then," Tim said, swallowing. "Well, if nothing else, at least you'll finally get a chance to try it out."

19

Tim was woken up early the next morning by his phone. When he saw his mother's face on the caller ID, he groaned, but decided to answer anyway. She would only keep calling until he did.

"We want you to come over for dinner tonight," his mother said, getting straight to the point.

Even in his groggy state, Tim knew that there was probably more to such an invitation than met the eye. It was his default assumption.

"Sorry," Tim said. "I have to work."

"But you have to come!" his mother insisted.

"I can come tomorrow," Tim suggested.

"That's no good," his mother said. "Tiffany's going out of town tomorrow."

"Ma," Tim sighed. "I don't think Tiffany and I are compatible."

"You're very lucky," his mother said. "I explained to Tiffany that the last time was a work emergency. A last-minute thing. No son of mine would be so inconsiderate. At least, not on purpose. She's willing to give you another chance."

"That's very kind of her," Tim said. "But I'm not interested."

"You should bring her a present," his mother continued, as always, as if she hadn't heard a word he'd said. "To make up for not showing the last time. I picked up a nice necklace she'll like. You can pay me back later. Don't worry. I got it wholesale. I know the manufacturer. Works out of her apartment. Really nice stuff."

"Wear it yourself," Tim said.

"Tiffany's going to be here at seven," his mother said. "You should be here when she arrives. Like around six thirty."

"I will not be there at six thirty," Tim said. "I won't be there at all."

"I don't understand why you need to make everything so difficult, Timothy," his mother scolded. "Your father and I are only thinking of you. We want you to be happy."

"I would be a lot happier if you'd stop doing this shit," Tim muttered.

"Language, Timothy," his mother said. "Your aunt Raylene will be here, too. You better not use such words in front of her. You know she hasn't been the same since they found out your uncle Michael had been possessed for all those years."

Tim's uncle Michael had recently been diagnosed as being inhabited by the ghost of a long-deceased transit commission candidate who had hung himself after getting less than two per cent of the vote in a municipal election that had taken place more than a century before. Michael had manifested almost none of the usual outward signs of identity theft beyond what doctors initially thought was just seasonal affective disorder and a strange desire to put signs with his name on them on his neighbour's lawns. Once the ghost had been exorcised, Michael had immediately snapped out of his five-year-long funk, bought a Corvette, left Raylene and ran off to Cabo San Lucas with his dental hygienist.

"Look, it's great that you're trying to help," Tim said. "But I don't need it, okay? You really want to help me? Then let Keef move back into your spare bedroom."

"We can't do that," his mother hissed. "You know our condo board has a strict prohibition against vampires. Technically, he's not even supposed to visit."

Tim shook his head silently. Sometimes, he suspected that his parents had moved into that particular building for that exact reason. He couldn't really pretend to be outraged by it, though. Most of the condo plans he'd been looking at lately had similar bylaw prohibitions. Tim was opposed to such discrimination on principle, but principles weren't going to help him shake off his freeloading brother anytime soon.

"Look, stop trying to set me up, okay?" Tim said.

"I just don't like the thought of you using those dating apps," his mother said. "You know Letitia from the salon? Her son Hayden uses them. He went out on what he thought was going to be a date last week. Only, the next thing he knows, he wakes up in an alley with half his blood missing. Didn't even have the energy to call the police! Doctors said half a pint more and he would have totally exsanguinated! Is that what you want to happen?"

Tim thought back to his experience with the baggers the previous day. He decided that there was nothing to gain by mentioning it in this context.

"No one's going to steal my blood, ma," Tim said.

"At least I know these girls," his mother said. "They're not blood junkies or sex demons like the ones all over the news these days."

Tim groaned. His parents watched HEX-TV news, a network that was not known for its subtlety when it came to reporting certain topics, especially supernatural-on-human crime. It was the only network that had an all-human on-camera staff and made it a point to editorialize rabidly against any attempt by spectral minorities to gain any additional rights on any level. From their perspective, humans were under siege by an unholy alliance of evil, bloodsucking and limb-shredding fiends. The fact that her oldest son was one of those supposed creeping destroyers of civil society had long been a source of great personal unease and embarrassment for Regina Lovecraft.

"Ma, a succubus is not a sex demon," Tim said. "It's a misconception that's developed over centuries. They have mind control abilities and humans are just naturally attracted to them, that's all."

"So *you* say," his mother said. She had long ago become immune to what she regarded as his naively well-intentioned liberal bullshit. "Try explaining that to poor Hayden! Letitia said he might not be able to go back to work for weeks. Doctors said they might have to transfuse all of his blood because the needle might have been cursed. What kind of sick creatures are these?"

"All of that aside," Tim said, eager to stop the conversation from taking another unpleasant political turn. "I still won't be able to come to dinner."

"You can't stand Tiffany up again," his mother said. "She's already giving you a second chance. It's the weekend. Surely you can reschedule. What is this work thing, anyway?"

"It's an internal investigation," Tim said. Technically, that was a lie. He wasn't really doing this for work. But, from a certain perspective, it was all about work. "I can't discuss details."

"Oh, Timothy," she said. "I'm your mother. Who am I going to tell?"

"You run a psychic salon, ma," Tim said. "You tell everyone everything. If you ever signed an NDA, you'd be sued into insolvency before the ink was dry."

She sighed. "Well, maybe I can ask Tiffany if she can change her plans for tomorrow. But you had better-"

"Don't ask her to change her plans," Tim said, exasperated. "I am not going out with Tiffany, okay? We have nothing in common. She watches *The Satyr*. She reads those stupid gossip mags like *Undying Lives* and *Wolf World*."

"I read those magazines," his mother said in a huffy voice. "I watch that show. What are you implying?"

"I don't think it would be appropriate for me to date my mother, either," Tim said.

"Don't be a smartass," his mother said, then held the phone away to yell at Tim's father, who was evidently in another room. "Thaddeus! Explain to me how we managed to raise such an incredible snob!"

"Look," Tim said, keen to cap the conversation before it went further off the rails. "It's not that. Well, not just that. I can't date Tiffany because I met someone else."

He could feel the bomb bay doors opening and feel the silence as this particular payload dropped through the clouds towards its target. It wasn't strictly true. He and Tabitha were not back together. But until that situation resolved itself one way or (hopefully not) the other, there was no way on earth that he was going to be able to pay any kind of romantic attention to any other woman.

"Who?" his mother said.

"I'd rather not say," Tim said. His mother and Tabitha had not gotten along particularly well in the few times they had met in the past. Regina did not think that women were well suited to what she regarded as more traditionally masculine occupations, a position against which Tabitha naturally bristled. Their first meeting had been prickly and subsequent ones frosty.

"Is it a man?" his mother asked. "Oh god, it's not a demon, is it?"

"No," Tim said, rubbing his temples. He could always count on his mother to supplant one prejudice in favour of a deeper prejudice.

"So it's a woman?" his mother said. "Why can't you tell me her name? Is she married?"

"For crying out loud!" Tim snapped. "I'd rather be back in the basement with the djinn!"

"The what?" his mother asked.

"Nothing," Tim muttered.

"C'mon, Reg! Give the kid a break!" Tim heard his father shout from the other room.

"Are you going out with this other woman tonight?" his mother asked. "Is that really what this secret work thing is?"

"No," Tim said. "I really do have a secret work thing." *I'm going out with a man-boy in a homemade superhero costume to spy on the headquarters of a secretive group of demon-worshipping cultists. Does that make you feel better?*

"Hmmm," his mother said, clearly skeptical. "If you say so."

"Anything else?" Tim asked.

"I worry about you, Timothy," his mother said. "Ever since you got dumped by that horrible lawyer-"

"I wasn't dumped," Tim said. "She went to law school. And she's not a lawyer. She's a cop now." He was about to also state that Tabitha was not horrible but realized that might come off as too strident. If he defended Tabitha too forcefully, his mother would get suspicious. And if she got suspicious, she would get curious. And if she got curious, she would not let up until she had gotten to the truth. It was one of her few truly admirable qualities. Had she been an investigator, she would have been an excellent one.

"A cop?" his mother said. "Even worse."

"How is that worse?" Tim asked. "Worse than what?"

"You know my feelings on that," his mother said. "Anyway, since then, you just haven't been the same."

"I'm the one with the stable job and his own apartment," Tim said. "You want to hassle one of your kids? How about you try the one hiding behind blackout curtains in what should be my office who pays no rent and leaves Scabs crumbs and old blood bags all over my living room couch?"

"You know Keef pays no attention to anything I tell him," his mother said.

You're not the only one, Tim thought. The idiot had played VR all night and passed out on the couch with the blinds open. The only reason he hadn't burned himself to a crisp was because Tim had forgotten to turn off his alarm and had gone out for a glass of water just as the sun was starting to prick the horizon. Tim had closed the blinds and dragged him back to his room, where he had slunk back into his double-wide coffin and started to snore like a backfiring diesel engine.

"Tell me about it," Tim said.

He finally managed to get his mother off the phone. He checked his email quickly and was about to get in the shower when his phone rang again. He answered without checking the caller ID, as he was sure it was his mother calling him back to say that Tiffany could re-schedule and Sunday was fine.

"What now?" he snapped.

"Uh … did I catch you at a bad time?"

It was Tabitha. Tim slapped his forehead and cursed under his breath.

"Hi, Tabitha!" he said. "Sorry. I just got off the phone with my mother and assumed she was calling me back. She's driving me bananas. How are you?"

"I'm good," Tabitha said. "Listen, I might have some information on that wandering psychic you mentioned."

"Really?" Tim said, sitting up straighter.

"Yes," Tabitha said. "But I can't really talk right now and I'm working tonight. Are you around tomorrow?"

"Absolutely," Tim said. "All day."

"Great," she said. "I'll call you. How are things going on your end?"

"Good," he said. "Been making a lot of progress. Got some interesting things to show you."

"And I look forward to seeing those interesting things," she said. "Just remember, you promised me you wouldn't do anything ridiculously dangerous."

"Scout's honour," he said, crossing his fingers behind his back. Now was probably not a good time to mention the Crypt Network. Or the baggers. Or his plan to infiltrate the Sons of Darkness with a mall cop who talked like Batman.

"That's my Gurg," she said, hanging up.

After he was out of the shower and dressed, Tim went through his investigation kit and pulled out a few select items that he thought he might need. Having encountered the Sons of Darkness a few times already, he decided that he wasn't about to go in unprepared. He had no idea what kind of weaponry Stake was going to bring on this expedition. Whatever it was, hopefully they would have no reason to use it.

And if they did, hopefully he would be nowhere near it when it went off.

20

"*This place*?" Tim said in disbelief as he crouched behind the dumpster. The building he was staring at looked more like a modernist art gallery or the headquarters of a technology company than the dark and secretive bunker that he had been envisioning. It was circular and occupied the entire block, with three-storey high walls made of smoked glass. There was no door—or at least not one that he had been able to see during their circuit.

"That's it," Stake said, crouching next to him. He was busy strapping a long black combat knife to his right leg. The buckle kept snapping loose and he had given up and just decided to tie it, although that wasn't working so well, either.

"It's not exactly what I pictured," Tim said.

"They never are," Stake said.

What does that mean? Tim wondered. Has he seen dozens of secret cult headquarters buildings in his time? What in the hell am I doing here?

"Incoming!" Stake hissed.

The two of them ducked down as a car approached from the north side. Like the others they had seen, it was a black four-door sedan with heavily tinted windows, which made it impossible to see who might be inside. The car turned off the road and went down a ramp on the north side of the building, disappearing below ground. Tim could see the security camera mounted at the top of the ramp. There had to be some sort of scanner or licence plate identifier, because the car only paused for a moment before the barriers at the top of the ramp dropped into the ground and allowed it to pass through.

"It's got better security than an embassy in a hostile foreign country," Tim said, watching as the tail lights disappeared down the ramp.

"Yeah, it's good," Stake nodded. "But not good enough to keep us out."

Tim had not seen anyone coming or going to the place on foot. That made sense, he supposed. If you had a secret headquarters, you didn't want anyone to see you entering or leaving. Based on what he had seen so far, however, it looked extremely unlikely that they were going to be able to sneak in.

"And how do you propose we do that?" Tim asked. "I don't see a door. And they have cameras set up everywhere. We try to make it down that ramp and they'll probably have guards on us before we even get within 50 feet of the barrier."

"True," Stake said. "But that's not the only way in."

"What are you talking about?" Tim said.

"They have their own secret entrance underground," Stake said. "Connects right to the subway line."

"Oh," Tim said. "Then what are we doing up here?"

"Just thought you wanted to see the place first," Stake said. "Get a better idea what we're up against."

Tim wasn't sure exactly how looking at the outside of a building was supposed to give him a better sense of who might be inside it, but he decided to let that go for the time being. Whoever was in there obviously had no shortage of money and didn't want anyone else poking their nose into what they were doing, but those were things that he figured he already knew.

"Okay," Tim said. "So where do we go?"

Stake waved for Tim to follow him down the alley to a metal door. He opened the door and they made their way through a 24-hour laundromat and back out onto the street on the other side of the block. There was a ghoul sitting on a plastic chair near the entrance as two tumble dryers rumbled along the wall, but he never even looked up from his phone as they went past.

Stake turned left and jogged down the block to the entrance to the subway station. There was a zombie standing at the top of the stairs holding a sign that read: "The End of High Cell Phone Prices Is Nigh!" There was a web address at the bottom of the sign. Zombies made up about 95 per cent of sign workers in the city. They could stand still for hours, rarely complained and weren't unionized, which were all big pluses for the kinds of employers who tended to gravitate towards the less glamorous side of the advertising business.

They jogged past the zombie and went down the stairs into the station. It was Saturday night and the station was not one of the busier ones in the city, so it was almost empty. The only figures Tim saw as they made their way up to the turnstiles were a couple of young vampires huddled in a corner sucking on what was either a large rat or a small dog. Stake vaulted over the turnstiles without paying. Tim stopped and got out his pass card.

"Don't pay!" Stake hissed.

"Why not?" Tim asked.

"You don't want any official record that you were here!" Stake said.

Tim glanced at the ticket booth, which was vacant, and then looked around for cameras.

"Don't worry about the cameras," Stake said. "They're just for show."

Tim stuffed his card back in his pocket and climbed over the turnstile. In all his time riding the subway, he had only ever seen a transit enforcement officer once. With his luck, he figured the next one would be waiting on the other side to give him a ticket, but Stake had a point. It was better not to leave an electronic trail if possible. As far as the cameras were concerned, he would have to take Stake's word on that.

"Where are we going exactly?" Tim asked as they jogged down the stairs and into the tunnel.

"Just follow me!" Stake said. "You're not gonna believe this! For a cult, these guys are actually pretty cool!"

Tim considered—not for the first time—simply turning around and ditching this mission. So what if these guys seemed to want him dead for some reason? Maybe he could move to a different city and get a job at a company where his coworkers weren't a part of some homicidal conspiracy. He could always just go back to working for his father's extermination business. It wasn't so bad so long as you remembered to wear breathing apparatus when using some of the more noxious anti-demon sprays. He was pretty sure that had been the reason he had been dumped by his last high school girlfriend. With some things, it just didn't matter how many times you showered or how many times you washed your clothes, the smell of Demonex just never seemed to come off. His mother still refused to allow his father to set foot in any of her salons or pop ups and had insisted that he install a chemical detoxification shower at his shop. Being a "happy wife-happy life" type of husband, Thaddeus had acceded to both demands without complaint.

The two of them reached the platform. Stake pulled him in behind an advertisement for synthetic brains and they crouched down. The platform was empty. Tim could hear the droning howl of air moving through the tunnels.

"What's so super cool?" Tim asked. "This looks like a pretty ordinary subway station to me."

"Just wait!" Stake hissed. "This is the last stop on the line. But not for them."

Tim was about to ask what that meant but stopped when he heard the rumble of the approaching train. The rumble grew steadily louder as the train got closer. Tim crouched down further as it pulled into the station in a blur of rusty red paint and windows. It slowed to a halt and there was a ding as the doors opened. Tim leaned out just far enough to see two figures step out of the front carriage and onto the platform. The first was a man in his 50s who looked vaguely familiar. He was wearing a black suit with a red shirt and tie and was carrying some sort of walking stick. He was bald with a pointy black beard. He looked like a magician in the middle of a low-rent residency in North Las Vegas. His companion was a woman in her early 30s. She had short blonde hair and was wearing a leather jacket and jeans. She was wheeling a carry-on size suitcase on a telescoping handle. Tim's first impression was that she was the man's daughter or assistant, but he knew he could be wrong about that.

The two of them stood to one side and waited as the doors closed and the train backed out of the station in the same direction from where it had come.

"They're waiting," Tim whispered.

"They don't want anyone to know where they're going next," Stake said. "Little do they know."

As soon as the train was gone, the man and woman turned and walked over to the far wall, where there was a large poster advertising the Stygian School of Business Management, a prestigious and extremely expensive private college. Stygian was currently being sued because it only admitted humans, a policy that had drawn the ire of various supernatural rights groups. The poster featured two fresh-faced and smiling graduates sitting on the hood of an expensive Italian sportscar in front of a castle. Most of the school's advertising was equally subtle. It didn't really matter, though. The only people who could afford to send their kids there tended to live in castles already.

The man and woman reached the ad. The woman tapped a wall tile next to the frame. It slid aside to reveal something that Tim was too far away to see. Stake, however, was leaning forward with his binoculars in place, watching intently.

"It's a keypad!" he whispered, watching as the woman tapped in a series of numbers. "Six … six … six … pound. I guess that makes sense. They haven't changed it since last week. That's lax security. That's how we're gonna get them."

The ad swept open, revealing a hidden corridor behind it. The man and woman stepped through and the door closed behind them.

"Come on!" Stake said, jumping up. "We need to catch them before they get to the monorail!"

"The what?" Tim said, standing up and following along.

Stake raced down the platform and tapped the tile, which slid aside. He quickly tapped in the code and the door opened. Stake reached into his bag and pulled out what looked like a handgun.

"What the hell is that?" Tim asked.

"Just come on!" Stake said. He turned and ran down the corridor as Tim reluctantly followed. The walls were plain gray concrete blocks. Their way was lit by triangular sconces placed every 20 feet. The top corners of each light were shaped like horns that curved up at a slight angle. The hallway angled down at about a five-degree slope. Tim could hear the wheels of the suitcase as they got closer to the pair at the front.

"What are you doing with a gun?" Tim said. "You never said anything about a gun!"

They reached the end of the hall and found themselves on a smaller platform. There were metal-frame leather chairs along one wall and a glass barricade on the other. The barricade appeared to block off another set of tracks. The woman was sitting on one of the chairs while the man knelt down to unzip the suitcase.

"Hey," Stake said, nodding at them. "Sorry to break up your demonic little double date."

"Who the hell are you?" the man said, starting to get up.

"Me?" said Stake. "I'm righteous vengeance. I'm the light in the dark. I'm the one whose name you whisper when you're shaking with fear, too scared to come out of your little rat's nests. I'm St-"

The man twisted the handle of his cane and pulled, revealing a hidden knife. He yelled and jumped to his feet to charge at Stake, moving with surprising speed considering his age. Stake raised his gun and shot the man in the chest. He staggered and fell to the floor. The woman screamed. Stake raised the gun again and shot her in the shoulder. The scream slowly died in her throat as her eyes rolled up in their sockets and she fell off the chair.

"What are you doing?" Tim yelled.

"Relax!" Stake said. "They're tranks."

Tim ran over to the woman and saw the tip of the dart sticking out of her shoulder. Stake kicked the man over onto his back and leaned over to pull out the dart, which had a red feather sticking out the back.

"Where on earth did you get tranquilizer darts?" Tim asked, feeling the woman's wrist to make sure that she still had a pulse.

"I know a guy who works for werewolf control," Stake said. "These babies are strong enough to stop a whole pack!"

"But they aren't werewolves!" Tim said, happy that the woman appeared to still be breathing. "You could send them into a coma! The kind they don't come out of!"

"Stop being such a grandma!" Stake said. "These people are demon worshippers!"

"So you think!" Tim said. "But what if they're not? What if they're coming into town to see the new history of vampirism exhibit at the museum and just took a wrong turn?"

Stake walked over to the suitcase and finished unzipping it, then flipped it open. He reached in to pull out a thick black robe.

"Still think they're just tourists?" Stake asked.

"Okay, maybe you've got a point," Tim said.

There was a hiss as a single sleek black and red monorail car pulled in behind the glass. It glided to a stop and sat there silently. Tim expected the doors to open, but they did not.

"Hurry!" Stake said. He stuffed the dart gun back into his bag and pulled out the phone. "Help me! I need you to hold his eyes open!"

Tim crouched down behind the man and reached down tentatively to pull his eyes open with his thumbs and forefingers. He was reluctant and a bit squeamish about touching the prone stranger's body. As a result, his fingers were sweaty, which meant that the man's eyelids kept slipping out of his grip.

"Hold them open!" Stake barked.

"Sorry!" Tim said, using slightly more force. It occurred to him that he remembered where he had seen this man before. This was Ottavio Syzstra, a city councillor whose ward consisted mostly of the Lower Styx. He had been in the news lately for proposing a bylaw amendment banning werewolves from city parks. It had never even made it out of committee and onto the council floor for a vote, which he had attributed to illegal campaign contributions from "soft-minded, pro-lycanthrope special interest groups." Syzstra had a long record of supporting measures aimed at marginalizing vampires, werewolves, zombies and ghouls. The only two demographics he didn't go after were humans and demons. Tim didn't know who the woman was. He guessed that it could be Syzstra's daughter, although there really wasn't much of a resemblance.

Stake held the phone up over the man's eyes and waited until there was a beep.

"I think we've got it," Stake said. "Let's get the other one just in case."

Tim held the woman's eyes open while Stake scanned those, too.

"Okay," Stake said once he was done. "We need to move them out of sight just in case anyone else comes along. Help me move them over there!"

Stake grabbed Szystra by the legs and started dragging him along the floor. Tim grabbed the woman and did likewise. The floor was smooth and the woman was relatively light, which made his work slightly easier.

"Down here!" Stake said, pointing to a door on the wall opposite the one where they had entered. He pulled it open to reveal a small maintenance closet with a large network of wires and cables running from the ceiling to the floor. Stake dragged Szstra in and propped him up in the corner, then stepped aside so that Tim could put his companion in next to him. Stake jogged back and grabbed the suitcase, pulling out he robes and doing a quick search of the rest. He found a couple of necklaces with a similar face to the one that had been on the statue Tim had found at Madame Zoudini's.

"Ever seen these before?" he asked.

"Nope," Tim said, shaking his head.

Stake put on one of the necklaces and tossed the other one to Tim.

"Here," he said. "Put this on."

Tim put on the necklace. It did not immediately cause nausea or him to black out, so hopefully that meant that it wasn't cursed. Stake tossed him one of the robes as well, then wheeled the suitcase into the closet and closed the door.

"How long will they be out?" Tim asked.

"Hard to say," Stake said, pulling the robe over his head. "An hour maybe? To tell the truth, I've never used those darts on a human before. Assuming a similar neurochemical reaction as a werewolf on a pound-for-pound basis, I would say at least an hour."

"Hopefully they're too out of it to be able to identify us when they wake up," Tim muttered under his breath. He did not want the next time he saw Tabitha to be her showing up at his apartment to arrest him for assault, trespassing and whatever else they might end up doing before this night was over. He wondered how many other politicians and other assorted VIP types might be involved with the Sons of Darkness. Based on the size and security of their headquarters, their top dog was probably more highly placed than a populist city councillor.

Tim put on the robe. The fabric felt rougher than it looked and smelled faintly of sulphur and Demonex. He didn't know if this was Szystra's uniform or the woman's, but he supposed that it didn't really matter. The Sons of Darkness appeared to be a one size fits all kind of evil cult.

"Ready?" Stake said.

"I guess," Tim said, adjusting the hood so that he could still see.

"Be prepared," Stake intoned. "There's no way of knowing in advance what kind of horrible demonic perversions we might witness on the other side of this ride. The important thing is to keep your cool. Don't freak out under any circumstances, no matter what."

"Relax," Tim said. "I've seen some pretty freaky stuff in my time."

"Just saying," Stake said. "Be ready for the worst. If we want to get out of there alive, it's important that we don't lose our shit."

"Got it," Tim said. "Let's go."

The two of them jogged over to the barrier. Tim pushed a button and there was a hiss as two glass panels slid out and open to allow them to enter the train. Tim took a deep breath and stepped aboard. There were eight black leather chairs at either end of the compartment, but he didn't feel like sitting.

The doors closed and the monorail began gliding silently out of the station and into a darkened tunnel.

Okay, Tim thought. Time to see what these Sons of Darkness were really about.

21

The train continued through the darkness for several minutes. It was a strange experience. There were no lights of any kind and the monorail was so smooth and quiet that it was almost like they weren't moving at all. Tim imagined that this was probably what it felt like to ride in a submarine.

"Where the hell are the lights on this thing?" Stake muttered. Tim heard him take a step and almost fall down. "I can't see a damn thing!"

"Maybe they're not working," Tim suggested. "Or maybe they left them out for thematic reasons."

"What?" grunted Stake, bumping into the wall.

"Nothing," Tim said, unable to remember the specific Paradise Lost quote he had been thinking of.

The train made a barely perceptible turn as they entered what seemed to be another station. Ruby red light seeped through the windows. Stake climbed back to his feet. Tim looked out and saw a line of flame burning just beyond the edge of the track.

That's got to be some sort of transportation safety authority violation, he thought before realizing how ridiculous the notion was.

The train came to a stop and the doors opened. Tim peeked out and saw that their train appeared to be just one of many. All of the tracks fanned out like strands in a web from a central point. He counted at least a dozen other trains and as many more arrival points where no monorail had yet arrived.

"Wow," Stake said. "They must have secret departure points all over the city."

"Yeah," Tim said. It was the literal definition of an underground network. "Looks that way."

The platform next to the train led to a circular building in the middle that looked like an extension of the one visible aboveground. The exterior appeared to be made of black glass, making it impossible to see what was happening on the inside. Each platform had its own door, and each one of those was guarded by two enormous demons. The demons all had huge horns, which was an uncommon sight. Demons aboveground tended to trim their horns as most cars, buses, trains and doorways weren't really designed with an additional three feet of headroom in mind. Each demon was armed with a large golden pitchfork that looked long and sharp enough to kill and slow roast a wild boar.

"Any thoughts on how we're supposed to get past these guys?" Tim said.

"Just walk right on by," Stake said. "As far as they know, we're members."

"Right," Tim said with no conviction whatsoever.

"Okay," Stake said. "Let's do this!"

He pulled up his hood and stepped out onto the platform. Tim swallowed and did likewise. This might not be the stupidest thing he had ever done—possibly not even the stupidest thing he had done this week—but it was still more dangerous than staying home watching vampire skin-flicks on late night cable with his brother.

Tim could see other figures approaching on other platforms. As they got closer to the demons, each of them held up their pendants. In each case, the demons nodded and waved them through.

"Show them your necklace!" Tim hissed.

"Copy that," Stake said.

Tim fished around under the robe and grabbed hold of the necklace. He also used his other hand to surreptitiously pull the hood a little tighter around his face. He didn't want to take the chance that the pendants had some sort of advanced photo ID system that only the demons could see. He was so busy trying to do this that he stepped on the back of Stake's robe, almost pulling the hood off and causing Stake to fall over.

"Watch where you're going!" Stake hissed, recovering quickly.

"Sorry," Tim whispered.

They reached the demons, each of whom were at least nine feet tall. They were also naked, which was also something of a rarity aboveground. Tim did his best not to look at the giant red phallus, but this was difficult as it was right at eye level and as thick as a fully-grown boa constrictor. Everyone had heard the expression "hung like a demon" but it was still disconcerting to see the reality of it up close. The demon glanced at their necklaces and waved them ahead as casually as a night club bouncer.

Tim and Stake moved forward and arrived at a golden door. Tim looked around, but it had no handle and no obvious way to open it. It also didn't open automatically as they approached.

"It's got a retinal scanner!" Stake whispered gleefully, pointing at a small display panel set roughly at eye level to the right of the door. "Good thing we came prepared!"

Stake leaned forward to make it look like he was bringing his eyes closer to the scanner while unobtrusively raising the cell phone up to rest on the bridge of his nose. He was careful to keep the device hidden within the folds of his hood as he did so. A moment later, there was a beep and a click as the door slid open.

Stake turned, grinning, and gave a barely perceptible first pump of triumph.

"Knew it would work!" he whispered.

"Totally," Tim whispered back.

Stake handed Tim the phone and stepped through the door, which closed again almost instantly.

Okay, Tim thought. Here goes nothing.

He was acutely aware that if the scan did not work this time, that the chances of him making it back to the train before being impaled by one of the enormously endowed demons was, at least statistically, on par with winning the lottery three times in a row.

Tim leaned forward and held the phone up in front of the scanner. There was a pause and then an electronic buzz of discontent as the message "Invalid Scan" displayed on the readout.

Tim felt a stab of panic, convinced that it was the first of multiple, far more physical, stabs that he was about to experience. He looked down and realized that the phone was facing in the wrong direction. He quickly turned it around and held it up to the scanner. This time, the system scanned for a moment and then beeped, flashing a green message on the readout: "Welcome, Dr. Carmichael".

The door slid open and Tim stepped through quickly. Stake was waiting for him in a narrow hallway lit by torches. Looking closely at the torches, Tim could see that they were burning with real Hellfire. He had never seen it used in a controlled setting like this. It sparkled as it burned, as if it was full of flickering dust-like specks of pure white tinder. It gave off a ruby red light but no heat, although he knew better than to get too close to it to really check.

"Do you believe that?" Stake said, punching him in the shoulder. "Did that mother work or what?"

"It worked," Tim said, handing back the phone. "Nice job. You ever want to sell that, you could probably quit your day job."

"Actually, it's not entirely my technology," Stake admitted. "But I did make some premium modifications. For example-"

"Tell me later," Tim said, grabbing Stake's arm and propelling him forward. "I have a feeling we may already be late for whatever's going on in there."

The two of them made their way down the hall and emerged in what looked like a balcony with two large leather seats. Tim looked over the edge to see a massive amphitheatre with hundreds of similar balconies all arranged in a circle. They appeared to be in the top row of six. Some of the ones closer to the floor were larger, seating as many as a half a dozen people. All the seats appeared to be occupied by figures in black robes. Tim estimated that there had to be at least a hundred of them in the room ... if not more. He was not good with crowd numbers.

"Holy shit!" Stake whispered. "It's like having box seats for an Undead game!"

"Yeah," Tim said. "Each door must lead to a different private box."

Tim looked down at the floor, which appeared to consist of a massive hexagonal wooden stage with six black iron rails that converged in the centre, where there was a six-sided red seal. Tim recognized the seal as the same one that had been on the back of the statue he'd found at Madame Zoudini's. The entire room was lit by large Hellfire torches spaced throughout. He looked up and saw the roof consisted of a glass dome that was open to the floor of the building above and in turn to the sky.

"I've never seen anyplace like this before," Tim said.

"You should see my workshop," Stake said. "It's not quite as big, I'll grant you that. But it's totally badass."

The rumble of conversation in the room suddenly stopped. It didn't slowly peter out the way it did in most situations but simply stopped, as sharply as if someone had unplugged a speaker. Tim looked down and saw a figure in black walk to the centre of the stage. The leader was followed by three more. The two on the outside appeared to be leading the one in the middle forcefully by the arms, giving Tim the feeling that, whoever it was, they weren't there voluntarily.

"Oh, mighty Belial!" the first figure said, raising its arms. "The hour of your return is almost nigh! We call out to you in the darkness!"

The voice was unmistakably female and, although she was speaking with a loud and exaggerated formality, familiar.

I've heard that voice before, Tim thought. But where?

"We call!" repeated the crowd in rumbling unison.

"Oh, great and terrible ancestor," the figure continued. "Father of us all! Unjustly imprisoned! Rise up and destroy your enemies! Let the streets run with their blood!"

"Let them run," intoned the crowd.

The figure knelt down and put a hand on the seal.

"We shall break the red seal!" she said.

"Break the seal," said the crowd.

"We shall open the door!" she shouted.

"Open the door," repeated the crowd.

"We shall behold the glory of thy restored kingdom!" she said.

"We shall behold," parroted the crowd.

Tim leaned forward and looked more closely at the stage. He realized that it wasn't a stage at all. The large iron cylinders on either side weren't supports.

They were *hinges*.

The thing they were standing on was a massive door. The seal in the middle looked like some sort of lock.

"It's a door," Tim whispered.

"I think you're right," Stake whispered. "What do you suppose is on the other side?"

Tim swallowed. "Probably not somebody who wants to know if you have two minutes to talk about a truly fantastic deal for a premium cable upgrade."

"True that," Stake muttered.

"We must prepare for the coming of the great king!" said the woman. "We must sanctify his temple with the blood of the nonbeliever! And of those whose loyalty is found wanting!"

She turned and pulled the hood off the figure standing between the two demons. Tim felt a jolt.

It was Carmilla.

"Oh shit," he whispered.

"What?" Stake hissed. "You know her?"

Tim nodded. "She works in my office."

"Did you know she was one of them?" Stake whispered.

Tim shook his head.

"Well, maybe she isn't," Stake whispered. "Maybe they're just gonna use her as some sort of, you know, sacrificial offering or something."

Tim watched as two enormous demons walked out carrying what at first looked like some absurdly large and complicated piece of exercise equipment. It had a star-shaped platform tall enough for a person to lie on in the middle of a pentagonal wooden frame. The frame was ringed with a row of what looked like claws that angled up into the air. At the tip of each was a long, shiny steel blade.

"It's a Bloody Morningstar!" Stake whispered.

"A what?" Tim gulped.

"They strap you in and then it starts slicing through the victim from the tips of the extremities and keeps going until it gets to the heart!" Stake whispered. His expression indicated that he was equal parts horrified and impressed. "Depending on how slowly they crank it, the subject can take up to six days to die!"

"That sounds like it would be about their speed," Tim whispered.

"Prepare the sacrifice!" said the first hooded figure as the other two led Carmilla to the device and began to strap her in. She had to be under some sort of trance, Tim figured, because she was putting up no resistance whatsoever.

"We have to do something," Stake hissed.

"What do you suggest?" Tim asked. "There are hundreds of them and only two of us!"

Stake reached into the bag under his robe and pulled out his dart gun.

"Not sure," he grunted. "But there's no time like the present."

Stake leaned over the balcony and extended both arms, taking careful aim. His targets were at least 50 feet away. Tim had no idea what the range on the gun was, but it didn't matter. Before Tim could do anything to stop him, he heard two small pops. At least one of them seemed to find their mark, as the figure on the left side of the platform staggered and fell to the ground.

"What was that?" said the leader. "Who's there?"

Stake fired two more shots. Tim heard one ping off the side of the machine, but the other one hit the second hooded figure, who collapsed against the frame and tumbled to the floor.

"Come on!" Stake said, standing up and throwing off his hood. "It's time to kick some demon cult ass!"

"Wait!" Tim said.

But Stake had no intention of waiting. He pulled off his robe and grabbed the silver bat off his back, then vaulted over the edge of the balcony and began running down the sloped arena to the stage.

"Eat righteous justice, you demon-loving pukes!" Stake yelled, getting halfway down before tripping over his feet and rolling the rest of the way to his target as a clanking and grunting black ball of moral fury.

"Of course," Tim muttered, pulling off his own hood. He grabbed a couple of items out of his backpack and stepped over the balcony, careful to move more slowly than his companion. The stone was slick and damp with condensation, so he did more sliding than running.

Tim reached the bottom just as Stake was getting to his feet. The leader, he noticed, had disappeared. Three more hooded figures came running out of the shadows along with two extremely large demons, both of whom were carrying enormous black pitchforks. Stake clocked the first one over the head and executed a neat spin move to hit the second one in the middle of the chest with the tip of the bat. The third one tried to jump on Stake's back and grab his arms. Stake wrenched them free and swept the bat straight back over the top of his head, hitting his attacker square in the face. There was a crunching sound as the bat connected with the hooded attacker's nose.

Tim turned towards the closest of the charging demons. Despite their size, they were only Serrabluks. That meant they were big and scary looking, but not gifted with great reasoning ability or curse power. Most of them worked as bouncers, doormen and low-rent bodyguards. You couldn't overpower them, but you could still incapacitate them with the right tools.

Tim raised his hand and squeezed the nozzle on the canister, aiming the jet of green spray straight at the demon's face. The demon screamed as the stream hit it in the eyes, which started to smoke as it went down on its back. The second demon, completely failing to learn from the first, went down the same way.

"Holy shit!" Stake said. "What is that?"

"Demonex," Tim said. "Military grade. My father buys the stuff by the gallon with his contractor's discount."

"Nice!" Stake said. "You've gotta hook me up with some of that!"

"Let's get Carmilla out of here!" Tim said, nodding towards his prone co-worker.

The two of them raced over and pulled Carmilla back up to her feet.

"Where the hell am I?" she said, shaking her head.

"We'll explain as soon as we leave," Tim said. "Come on!"

"Which way?" Stake said, looking around.

Tim pointed back down the way the demons had come. "This way, I guess. If they got in, there must be a way to get out."

Two more hooded figures came charging at them. Stake knocked one over with a line drive to the side of the head, while Carmilla instinctively grabbed the second and flipped them over with a neat judo move. The hooded figure went flying into the torture machine, which kicked in with a rumble and began to spin. The sleeve of the figure's robe got caught in the mechanism and lifted them up like a rat caught in a lottery machine. The figure let out a surprised squawk as the blades flipped around and came down with frightening speed, slicing the individual into six equal pieces with lethal efficiency.

"Well, they wanted blood, they got it," Stake observed.

"Yeah," Tim said, trying not to look as his ears filled with the damp splat of severed body parts hitting the stone floor. "Let's go."

They raced down the dark corridor and found a curving stone staircase that led up. Tim could hear footsteps clacking overhead. That had to be the leader, he thought, but that was a matter for another day. They made their way up and reached a level that looked like the lobby of a large corporation. The walls were black marble lit by sconces glowing with Hellfire. A smoked glass dome rose up in the centre. The outer perimeter was lined with five statues, each depicting the same, monstrous demonic form. All of them had six arms and two heads, but each of the statues depicted the demon in question in a different pose. One showed it eating what looked like six screaming humans. Another showed it breathing fire on a group of screaming humans who were trying to flee. Still another showed it holding at least six anguished humans, each of which was impaled on a large pitchfork.

"I hate to say it, but this place is actually pretty cool," Stake said, looking impressed.

"Yeah," Tim said. "They at least have a consistency of motif."

"Who is that?" Stake said.

"Probably Belial," Tim said. "I'm guessing he's the one trapped behind the giant door in the basement."

"So how do we get out?" Stake said. "I don't see any actual doors."

There was a click and a humming sound. They rounded the edge of the dome to see a hooded figure escaping through a door that appeared to be built into the wall behind one of the statues.

"That looks like a way out," Tim said.

The three of them took off across the floor, reaching the door just as it was starting to close. Stake jammed his bat underneath it, stopping the door before it dropped back down into the floor.

"Hurry!" he said, waving the others through.

Tim and Carmilla dropped down and crawled under the door as the mechanism screeched and smoked ominously. Stake followed right behind and pulled the bat back out once he was clear, allowing the door to grind mechanically back into place. They got up just in time to see the hooded figure disappear into a limousine that was waiting by the curb. As soon as the figure was in, the car screeched away and raced down the road.

"Rabbited," Stake said. "Typical."

"We need to get as far away from this place as possible," Carmilla said. "Now."

"Good idea," Stake said. "Get off the street. Hide out until this blows over. I have a workshop I use. More like a headquarters, really. For my operations. Secret. Can't tell you where it is."

"Okay," Tim said.

"I'll be in touch," Stake said. He checked the Hammer of Helsing, which was dented where the bottom of the door had lodged against it. He frowned and spun it over his head and on to his back with a flourish, then ran across the street and disappeared into an alley.

"You know that guy?" Carmilla said.

"Sort of," Tim said. "I'm kind of waiting for him to get a less-gritty reboot with a sunnier origin story."

"Listen," she said. "Thanks for getting me out of there. I'll talk to you at work!"

She turned to run.

"Wait!" Tim said. "What the hell are you doing with those guys?"

"No time!" she said. "Watch your back!"

Carmilla jumped off the curb and ran down the street, cutting through a vacant lot and disappearing between two buildings.

"Why do I get the feeling that taking this new job might not have been one of my better ideas?" Tim wondered to himself.

He heard a rumble that he recognized as the sound of the huge underground garage doors opening. He realized that his employment status was a question he should probably ponder elsewhere. He checked to make sure there was no one coming, then ran across the road and off through the night.

22

"We may have gotten lucky," Tabitha said. "A surveillance camera picked up a three-quarter view of a woman's face leaning out of a car that was westbound on Route 113 just yesterday morning. When I ran it through recog, it came back as a 72% likely match for your missing psychic."

It was early Sunday morning. The two of them were in Tabitha's car headed west out of the city.

"That is lucky," Tim said. "What are the odds she'd stick her face out of the car at that moment to smile for the camera?"

"Part luck, part planning," Tabitha said. "That point in the road is one of the few lookout points for the Styx Canyon Rapids. We stuck the camera there because the road became a popular stalking spot for feral werewolves and baggers looking to roll unsuspecting tourists. There's a wide spot at the side of the road where people often park to check out the view even though the signs warn them not to."

The Styx Rapids were popular with tourists and adrenaline junkies, especially the two times per year that they caught fire courtesy of a seasonal Hellfire eruption. In the spring, it burned bright green for six days. In the fall, the waters turned fiery purple. It was easily one of the most photographed wilderness scenes in the world. The Devil's Throat was the name given to the most perilous stretch of rapids, which ran roughly six and a half kilometres through the canyon pass. Twice a year, 13 boats entered it in the hopes of winning the Hellfire Invitational. There had never been a race where all 13 boats made it to the finish line intact. Incapacitating injury and death were not uncommon outcomes for competitors.

"We know some of the mid-level blood runners have been using the route to move their product in and out of the city less visibly," Tabitha said. "That's why we've been running scans on all the plates and, when the opportunity presents itself, faces. When the name Russenberger cropped up on yesterday's list, I thought I might take a closer look."

"Any idea where they went?" Tim asked.

"That's where it gets interesting," Tabitha said. "We've got another camera five clicks further down the road at the I66 interchange, but her vehicle didn't pass it."

"So they must have gotten off before that," Tim said.

"Right," Tabitha said. "There are only two places to exit the road before that point. One leads to the municipal water treatment plant. That's a secured entrance, though. Has a guard station and two-stage authentication. They installed it after that idiot tried to dump a compound into the water supply that was supposed to turn everyone into a werewolf. Remember him?"

"I do," Tim nodded. Lucian van Horn had been a notorious curiosity even before the water tampering attempt. A militant crusader for werewolf rights (despite not being one himself), he had actually earned the suspicion and ire of the were-community by campaigning in a wolfman Halloween costume and demanding things in which actual werewolves had no interest whatsoever, like city-funded grooming stations and a formal declaration naming January 24 (his birthday, it turned out) International Werewolf Day. The general opinion seemed to be that he was only doing it for the social media recognition, although his YouTube channel only had 150 subscribers. Real or feigned, his activism came to an end when he broke into the sewage treatment plant and tried to dump 40 gallons of what he called "Wolf Juice" into the city water supply. Not having planned his mission to lycanthropize an entire metropolis too carefully, all he managed to do was fall into a vat of untreated waste, where he was quickly overcome by fumes and would have drowned had a quick-thinking city employee not hit the emergency discharge switch.

"There's only one other place to get off the road before that," Tabitha said. "It's so obscure that it's not even on any of the digital maps. It's a service road leading up to the old Stygian Hotel."

"Wow," Tim said. "I didn't even know that place still existed."

The Stygian Hotel had been part of the landscape since the time the city was little more than a trading outpost. Perched on a remote outcrop high up on the ragged edge of the Bloodmoon Mountains to the west, the place had originally been some sort of pagan temple before the extremely wealthy and reclusive Tantalus family snapped it up and controversially built their estate on the ruins. Although it was not unusual to tear down and rebuild on such sites within the metropolitan area where space was at a premium, the remediation costs made it prohibitively expensive for all but the most deep-pocketed developers. To do it outside the city centre where uncursed land was relatively plentiful and cheap was considered insane. The general consensus was that the approval had been obtained via copious bribery, blackmail and threats, concepts with which the Tantalus clan were extremely familiar.

Family patriarch, Solomon V., had supposedly made his vast sums by selling his family's souls to the devil himself, although he also had sizable holdings in several banks, which was the source more commonly cited by historians of the period. The spot was also in close proximity to an old silver mine that had collapsed a century earlier, killing more than 200 workers, many of whom were children. The five-kilometre zone around the place had one of the highest non-insure scores on the exclusion charts that Tim had ever seen.

Solomon, however, did not get to spend a single night in the house. He was killed during one of his periodic inspections of the construction work when a stone gargoyle weighing 3 tons came loose from its mounting above the north entrance and fell on him from three storeys up. Reporters had joked that the deceased owner, so keen to make an impression on the landscape, had done so in a manner rather more permanent than he had intended (Solomon also owned a lot of newspapers and was notoriously unpopular with his employees).

Internecine wars over his fortune left the house in a state of physical and legal limbo for much of the next ten years before it was snapped up by his second-oldest son, Rupert, who had the idea to turn it into a hotel. The project was, not surprisingly, plagued with problems and cost overruns. Workers reported seeing the ghosts of small, ravenous children coated in dust who chased them through the halls. Others reported sightings of the late Solomon himself, who apparently was fond of haranguing architects and interior designers about some of the design and décor changes made by his son.

The hotel was only open for a few months when a fire destroyed much of the main hall during a large and elaborate All Hallows Ball. Many of the guests were trapped and either suffocated in the smoke or were incinerated in the flames, the cause of which was never determined. Rupert survived the blaze but was found dead less than a week later, having apparently jumped to his death from the window of his private suite on the top floor. He had borrowed heavily to finance construction and was more than $100 million in debt at the time of expiry. With no other family members stepping forward to assumer ownership of the place, it rapidly fell into decline and eventual ruin. The forest that had been chopped down to make room for it slowly reclaimed the space and overgrew the site, speeding the hotel's decline into historical oblivion. A few ambitious or delusional developers had made noises in the intervening years about revitalizing the place, but none of their plans had amounted to anything more than talk. Most people thought of the Stygian as a remote and desolate monument to hubris; a cursed wreck best left rotting in obscurity.

"Did you manage to find out anything more about these Sons of Darkness guys?" Tabitha said, steering on to the exit ramp from the main highway. It was Sunday and traffic was light. By Monday morning, it would be a very different story. Not for nothing was the ring road around the city nicknamed Purgatory Circle.

Tim told her about his visit to the underground temple with Stake the night before.

"Didn't I tell you not to do exactly that sort of stuff?" Tabitha said in an exasperated voice. "Is living with your brother that bad? Are you trying to get yourself killed?"

"The plan was just to sneak in for a look," Tim said. "Stake was the one who decided to jump right into the middle of proceedings."

"That's another thing," Tabitha said. "This new friend of yours."

"You know anything about him?" Tim asked.

"Oh yes," Tabitha sighed. "You could say that the wannabe vigilante calling himself 'Stake' is well known to police."

"He told me his parents were killed by a vampire," Tim said.

"That is true," Tabitha said. "But probably not in the way you think. They weren't attacked and drained. It was a car accident."

"A what?" Tim said.

"Yeah," Tabitha said. "Perpetrator was a bartender who stayed out a little too early at the club and was racing to get home before the sun came up. The family was crossing the street in front of their apartment when he came racing around the corner and hit them. Father managed to push the kid out of the way onto the sidewalk. Father was hit head on and killed more or less instantly. Mother lingered for a few days in hospital before she died, too. Kid was only eight years old and passed to the custody of his aunt."

"Shit," Tim said. "That's rough."

"It is," Tabitha agreed. "He didn't adjust well. Lot of misdemeanor stuff. Fights with other kids. Got expelled a couple of times. Dropped out of high school in his second year, if memory serves. That's when he stepped things up a notch. Started getting picked up for more serious harassment and assault complaints. Most of the time, nobody bothered to press charges, but he's spent more than a few hours in a holding cell. Most of the cops know him on a first-name basis."

"What is his real name?" Tim asked. "He only ever refers to himself as Stake. Sometimes in the third person. It's like he's narrating his own graphic novel as he goes along."

"His real name is Harlan Oddler Murnau," Tabitha said. "I think he's 22 or 23 years old. Works for Cerberus Security Services, mostly on daytime mall duty. He's racked up a few harassment complaints while on the job—mostly from vampires and werewolves—but not enough to get him fired. I think they like him because he keeps the baggers and junkies away, so mostly they just look the other way on the other stuff. He got the job though one of those pathways to employment programs and settled right in. Although it's pretty clear that he believes his real job is keeping non-humans off the streets."

"He is pretty handy with a bat," Tim said. "He helped me out when I got mugged by a couple of baggers down in the Crypt Network a few days ago. That was how I met him. Although I did see him getting kicked out of Circle 9 before that."

"What the hell were you doing down in the Crypt Network?" Tabitha asked. "Not even cops go down there!"

Tim explained finding the key in the bookstore underneath Madame Zoudini's.

"I have no idea what it opens," he said. "We got swarmed by more Sons of Darkness goons before I could do any more poking around."

"So that giant building they're in is their headquarters?" Tabitha said.

"Not sure about that," Tim said. "I didn't see offices or anything like that. But it's definitely where they hold their rituals."

"Did you actually see them kill or injure anyone?" Tabitha asked.

"Er … no," Tim admitted. He decided not to mention the cult member that Carmilla had tossed into the slicing machine.

"Which means we would have absolutely no legal pretext to go in there," Tabitha said. "Warrant-wise, anyway."

"What about kidnapping?" Tim suggested.

"Too much of a stretch," Tabitha said, shaking her head. "We'll need something more concrete before we go charging in with a Tac team."

"Probably a good idea," Tim said. "I wouldn't be surprised if the mayor, the chief of police and half of the city council are members."

"Based on their HQ and the fact that they've been able to grow so quickly with practically nobody noticing, you might have a point there," Tabitha said. "All the more reason to tread carefully."

She slowed the car to a stop next to a gap in the trees that was barely wider than a path.

"I think this is it," she said, turning the car slowly onto the narrow gravel road.

"Are you sure?" Tim said, ducking down involuntarily in his seat as the tree branches scraped along the roof.

"According to my phone it is," she said, nodding to the cell phone in the mount on her dashboard. "I pinned it before I left."

They made their way slowly down the narrow path, which curved and angled sharply up the side of the mountain. After about 100 yards, they came upon a decrepit-looking, single-storey wooden frame building on their left. In front of it was a small booth with a swinging attachment for a security arm that was no longer there.

"Looks deserted," Tabitha said.

She was about to pull in and park next to the building when Tim raised a hand to stop her.

"Wait," he said. "Let me just check something first."

Tim reached into his pack and pulled out his goggles. He fixed them in place over his glasses and did a scan of the building. As far as he could see, there was no one there, supernatural or otherwise.

"What are those?" Tabitha asked.

"PSV glasses," Tim said. "They pick up entities that might not show up in the visible spectrum."

"They also make you look like a dork," she snickered.

"Go ahead and laugh it up," he said. "You'll be laughing out the other side of your face if I spot an Onyxite before it bites a hole in your skull and starts eating your amygdala."

"Okay, I take it back," she said. "What else you got in that little bag of tricks of yours?"

"Wouldn't you like to know," Tim said, winking.

"Just remember," Tabitha said. "We see Russenberger or anything else weird up there, you let me do the talking, okay?"

"Fine with me, sergeant," Tim said.

Tabitha shook her head. "How did I let myself get talked into this?"

"Don't ask me," Tim said. "This was your idea."

"Seriously," Tabitha said. "We have no official excuse to be here. I don't even know if anybody still owns this place. But if they do and we run into them and they decide they'd rather we not see what they're up to, then leave it to me. If things get crazy, then stay low and try to get back to the car to call for backup on the radio."

"Relax," Tim said. "I've been in the occasional tight spot in my time. I promise I won't freak out."

"Okay then, tough guy," Tabitha said. "Let's go."

23

They checked the building and the booth first. Both looked like they hadn't been used for at least a century. The roof had either collapsed on its own or been pulverized by some sort of mini-avalanche that had rolled down from higher up. The floor was covered with boulders and plants growing up through the cracks in the wooden floor. The booth appeared to have been occupied by several generations of wildlife, none of which had been conscientious tenants.

Behind the building was a staircase winding up the side of the rock. They decided to take it since it appeared to be a more direct route than the road. Tabitha took the stairs two at a time in a steady jog, while Tim was reminded that he had allowed his gym membership to lapse more than a year ago. He huffed and puffed up the last couple of flights to where Tabitha was already crouched, peering over the top stair. He sat down heavily next to her, trying to catch his breath.

"You're out of shape, Gurg," she smiled. "You need to get out from behind your desk more often."

"Thanks for the tip," he gasped. "You see anything?"

"Nope," Tabitha said, shaking her head.

Tim peered over the top stair. He could see the road curving past from the right towards two structures. The first was obviously what had once been the hotel. It was a five-storey neoclassical behemoth of black stone. The original lines were still evident, but it had become so rundown and decrepit that it was hard to imagine that anyone would be keen to walk through the front doors. There were no signs of life or movement in any of spectrums he dialled into with his goggles.

The second building was smaller and off to the left. It looked like it had at one time been used as a stable or garage. Unlike the checkpoint down below, the walls and roof of this one were intact and even looked like they might have been recently replaced.

"See anything?" Tabitha whipered.

"Not off the top," Tim said. "It looks-"

He heard a clank and dropped down just as a door on the side of the secondary building opened. Two figures emerged and began moving across the grounds towards the main building. Tim zoomed in on them. They both floated about five feet off the ground and trailed a large number of dangling tendrils, which made them look like jellyfish. Both of them appeared to be carrying something.

"What are those things?" Tabitha hissed.

"Osmanibaks," Tim said.

"Osmani-whats?" Tabitha said.

"Osmanibaks," Tim said. "It's a type of demon. It's basically just a floating mouth with arms."

"Ugh," Tabitha said. "I think I've dated a few of those."

Tim laughed. He hoped that she wasn't referring to him.

"So what are they doing up here?" Tabitha asked.

"No idea," Tim said. "They're actually supposed to be incredibly intelligent. Some scholars even think they were responsible for the first spoken and written language. Although that is, naturally, disputed."

"Naturally," Tabitha said.

They watched as the two demons reached the main building. One of them held something out to a scanner next to the door. It opened and the two of them glided through the opening and disappeared. Less than a minute later, the door opened again and three more Osmanibaks emerged from the secondary building and headed for the main hotel. Tim zoomed in as much as he could. The one in front was carrying a large glass vial full of what looked like a glowing blue liquid.

"What are they carrying?" Tabitha asked.

"Not sure," Tim said. "But I have a feeling it's not a pitcher of Dr. Apocalypto's Crypt Berry Buster energy drink."

"You see any humans anywhere?" Tabitha asked.

"No," Tim said. That gave him an idea. He reached into his bag and pulled out a clip with a small transmitter attached to it. He handed one to Tabitha and clipped the other one to his jacket. "Here, put this on."

"What is it?" Tabitha asked.

"It's a scrambler," Tim said. "You wear it and it makes it pretty much impossible for certain types of demons to see you."

"Does that include this type of demon?" Tabitha asked.

"It does," Tim said.

"Are you sure?" Tabitha asked, attaching the clip to the lapel of her overcoat.

"Positive," Tim said. "They won't be able to see us. But they will still be able to hear us, so try to be as quiet as possible. The adjusters use them when they're reviewing poltergeist claims. You can never count on the remediation team to get every last entity out of a place and it's better safe than possessed."

"And what happens if we run into a type of demon that this doesn't work on?" Tabitha asked.

Tim smiled. "Then I believe you mentioned something about getting out of your way and letting you handle the situation?"

"Smartass," Tabitha muttered.

The two of them got up and jogged across the ground to the corner of the main building. The windows were dark and too high up to see through. Tim's curiosity was peaked. What were a bunch of hyperintelligent demons of a type normally not found outside of east Asia doing in an abandoned and derelict hotel on the outskirts of the city?

They reached the main building just as the door opened and two more demons emerged from the other and began moving towards them.

"You're positive those things can't see us?" Tabitha whispered.

Tim nodded.

"And what would they do to us if they could?" she asked.

Tim grinned. "You probably don't want to know."

"So what's our plan?" Tabitha whispered.

"That depends," Tim whispered back. "Do you want to see where they're making that blue stuff or what they're doing with it?"

Tabitha thought for a moment. "The second one."

"Yeah," Tim whispered. "Me too."

"So how do we get in?" Tabitha whispered.

Tim dug into his pocket and pulled out his cell phone.

"Need to make an urgent call?" Tabitha whispered sarcastically.

"No," Tim whispered. "I'm going to disable our one-eyed friends."

"With a phone?" Tabitha hissed.

"There's an app for that," Tim whispered, smiling. He brought up the application he was looking for and scrolled through the options looking for Osmanibaks. He was not surprised to see that they weren't on the default list. They really didn't exist in North America, after all. He went to the app store and quickly downloaded the add-on he needed. Once it was loaded, he stood up and walked around the corner so that he was standing directly between the demons and the entrance to the main building. "Get ready."

"Get ready for what?" Tabitha hissed. "What are you doing?"

Tim raised his phone and pointed it at the approaching Osmanibaks. He could hear them chattering to each other in their language. To human ears, it sounded oddly like the squawking of large birds. He remembered reading in university that some demonolinguist from Cambridge University had studied the Osmanibak language and determined that it had more than 231 million words, or roughly a thousand times as many as were in existence in English. This apparently gave them a tremendous facility for specificity and meant they were never misinterpreted amongst their own kind. It also meant that they could talk about things with a level of precise detail that no human could hope to match, but that it could also take them hours just to say hello.

Tim waited until the demons were close enough. He had never actually seen an Osmanibak in the flesh before—only in textbooks, and those reproductions had not been greatly detailed. Osmanibaks tended to shun humans, which they considered primitive and volatile. These ones were more wild looking than he had expected. Their eyes were veiny and filled with floating gloop, giving them the appearance of a living lava lamp. That was their brains, he supposed. Their arms hung down below them like the clenched claws of a bird of prey in flight. Each one was tipped by a gnarly knot of spines that the demon would use to defend itself if threatened. Although they looked fierce, they didn't use them for slicing. Instead, victims would be subjected to a spectral current that would essentially cook them where they stood. Osmanibaks rarely attacked humans, but when they did, the general consensus was that it was better not to survive such an event.

The flipside of their tremendous power was that they were remarkably sensitive to even the weakest signal frequencies, which was another reason they tended to stay as far from humans as possible. Something as simple as a garage door opener could put one of them into a coma. Tim didn't want to kill them, but he didn't want to end up on the wrong end of those tentacles, either. He waited until the two demons were in range and then tapped the large red "Activate" button on his screen. Both demons froze, shivered in mid air, and then slowly collapsed on the ground, dropping their glowing blue containers.

"How did you do that?" Tabitha said, running up behind him.

"Easy peasy," Tim said, tucking his phone back into his pocket. "I have an app that incapacitates 55 different kinds of demons. Some of them require specialist curses, but these guys are hypersensistive to certain frequencies. You could probably knock them out with a dog whistle if you had one."

Tim leaned down and picked up the blue glass tube. The liquid inside was thick and glowed like a blue neon bulb.

"What is that?" Tabitha asked.

"I'm not sure," Tim said, studying the tube carefully. The liquid appeared to be sparking, like it was conducting some sort of electricity. "It looks kind of like some sort of liquid Hellfire."

"Like what?" Tabitha said, leaning closer.

"Almost like napalm," Tim said. "Except a lot more destructive."

"Napalm?" Tabitha said. "Maybe you should put it down."

"Seems stable enough in here," Tim shrugged.

"What are they using it for I wonder?" Tabitha said.

"Good question," Tim said. "Why don't we take a look and see?"

Tabitha nodded to the unconscious Osmanibaks. "Are they dead?"

"I don't think so," Tim said. "I didn't stun them that hard. But I don't exactly know how to check for a pulse on these things, so I suppose it's a possibility."

Tim leaned over and pulled the ID cards out of the claws of each. They were plain white cards with no photos or other identifying characteristics. He supposed that made sense. Osmanibaks were pretty hard to tell apart, except possibly to each other.

"Do we just leave them here?" Tabitha said.

"Help me move them into these bushes," Tim said. "Just be careful not to touch the arms. They might still have some juice in them."

Tim bent down and rolled the first demon into the bushes next to the main building. Its skin was smoother than he had been expecting, but touching it still gave him the creeps.

Once they had done that, he and Tabitha turned and made their way to the metal door. Tim held the card up to the reader and a moment later the door slid open. The two of them stepped inside and descended a flight of stone stairs. They emerged in a narrow hallway of pristine white walls lit by greenish overhead fluorescent bulbs. There were doors on either side spaced about 20 feet apart. Osmanibaks drifted in and out of the rooms, some of them carrying blue vials and others carrying empty glass tubes.

"This looks like a hospital ward," Tabitha whispered, looking puzzled.

"It does," Tim nodded.

"Are you sure those things can't see us?" Tabitha asked.

"Positive," Tim whispered. "But the scramblers don't work against cameras or humans. Or other things that might happen to be down here, so be careful."

Tim and Tabitha moved slowly down the hall, careful to avoid the oblivious Osmanibaks. They reached the first door and peeked in through the window. Inside was a woman lying on a table. She had dozens of sensors attached to her head and body, the wires snaking across the floor and into the back of a large set of machines being monitored by a group of five Osmanibaks. Tim felt a stab of recognition as he saw the woman's face.

"It's Anita Browdley!" Tim gasped.

"Who?" Tabitha asked.

"She was a client of Zoudini's," Tim said. "She was with her when the possession happened! I went to talk to her after as part of the investigation. When I tried to go back to talk to her again after Zoudini disappeared, her house had burned down. They told me she had been killed in the blaze."

"Who told you?" Tabitha asked.

"Neighbour," Tim said.

"Well, if that's her, then it looks like they got it wrong," Tabitha said. "What are they doing to her?"

"No idea," Tim said. "Maybe they're scanning her brain. Looking for some clue that'll help them decode the message."

"Didn't you already decode it?" Tabitha asked.

"Yes," Tim said.

"So if you could do it, chances are these things would have been able to do it too?" Tabitha said.

"Thanks, Tab," Tim muttered.

"I didn't say you're not smart," Tabitha said. "But didn't you say these things are basically just giant floating brains?"

"Yeah," Tim admitted. "Point taken."

They moved on. The next two rooms were full of similar equipment but appeared to be unoccupied. They pushed themselves up against the wall as two Osmanibaks passed them carrying blue vials. The demons continued straight to the end of the hall and disappeared down another flight of stairs.

"Looks like that's where the action is," Tabitha said. "Come on."

The two of them jogged to the end of the hall and down the steps. The air grew sharply cooler and the pristine white walls gave way to dark black stone as the stairs curved around into a spiral. They reached the bottom and followed the demons through a low stone archway into a massive chamber. At first glance, it appeared to be as large as the entire building aboveground. The ceiling was supported by thick stone pillars that were evenly spaced down the length of the room, which To Tim looked to be at least as large as two football fields placed side by side.

"Holy shit!" Tabitha gasped. "What is this place?"

The most striking feature of the room were the hundreds of cylindrical glass tanks arranged in neat rows from one end of the floor to the other. Each one appeared to be full of the glowing blue liquid, which seemed to be the only source of light. Hundreds of Osmanibaks moved back and forth between the tanks. Tim watched as they attached the glass vial to a port on the side. Once it was in place, the fluid was sucked into the tank and the vial was emptied and removed. This happened constantly; a never-ending process of constant motion that reminded Tim of the floor of a factory or assembly plant.

"I have no idea," Tim said.

The room vibrated with the low hum of electricity. Each time a vial was loaded, the tank in question would glow briefly brighter and flicker with what looked like internal lightning. The lightning momentarily illuminated the shadow of something floating inside.

"Did you see that?" Tabitha said, pointing at one of the tanks as it briefly lit up. "There's something in them!"

"I saw it," Tim nodded. "Let's try to get a closer look."

The two of them stepped out onto the floor. It was much more crowded with demons in here, which made it difficult to move without bumping into one of them. Tim and Tabitha approached the nearest tank just as an Osmanibak was attaching the vial. The two of them snuck up to get as close to the glass as they could when the fluid passed through. There was a flicker and a flash as Tim peered through the blue ooze. When it lit up, he could see the outline of a large demon with six arms and two heads. Each one of the heads had a large set of curved horns attached at the forehead. All six of its eyes were closed and its arms were wrapped around its body in a perversely fetal pose.

"What is that thing?" Tabitha gasped as the light flickered out.

"It's a Serrabluk," Tim said.

"A what?" Tabitha said.

"A Serrabluk," Tim repeated. "It's a type of demon. But they get to be up to 15 feet tall. This one is barely as big as me."

"Maybe they're growing them," Tabitha said.

DEMONIC INDEMNITY • 225

They made their way over to the next tank. When it lit up, they could see that it also contained a Serrabluk that was almost exactly the same as the first.

"You're right," Tim said. "It's like some weird demon nursery or something."

"Look at the wires," Tabitha said, pointing up at the top of the tank. "They all lead to the big one in the middle."

Tim looked up and could see that Tabitha was right. A thick coil of black wires led from the top of each of the smaller tanks to a much large tank in the middle of the floor. The central tank was about five times as large as the others and surrounded by an almost unbroken line of Osman-ibaks, who were recharging it with new vials almost constantly at dozens of access points. Because of this, the main tank was glowing much more brightly than the others. Tim thought he could see not one but two dark shapes floating inside.

"Wonder what they've got in there?" Tabitha asked in a manner that clearly communicated that she would prefer it if she didn't have to find out the answer to that question.

"Only one way to find out," Tim said.

The two of them made their way carefully through the crowd to the main tank. It was difficult to see past the Osmanibaks, of which there were at least 50 crowded around waiting to load fresh vials. Tim waited until one of them moved out of the way and then stepped quickly into a space between two ports as Tabitha did the same on his left. Whatever was in the tank was on the far side and the fluid was too thick to see anything, but Tim could see that there was an odd sort of counter-clockwise current that was pulling it around towards them.

"Can't really see anything," Tabitha whispered.

"I think it's coming around!" Tim hissed back. He could feel the glass vibrating against his hands. Whatever was in there was putting out a tre-mendous amount of energy. Tim pushed his nose right up against the glass as the shape moved closer to them and gradually began to take on a recognizable form.

"Oh my god," Tabitha gasped, putting a hand over her mouth.

Tim let his muscles freeze in horror as he realized what he was looking at. There were two distinct shapes. The larger of the two, near the bottom, was Madame Zoudini. Or had been. The top of her skull had been removed, leaving most of her brain exposed. Her arms and legs had also been removed, and not with surgical precision. Tim could see protruding bone and tiny wisps of loose flesh and tendon floating loosely around the wounds. Her jaw was also missing, although most of the skin around the chin was still there, swelling in and out like a puffer fish.

Some kind of cable had been attached to the late psychic's exposed brain, but it didn't look like electrical cable. It looked more...fleshy. Whatever it was, it was attached to the second object, which at first glance looked perversely like a balloon. As it got closer, however, Tim could see that it was a translucent bag containing some sort of humanoid form. It was only when the thing was practically level with his eyes that he could see that the thing inside the bag was a demon, or at least, a demon in the making.

Tim had heard about the process of Demonorecombinant Engineering—of using a possessed individual to actually grow a physical demon—but had never seen the results of such an attempt or even heard of anyone who had tried it. The practice was internationally banned by the United Nations Declaration of Universal Supernatural Rights, which included a clause forbidding any attempt to meld human and demon DNA and had been signed by more than 120 countries (Syria, the Philippines and the United States were the only major nations who had refused to add their signatures). It was rumored that the Nazis had experimented with it during the Second World War, but there was no proof of this beyond the ravings of the usual nuts on the usual conspiracy websites. Leading geneticists balked at the process, claiming that it was not only unethical, but completely impossible.

Dr. Theresa Lighthizer, who had won the Nobel prize for Physiology or Medicine only a year previously, had said in her acceptance speech that: "The notion of a human-demon hybrid is one that belongs in science fiction, not science fact."

Well Dr. Lighthizer, Tim thought, medal or no medal, it appears that you don't know shit.

Tim staggered back from the glass, his brain focused solely on the idea of getting as far away from what was in there as he possibly could. He staggered as something bumped into him from the right. He spun sideways and heard a clink as something metal hit the stone floor. He reached up instinctively to feel for his scrambler, but it wasn't there. He was shoved forward and felt his shoe come down with a crunch on something small.

Uh oh, he thought.

The Osmanibak closest to him lit up and raised its arms in alarm as others did likewise. He could hear their chatter rise to a twittering cacophony as they became alerted to his now visible presence.

"Tim?" said Tabitha. "What the hell are they doing?"

"I lost my scrambler!" Tim said, grabbing for his cell phone. "Run!"

Three Osmanibaks charged at him at once. Tim unlocked his phone. Luckily, the app was still open and live. He hit the button. Two of the demons dropped, but the third kept coming, quickly joined by six more. Tim turned and ran with Tabitha for the stairs. Fortunately, she was still invisible to them.

"I'll draw them off!" he shouted. "They still can't see you! Just go!"

"The hell with that!" Tabitha said, pulling something out of her jacket. "Do Tasers work on these things?"

Instead of waiting for an answer, she jabbed the device in the back of one of the creatures that was chasing after Tim and hit the button. The creature lit up and started to smoke, then dropped to the ground and caught fire.

"Never mind!" she said. "They do!"

The two of them ran for the stairs as every demon in the place chased after them. One of them grabbed the back of Tim's jacket and almost pulled him over before Tabitha kicked it off and electrocuted it. Tim noticed that the other demons were extremely careful to avoid the flames, especially if they were carrying a blue vial. That gave him an idea.

As soon as they reached the stairs, Tim raised the vial he was carrying and smashed it against the floor, sending thick blue goop everywhere.

"Light it up!" he yelled.

Tabitha bent down and touched the prongs of the Taser to the puddle, which immediately burst into wild blue flames. The flames quickly reached one of the tanks. Tim watched in amazement as the liquid inside started to bubble and boil almost instantly. A moment later, it exploded, sending liquid fire in all directions. The flames quickly reached the next tank in line, which did likewise.

"It's a chain reaction!" Tim said, watching in disbelief as another tank exploded. The blue flames landed on a tight pack of Osmanibaks, which screeched and tried desperately to flee even as they burned.

"Yeah," Tabitha said. "And as soon as it reaches that main tank, this whole place is gonna go with it! Come on!"

The two of them raced up the stairs to the sounds of more explosions. Tim could feel the building shaking more and more with each one. Well, he thought, at least we know why they moved the stuff in such small quantities.

They reached the top of the stairs and ran down the hospital corridor. Three Osmanibaks came out into the hall to investigate what was going on, but Tim stunned them before they could move to block them.

"We need to get to your witness!" Tabitha said, pointing at the room where they had seen Anita Browdley strapped down and wired up to machines.

"Anita!" Tim nodded. "Right!"

They were almost at the door when a series of eight explosions went off so close together that they almost seemed like a single blast. Tim and Tabitha were knocked off their feet and thrown against the wall. The lights flickered and went out. The ground didn't stop shaking as there were smashes and bangs all around them. To Tim, it felt like they had stepped into the middle of an avalanche.

Tim wiped the dust out of his eyes. As the lights flicked back on, he could see that the space where Browdley had been was now just a pile of rubble.

Tim staggered to his feet and helped Tabitha up. They made thier way over to where the window had been and peered inside. Not only had the ceiling come down, most of the floor had gone, too. Tim wasn't sure, but he thought he could see the outlines of a group of children wearing overalls climbing around and appearing to dance on the wreckage.

"It's the ghosts of the underage miners!" Tim said, pointing.

"Right," Tabitha said, pulling him back. "And if we don't get out of here now, we'll be stuck wandering around this place forever, too. Come on!"

The two of them made it to the end of the hall and up the stairs. The key card reader wasn't working. Tabitha got out a telescoping baton and knocked it off the wall, at which point the door opened. The two of them ran outside and across the field to the steps, followed by the sound of muffled booms. Tim looked back to see the lower windows of the old hotel lit up blue with each one.

They had just reached the bottom of the stairs and gotten into Tabitha's car when they heard a massive boom. Tabitha swung the car out onto the path and raced down the drive. Tim looked back to see the sky light up as the hotel vanished in a flash of blue light.

"Whoa," he said.

A massive stone gargoyle tore through the trees and landed in front of them just as they pulled out onto the road. Tabitha screeched around it and hit the gas, fishtailing the car back onto the road.

"How about for our next date we just go someplace quiet for a nice dinner?" she said, rounding the corner at twice the speed limit.

"Yeah," Tim said, nodding. "That sounds great."

24

The following day was completely taken up with the company-wide town hall meeting to present the CEO's grand strategic plan for the next five fiscal years. Although the SIU did not report directly to anyone within the executive hierarchy, it was strongly suggested that all staff show up for the seven-hour-long series of slideshow presentations, which was held in the grand ballroom of the King's Hotel in the heart of downtown.

After the adrenaline overload of excitement from the night before, Tim actually didn't mind the chance to just sit at a table and quietly doze off as a variety of speakers of wedding-speech-level charisma droned on about risk granularity and big data. His fellow employees, however, did not feel quite the same way.

"It's a dumpster load of buzzword-loving corporate dickheads," Volkerps muttered. "At least I only have to pretend to watch it from my office."

Volkerps had special permission to attend remotely as he had a tendency to fall asleep and fart lightning bolts. The first time he had attended the event in person, he had dozed off and accidentally set fire to the buffet table in the middle of a speech about how automated curse detectors were going to revolutionize the field of risk appetite analysis. The same allowance was granted to employees who could not be out in daylight and had to watch from the secure confines of their crypt or coffin.

"At least we get food," said Lonnie, scarfing a cherry Danish, bran muffin and fruit cup in short order. "Let me know if you see any more of those little eclairs. The damn actuarial department is swallowing all the best grub."

"Will do," Tim said, yawning. He had not gotten much sleep the previous night and was in serious doubt about his ability to remain conscious for the duration of the speeches.

The first presentation was given by Anderss Lupo, the company's CFO. Her presentation was mostly bar graphs and pie charts laying out earnings projections based on the last six months. Tim did his best to follow along, but the financial side of the business was not his strength. Terms like Pre-tax Ameliorated CED Reserve Income and Investment Abasement Derivative Coefficient were so strange to him that they were essentially a foreign language. As far as he could tell, the company was making money, although it would have made slightly more if not for the Fort Acheron major claims event of the past quarter. Fort Acheron was a city of some 3,400 residents that had been forced to evacuate when a company digging a natural gas pipeline hit an unmarked mass grave. The grave contained the bodies of roughly 200 factory workers killed in a gas explosion a century before. Their deaths had been quite literally covered up by the company, which essentially just filled in the crater and fled town. Many of the town's current residents were descendants of the company's owners, which meant that the resulting spectral intrusion was even more violent and destructive than usual.

Tim wasn't the only one who found the endless graphs and spreadsheets to be a bit on the dry side.

"Nobody cares," Lonnie muttered under his breath. "Just tell me if I'm getting my bonus this year. I need to replace the wolf screens on my windows. Those damn things are expensive!"

Next up was the VP of pricing, who gave a profoundly enervating presentation about a new predictive algorithm that was going to lower their loss ratios on poltergeist claims by at least seven per cent over the next two years.

Tim was actually starting to drift off to sleep when he was startled awake by the sound of a familiar voice through the sound system. His eyes snapped open to see claims department VP Lilith Warwick standing at the lectern. What's more, she was staring straight at him.

"Stand up!" Lonnie hissed, elbowing Tim in the ribs.

Tim got up and looked around the room. He smiled, trying to look like he'd been expecting this all along.

"Tim is the first human to work in the Special Investigations Unit in the history of the company!" Warwick said proudly. "Isn't that terrific?"

There was polite applause from the crowd. Tim felt his face go red. He hated being singled out for attention in front of a large group. Or even a small one. She thanked him and went back to extolling the virtues of the new diversity in hiring program as Tim sat back down, now more alert than he had been moments before.

That's the voice, Tim thought. It was the same one he had heard coming from under the hood of the leader of the Sons of Darkness. It appeared that the new vice president of the claims department moonlighted as the head of a demon-worshipping cult.

But how was that possible? On the surface, it appeared to make no sense. Warwick was widely known throughout the company for her inclusion initiative, the unspoken purpose of which was to get humans working in departments from which they had traditionally been excluded. That hardly seemed like the kind of thing that would be introduced by somebody who was working to bring back an ancient demon king capable of wiping out most of humanity.

Maybe it was just a cover, Tim thought. Warwick often dropped references about her volunteer work with Vamp Vocations, a charity focused on getting homeless vampires off the streets and back into the work force.

Her corporate profile showed that she was also on the board of an organization called WereCare, which worked to preserve urban werewolf habitats. Demons had a long and contentious history with vampires and werewolves. Altruism and unity were not qualities to be found in abundance in their interactions with each other. Because of their perceived disproportionate involvement in organized crime (although the numbers were far from conclusive), demons were often portrayed as the literal root of all of society's evils. Vampires were most frequently portrayed as oversized parasites, sucking not just blood but also far more than their share of scant public resources. And werewolves were usually viewed as mindless savages.

Things were slowly starting to change, but these views were still rampant in popular culture and not just with humans. There was easily as much if not more infighting and prejudice in the supernatural community as there was outside of it. If Warwick was a secret demonic nationalist, she was doing an excellent job of hiding it.

Had she seen him the other night or had she left before things went sideways? Or did it go back further than that? Had she already decided that he knew too much about the Zoudini case? Had she been the one who had somehow engineered his encounter with the djinn? If so, did she have somebody working for her inside the SIU? Carmilla, maybe?

Once Warwick was done, the seminar took a 15-minute break. Tim made immediately for the coffee table and poured himself an extra-large cup. His mind was racing and he wanted to keep it sharp. He was in the process of trying to figure out which of the tall silver jugs contained cream when he felt a hand on his elbow and turned to see Warwick standing behind him.

"Sorry to put you on the spot like that," she said, smiling.

"That's okay!" Tim said in a strained voice. "No problem!"

"I just think it's important that everyone can put a human face on the program," Warwick said, hitting the word *human* with subtle but unmistakable emphasis. "Otherwise it can just seem like so much corporate gobbledegook."

"Right," Tim said.

"I've heard that you're doing an absolutely fantastic job over there," Warwick said.

"That's always nice to hear," Tim said. He wondered how she could have heard such a thing, since his boss did not report to her. Maybe she was just being polite.

"So what are you working on now?" she asked. "I hear you had a very interesting identity theft."

"Right," Tim said. He was unsure how to respond. Because of the secretive nature of the SIU, no one outside of the department was supposed to be made aware of the subject or contents of any of their investigations, including the CEO. Under the terms of his employment agreement, he was strictly forbidden from discussing his cases with anyone other than his boss, Volkerps. Warwick knew that. What was she doing? Baiting him? Subtly suggesting she knew a lot more than she was letting on? He reminded himself to be careful. It was entirely possible that Warwick knew nothing about what he was up to.

"Don't worry," she said. "I know you can't say anything here. But do come and see me when you get the chance. I may be able to assist in ... other ways. The survival of this company—of humanity itself—would be in serious danger if certain events were to come about."

She smiled and turned away to talk to the director of underwriting, whom she greeted like an old friend she hadn't seen in years. Tim was left holding his coffee and staring off into space with a blank expression.

He was still trying to make sense of this when he heard somebody hissing his name and looked up to see Carmilla gesturing to him from the door. He followed her out into the hall, which was otherwise empty.

"Just wanted to say thanks for saving my ass the other night," she said.

"No problem," Tim said. "How on earth did you end up getting grabbed by those guys in the first place?"

"I was undercover as part of an investigation," Carmilla said. "Somebody must have ratted me out. If you guys hadn't come along they would have sliced me up as another blood offering for their demon god."

"What do you know about these guys?" Tim asked.

"I know they're looking for the thing they need to open up that door," Carmilla said. "But somebody beat them to it."

"Yeah," Tim said.

"Probably won't be long before they figure out it was you," Carmilla said.

"I get that impression," Tim said, looking around nervously.

"What did you find?" Carmilla asked.

Tim hesitated. It was a strange experience to find himself unsure of what he should or shouldn't say for the second time in as many minutes.

"Relax," Carmilla said. "You just saved my life, I'm not about to screw you over. Besides, if I was one of them, I'd have probably zapped you and stuck you in that human tenderizer ages ago."

"It was a file," Tim said. "A really old file."

"File?" Carmilla said, furrowing her brow.

"Yeah," Tim said. "A Crimson Seal file."

"As in, the Crimson Seal that we work for?" Carmilla said. "That one?"

"I think so," Tim said. "But the company name was in Latin."

"Latin?" Carmilla said. "Do you have a picture of this?"

Tim pulled out his phone and showed her the picture he'd taken of the file. "That's it."

"Whoa," Carmilla said. "That's a claims file."

"A what?" Tim said.

"A claims file," Carmilla repeated. "An insanely old claims file. The SF 666. That's a claim number. SF is *Sis Facis*. It's basically Latin for claim number. They used to catalog them that way before they switched to the automated system. Numbers are, like, twelve digits long now. Ars Azazel was probably the adjuster assigned to it."

"Holy shit," Tim said. "So the thing they're looking for is buried somewhere in our system?"

"Buried yes," Carmilla said. "But not in any database you can access on your laptop. Whatever that is, if it's that old, it's in the archive."

"Archive?" Tim said.

"Long before your time," Carmilla said. "Or pretty much anybody's."

"Where is this place?" Tim asked.

"Underground," Carmilla said. "Way, way underground. It's restricted, but we might actually be able to get in. Was there anything in the file?"

Tim nodded. "A key."

"Bingo," Carmilla said. "Our best bet is to go after hours. Security will be at a minimum, and the fewer eyes, the better."

"Okay," Tim said.

"Where's the key?" Carmilla asked. "You got it on you?"

"No," Tim said. "It's … someplace safe." He had put the key in the secret storage space under Keef's coffin. He figured it was safe there as not even Keef remembered that the drawer existed. Day or night, few B&E specialists were inclined to try to sneak in and rob a vampire.

"Good," Carmilla said. "I'll see you later."

Carmilla left. Tim turned and went back into the hall, where the director of loss prevention was talking enthusiastically about a new piece of wearable technology that would automatically detect when the wearer was being subjected to an identity theft and alert their bank to temporarily block access to their account and suspend any credit cards. Early trials with minor demons had been quite successful, although there was a shortage of volunteers willing to try it out with higher-level entities.

"Everything okay?" Lonnie asked when Tim sat down. "You look a little green."

"Fine," Tim said. "What did I miss?"

"Synergy," Lonnie said sarcastically. "Core competency maximization. Granular ass mastication. Blah blah blah."

Tim leaned in closer. "Have you ever been to the archive?"

"Archive?" Lonnie said.

"Yeah," Tim whispered. "The old claim file archive."

"Nope," Lonnie said. "I've heard about it, but I don't think I've ever met somebody who actually set foot in the place. You'd have to be nuts."

"Why?" Tim asked.

"Just think about what's locked up in there," Lonnie said. "Cursed artefacts so old that the counter curses are long lost to the mists of time. Demons that have been trapped in mirrors and music boxes and pens and whatever for thousands of years. You think being jailed in a porcelain doll for ten thousand years might make you go just a little bit stir crazy? Who in the world would be crazy enough to open the door and go randomly poking around through all of that?"

"Yeah," Tim said sitting back uneasily. "Who would be crazy enough to do that?"

25

Tim got home just as Keef was waking up.

"Tell me honestly," Keef said as he climbed out of his coffin. "Do I look like I'm porking up a bit?"

"Say what?" Tim asked.

"Do I look like I'm getting fat?" Keef asked, holding out his arms like an emcee for a children's magician. "I feel like I'm bulking up a bit."

Tim looked at his brother, who did not appear to have gained so much as a gram. "No. Is that even possible?"

"Well, I didn't think so," Keef said. "But you know, *she who must not be named* said it was one of the reasons she was throwing me out. Said all I did was sit around on the couch eating Scabs and watching TV."

"Well," Tim said. "She might have a point about that. But I don't think you've gained any actual weight."

"Thank you," Keef said. "People just don't understand what a curse it is to be permanently young and beautiful."

"Only to live with them," Tim muttered under his breath.

"It just got me thinking," Keef said. "You know how mom's always moaning at me to make something of myself. Like get a job or whatever.

It's not like she cares. It's just so that she can have something to brag about to all the women at her salon. Oooh! My son won the Nobel prize for plasma extraction!"

"Maybe there's a middle ground between getting a job and winning one of the most prestigious awards in the world," Tim suggested.

"Not for her there isn't," Keef said. "Dad doesn't care. He just wants to be left in peace to watch zombie baseball. Hey, did I ever tell you my theory about synthetic blood?"

When he wasn't watching TV, Keef also filled many of his hours surfing conspiracy websites. Tim had long ago given up on trying to talk sense into his brother about some of the more outlandish ones, like Keef's deeply held conviction that certain synthetic blood manufacturers were spiking their product with a secret chemical compound designed to induce bizarre hallucinations.

"Many times," Tim said. Keef was often excessively chatty as soon as he woke up. "But I'm still not sure why they want their customers to think it's nighttime when it isn't."

"All part of their secret vampire extermination plan!" Keef said. "The whole thing's funded by a secret werewolf cabal! Everybody knows this!"

"Uh huh," Tim said, making his way around to the other side of the coffin and pulling open the secret compartment.

"Hey!" Keef said. "What's that?"

"Secret compartment," Tim said, removing the file and key.

"Well I didn't know about it!" Keef said.

"Hence the secret aspect," Tim said, closing it up again.

"What is that?" Keef asked.

"It's an old claim file," Tim said. He figured that if Keef thought it was something to do with insurance, he would lose all interest in it immediately.

"Oh," Keef said. "Why are you sticking your work stuff in the secret compartment in my bed that I didn't even know was there?"

"It's a sensitive file," Tim said.

"What else have you stuck in there that I didn't know about?" Keef asked.

Tim smiled. "Wouldn't you like to know."

"Ugh, fine," Keef said, waving a hand. "I don't know how you can work in insurance, man. I mean, is it possible there's a more boring job in the world? I thought you wanted to be a cop just like your girlfriend."

"She's not my girlfriend," Tim said. "And speaking of expectations, for somebody who was just complaining about mom, you're starting to sound a hell of a lot like her."

"Whatever, bro," Keef said. "You two looked pretty friendly when I walked in, that's all I'm gonna say."

"Yes," Tim said. "Your timing was, as always, impeccable."

"I knew it!" Keef said. "Like you make the one dish you can actually make that isn't terrible unless it's a special occasion."

"I can make other things!" Tim said.

"You let this one slip away once," Keef said. "If you do it again, I'll turn you into a vampire. And I'm not even kidding. I don't care what mom says."

The buzzer sounded. Tim assumed it would be Carmilla and was surprised to see that it was Stake.

"Well, if it isn't Weaselly Snipes Junior," Keef said when Stake walked in. "Aren't you a bit on the old side for trick or treat, little man?"

"Aren't you a little on the dead side to still be walking?" Stake said, pulling out his bat and waving it at Keef.

"Boys!" Tim said. "Play nice!"

"Whatever," Keef said, smiling to reveal his fangs. "If you'll excuse me, I should probably go brush my teeth. I might need to use them later."

Keef wandered back to his room and closed the door.

"Sorry about that," Tim said. "My brother is just a little touchy on the subject of vampire hunters."

"Don't worry about it," Stake said, dropping the bat into the sling on his back. "I'm used to it. Many of my enemies fail to take me seriously. Until it's too late. For them, that is. Not me."

"Right," Tim said. "So, uh, what brings you by?"

"Intel," Stake said. "Somebody blew up a top-secret Sons of Darkness lab up on the site of the old Stygian Hotel last night."

"Yeah . . . " Tim said.

"Apparently they were growing some sort of demon army," Stake said. "And doing some other unrighteously horrible shit. Until somebody came along and rained on their little Island of Dr. Moreau parade, anyway."

"Yes . . . " Tim said.

"No idea who it was yet," Stake said. "But don't worry, I'll find out."

"It was me," Tim said.

"What was you?" Stake said, confused.

"I blew the place up," Tim said.

"*You* did?" Stake said, taken aback.

"Yeah," Tim said. "Well, me and a friend."

"You and a friend?" Stake said. "I thought I was your friend!"

"You are!" Tim said. "It was a total last-minute thing. We didn't even know what it was when we got there. And the explosion kind of happened by accident, too. It wasn't like we knew what we were getting into and then went up there loaded with plastic explosive or whatever to take the place down."

"I'd really like to have seen that," Stake said, sitting down on the edge of the couch.

"It was kind of cool," Tim admitted. "Except for almost getting killed."

"I guess," Stake said.

"You were right about the army, though," Tim said.

"Really?" Stake said, perking up a little.

"Totally," Tim said. "They were growing them in these tanks full of liquified Hellfire."

"Cool!" Stake said, eyes widening.

"They were using demons to transport it in small batches," Tim said.

"Makes sense," Stake nodded.

"They were also trying to grow a demon or something out of the brain of the woman who had been possessed," Tim said. "I have no idea why."

"Out of her brain?" Stake said.

"Yeah," Tim said. "It was actually even more gross than it sounds." He closed his eyes and tried to shake the image of Madame Zoudini floating through the tank full of blue liquid, but it was permanently burned on his cortex and, he knew, always would be.

"Clearly these devil whores are even more ambitious than we thought," Stake said. "So what's our next play?"

The buzzer sounded again. Tim hit the button and allowed Carmilla in.

"Hey," she said. "You ready?"

As soon as he saw Carmilla, Stake's face went slack and his expression became as enraptured as an audience volunteer for a stage hypnotist.

"You're insanely beautiful!" Stake gasped.

Carmilla rolled her eyes, having heard this sort of response from the weak-willed countless times in the past.

"Who's the Morpheus wannabe?" she asked, pointing at Stake.

"That's Stake," Tim said. "He's been helping out a little bit with the investigation."

"I love you!" Stake said breathlessly.

"Take a breath and hold it, Romeo," Carmilla said. "Did you say his name is Stake?"

"Yeah," Tim said. "Presumably like the pointy wooden thing and not the restaurant variety. It's not his real name, it's just what he goes by."

"Marry me!" Stake said, dropping to his knees.

"Do you hang out with a lot of people who play dress up?" Carmilla asked.

"I admit that he looks a little odd," Tim said.

"Looks like he just got ejected from Comic Con for exposing himself to minors, more like," Carmilla said.

"He did actually help me out of a real jam a few nights back," Tim said.

"Oh yeah?" Carmilla said, smiling. "What was that? Needed help with the zipper on your wizard's robe? Dropped your wand? What?"

"Actually, I got grabbed by some baggers in the Crypt Network," Tim said.

"The Crypt Network?" Carmilla said. "What the hell were you doing down there?"

"It's a long story," Tim said.

"You are the most enchanting creature I have ever seen in my life!" Stake said.

Carmilla pulled a small silver cylinder out of her pocket and sprayed Stake in the face. He flinched and started coughing.

"What is that?" Tim asked. "Mace?"

"No," Carmilla said. "Werewolf repellent. Usually helps put off the more ardent ones."

"Gah!" Stake said, flopping on the floor and rubbing his eyes. "It burns!"

"He'll be fine," Carmilla said.

Tim went to the kitchen and got a wet cloth for Stake to rub on his face. He got back up a moment later, blinking.

"What happened?" he asked.

"Relax," Carmilla said. "You just got a little too enthusiastic for your own good."

"That's never happened to me before," Stake said. "It must be some sort of curse!"

"Only for me," Carmilla said.

"Now I get it!" Stake said. "You're a succubus!"

"And so another MacArthur grant is awarded," Carmilla said. "Can we go?"

"You didn't tell me your friend was a succubus!" Stake said.

"Actually, that was someone else," Tim said.

"Who is he talking about?" Carmilla asked.

"We were having a conversation before you got here," Tim said.

"Evidently," Carmilla said. "So, are we ready to do this or what?"

"Do what?" Stake said. "Where are we going?"

Carmilla frowned. "We're not bringing this guy along, are we?"

"You can't leave me out again!" Stake said. "You left me out of the demon factory explosion!"

"Okay," Carmilla said. "I didn't want to know what he was talking about, but now I definitely do."

"I don't think you want to be in on this one, Stake," Tim said. "Things could get nasty."

Stake stood up and puffed out his chest. "That's exactly why you need me there."

Tim realized that he'd spun this the wrong way. He tried to regroup.

"I mean, things could get complicated," Tim said. "Like, insurance-level complicated."

Stake smiled. "Sounds just my style."

"I'm not sure it's a good idea," Tim said.

"Let him come," Carmilla said. "I have to say I really want to see Stick or Branch or Twig or whatever the hell he calls himself here in action. Just make sure you wash that spray off before you get in my car. I don't want my leather upholstery smelling like ghoul crotch."

"That's your fault," Stake said, looking peevish. "Evil half-demon!"

"Keep up the sweet talk and I'll do it again," Carmilla said, waving the canister.

"All right," Tim said, grabbing his jacket. "But if we can't get him a visitor's pass, he'll have to wait in the car."

26

They made their way through the thinning rush hour traffic to a dull grey warehouse building in an industrial park on the northern edge of the city limits.

"*This* is the place?" Stake said, leaning forward in the back seat.

Tim shared Stake's sense of disbelief. The place looked like an electroplating factory. It did not look like the repository of thousands of year's worth of powerful and potentially deadly cursed and supernatural objects.

"Yep," Carmilla said, holding out her card to the scanner. The gate rose up and they pulled into the employee parking lot, which was otherwise empty.

"Not what I pictured," Tim said, getting out of the car.

"I think that's kind of the idea," Carmilla said. "Kind of like a missile silo. You really don't want to put up a sign out front that says: Danger–Nuclear Weapon Storage."

Tim couldn't argue with that. "You've been here before?"

"A few times," Carmilla said. "Some of this stuff doesn't exactly lend itself to digitization, if you know what I mean."

They made their way along the side of the building, heading for the front door. Tim looked up at the corners for surveillance cameras but didn't see any. That wasn't surprising. The company probably had more sophisticated means of guarding a place like this.

Carmilla held her badge out to the scanner, which flashed green and buzzed. She pulled the door open and motioned the other two in.

"Don't bother scanning in," she said to Tim. "It's probably better that there's no record of you setting foot in here."

Tim nodded and entered the front lobby. There was a reception desk, but it was empty.

"There's nobody at the desk," Stake observed.

"Maybe they went to the can," Carmilla said. "Looks like we caught a break. Come on."

The three of them made their way around the desk and through a door on the left, which led to a pair of black elevator doors. Carmilla pushed the call button and the doors opened immediately. They stepped inside. Tim glanced at the panel and was surprised to see that there were no buttons, only a keypad.

"Does this elevator actually go anywhere?" he asked, confused.

"What's the claim number?" Carmilla asked.

"Six six six," Tim said.

Carmilla entered '666' on the keypad. The doors closed and the elevator began to descend, picking up speed as it went.

"It's an old one, so it's probably in the sub-sub-basement level," Carmilla said.

"How far down does this place go?" Stake asked.

"No idea," Carmilla said. "The last one I looked at was only 74 years old, but the storage for that year took up three floors."

Tim tried not to think about the implications of that. The claim they were looking for was a lot more than 74 years old. Given the company's age, they could be descending to the rough equivalent distance of the cruising altitude of a transatlantic jetliner.

"Oh boy," Tim said, steadying himself against the side of the elevator. He didn't care for enclosed underground spaces.

"Relax," Carmilla said. "It'll be fine."

"Claustrophobic?" Stake asked, clapping him on the shoulder.

"Uh," Tim said. "I don't mind small-ish spaces. Provided I know that I'm going to be able to get out of them again."

"Don't worry about it," Stake said. "I'm afraid of antique furniture myself. Don't know if there's a name for that."

"Of what?" Carmilla said.

"Oh yeah," Stake said. "Goes back to the time I was living with my aunt and she bought this Louis the Sixteenth-era foot stool. She liked to buy old stuff and fix it up. Only this one was possessed by the ghost of the Marquis of Burgogne, who went to the guillotine on the same day as Marie Antoinette. His headless body used to rise up from the stool every afternoon when I would come home from school. I was there by myself because my aunt had to work. She was a bylaw enforcement officer."

"You were chased around the apartment by a headless ghost when you were just a kid?" Tim said.

"I was," Stake said. "He would accuse me of hiding his head and insist that I give it back. Not sure how he talked, exactly. Not having a mouth. But it was all in French, so I had to record and translate it so I knew what he was saying."

"That must have been traumatizing," Tim said.

"A little bit," Stake said. "We sort of became friends eventually. Or at least, he stopped spraying me with ghost blood."

"Just tell your aunt to get rid of the damn stool!" Carmilla said.

"She couldn't," Stake said. "She spent a fortune on it. The ghost made it worth three times as much as it would be without one, so she didn't want to bring in an exorcist, either."

"So how long did you live with this thing?" Tim asked.

"Only a year and a half," Stake said. "She got it recovered and sold it to a podiatrist for twice what she paid for it. So, you know. Good ROI, I guess."

Tim and Carmilla exchanged a look. Tim was about to ask if that had been the only piece of haunted furniture to which Stake had been exposed when the elevator beeped and the doors opened. They stepped out into darkness as motion-sensor fluorescent lights flickered on over their heads to reveal row after row of massive shelving units. The shelves were grouped together in clusters of six, radiating out from the centre like spokes on a wheel. As only the lights directly over their head had activated, it was impossible to say how long each of the rows might be as they stretched out into the dark.

"This is not what I expected at all," Stake said.

"What were you expecting?" Carmilla said.

"I dunno," Stake shrugged. "You guys ever see *Thor*? You know how Odin has this secret vault full of dangerous objects that he's collected over the course of his conquests? I was kind of thinking this place would be more like that."

"Dude, this is an insurance company, not a supervillain's lair," Carmilla said.

There were signs up at the end of each row identifying a range of claim numbers. Tim walked around the circle until he found one that read SF650-SF678.

"I think it's down here!" he said, pointing.

Tim began walking slowly down the aisle. The lights flickered on one at a time as he went. Many of them sparked and almost immediately died, leaving large areas in darkness. He wasn't surprised by that. He doubted that anyone had been down here for a very long time.

There was a flash and a muffled bang from one of the cabinets as he passed it, causing all three of them to jump.

"What the hell was that?" Stake said.

"These things are full of old claim files," Carmilla said. "Who knows how long some of these demons have been locked up?"

Tim stopped in front of one of the units. According to the catalog numbers on the side, claim SF666 was in the middle of the stacks.

"It's here!" Tim said.

"How do we get to it?" Stake asked.

"Turn the wheels," Carmilla said, pointing to the gear system protruding from the bottom of each unit.

Tim and Stake crouched down and grabbed the handles, which required all their combined strength before they finally started to move. The metal groaned as the cabinets slowly started to inch away from each other.

"Feel like these haven't been used in about a thousand years," Stake grunted as the two of them worked.

"Probably haven't," Tim wheezed.

The two of them cranked the gears to the point where there was enough space for a person to walk in between the stacks.

"That should be enough," Tim said, getting back up. He took a deep breath and stepped inside.

"Maybe you shouldn't," Stake said, putting a hand on Tim's shoulder to stop him. "We have no idea what's in there."

"True," Tim said. "But if we don't, then somebody else will. We need to get our hands on whatever's in there before the Sons of Darkness do."

"Fair enough," Stake said, letting go. "But I reserve the right to say I told you so should the opportunity present itself."

"Fair enough," Tim said.

Tim walked into the space between the stacks. Only one of the overhead lights was working, so he had to give his eyes a moment to adjust to the shadows. In front of him was what looked like a large metal post office box. It was about six feet long and at least four feet high and had a sliver handle in the middle and the number 666 neatly engraved in the bottom right corner.

What in the world could be in there? Tim wondered as he got the key out of his pocket.

"Here goes," he said, sliding the key into the slot. He held his breath and turned the key. The lock clicked. "It fits!"

"Open it!" Stake said.

Tim gripped the handle. He thought about the items from his inspection kit that he had stuffed in his jacket pockets on the way out the door. They were all designed to protect against minor demons and curses of the sort that a claims adjuster might encounter in the line of work. None of them were going to be of much use against what might turn out to be inside the drawer he was about to pull open. Not in a worst-case scenario, anyway.

"Come on!" Stake said. "Stop farting around!"

Tim pulled open the drawer.

Lying inside was what looked like a very old and elaborate sledge hammer. It appeared to be made of shiny volcanic glass, much like the key that he had used to open the drawer. The striking surface looked like a 10-pin bowling ball covered in spikes. Instead of a pair of curved arms with a slot to remove nails, it had three sharp spikes that jutted out like the horns on a triceratops and looked equally capable of spearing one. The handle was slightly curved and had grips carved into it for a pair of hands much larger than his own.

"Whoa!" Stake said, crowding in next to Tim for a look. "That is one badass piece of weaponry! What is it?"

Tim realized that he had seen this thing before. Not this one specifically, but a much smaller version of it. The statue that had appeared in Madame Zoudini's—the one stolen by Azmoda's goons and then Tim and then the Sons of Darkness—had been holding a hammer that looked exactly like this.

"I think it's the Hammer of Belial," Tim said.

"It is indeed," said a familiar voice. "And I can't tell you how grateful I am that you found it for us."

27

Tim spun around to see Lilith Warwick standing in the aisle smiling at him. Carmilla was next to her. Behind them were three large figures in black hoods.

"What the hell?" Stake said, grabbing for his bat.

Warwick held out her phone and flashed Stake in the face. He crumpled immediately to the ground, unconscious.

"I had a feeling you'd be showing up at some point," Tim said.

"Of course, you did," Warwick said. "You're one of our best investigators."

"You've been working with them all along?" Tim asked, looking at Carmilla.

"Of course, she has," Warwick said spinning her phone. "Although not entirely of her own volition."

Tim thought of the time he had encountered Carmilla at Azmoda's club. She had gotten a text message just before she had sent him out the exit where the Sons of Darkness had been waiting for him.

"Mind control?" Tim said.

"Yes," Warwick said. "You see, despite their reputation for putting spells on others, a succubus is one of the most easily suggestible creatures on the planet. Why else would so many of them end up in sex trafficking rings? I can't oversee the Special Investigations Unit directly, but it is useful to have an agent on the inside I can control."

"So why kill her?" Tim asked.

"We thought she had become compromised and outlived her usefulness," Warwick said. "But then you and your little comic book friend came along to rescue her and I thought, maybe we could use her to manipulate you into getting what we wanted."

"Great," Tim muttered.

"Oh, it was," Warwick said. "Absolutely exceptional work. You deciphered the message. You located the key. And now, you've found the one thing we've been seeking for centuries."

"Right here in the vaults of your own company," Tim said.

"Oh, we knew it was down here somewhere," Warwick said. "You see, Crimson Seal itself was founded on the banishment and imprisonment of the Great Fathers. Where do you think the company name comes from?"

Tim thought back to the massive door in the secret headquarters. Right in the middle of that door was a six-sided seal. A red, six-sided seal. It was so obvious that he wanted to smack himself in the forehead.

"That's the thing holding that giant door closed in your secret headquarters," Tim said.

"It is," Warwick said. "And in that drawer lies the only tool in existence capable of breaking that seal. With one swift stroke, we can set the great master free!"

"And wipe out most of humanity in the process," Tim observed.

"Only those who forgot to honour his word," Warwick said. "The ones who turned their backs on the old traditions. The ones who forgot where they came from."

"So not the Sons of Darkness, then," Tim said.

"When mighty Belial returns, we shall be the soldiers of the new order," Warwick said. "Our only purpose is to exercise his will."

"I guess it will be just down to you," Tim said. "Since I blew up your creepy little lab experiment."

"You did me a favour," Warwick said. "There have been many crackpot schemes to attempt to bring our lord back in one form or another. Including that ridiculous attempt at Demonorecombinant Engineering. The late Madame Zoudini had fulfilled her purpose and delivered the prophecy, so what happened to her after that mattered little. I never expected anything to come of it. If anything, it only put us at greater risk of discovery. Storing so much liquid Hellfire in one place? Idiotic. Seeing it all vanish in a flash was a welcome turn of events for those of us who see only one path to the future."

"Kind of ironic that you were the one who introduced the diversity hiring program," Tim said. "Considering that you so obviously seem to prefer demons to humans."

"Secrecy is often enhanced by appearing to be the opposite of who you really are," Warwick said. "And besides, if I hadn't done it, you wouldn't have started at the SIU, in which case we might not have found the means to liberate our master so quickly!"

"Glad to be of service," Tim said. "Does that mean I get a promotion and a raise?"

"Regrettably, no," Warwick smiled and motioned to one of the figures behind her, who stepped forward and lifted the hammer out of the drawer. Tim was sure he saw her eyes well up with tears as soon as Warwick saw it. The robed figure handed her the hammer, which she appeared to hold without much strain.

"That's a big hammer," Tim said. "You've got impressive core strength."

"I do a bi-weekly boot camp," Warwick said. "To me, the master's hammer is as light as a feather."

Light or not, she quickly handed the hammer back.

"Now," Warwick said, smiling. "If you'll excuse me, I have a destiny to fulfill."

She took out her phone and flashed it at Carmilla, who passed out and fell to the floor next to Stake.

Warwick raised the phone to Tim. "We are, however, going to need a sacrifice to complete the ritual."

"Pardon, Mistress Paimon," one of the robed figures said, leaning forward. "But the ritual does specify a virgin."

"That's true," Warwick said, tapping her teeth. "Okay, grab him."

The second robed figure leaned forward and grabbed Stake, lifting the unconscious vampire hunter up and tossing him over a shoulder as easily as a bag of potatoes.

"He might not be," Warwick said. "But he looks like a pretty good bet. Now is the hour where all prisoners will be set free. Which means the end of this little corporate archive, obviously."

Warwick turned and gestured to the other robed figures who were wheeling what looked like glowing blue tanks out of the elevator and rolling them down the aisles. The containers were roughly the same size as the ones Tim had seen the Osmanibaks carrying back at the hotel but were connected to some sort of electronic console attached by wires to a plate near the handle. Tim didn't have any doubt about what those were: bombs.

"Good thing we didn't store all of our liquid Hellfire in the same place!" Warwick chuckled. "Don't worry, though. You won't feel a thing. It's the least we can do in recognition of all your hard work."

She held out her phone and flashed it in Tim's face. He fell between the stacks and landed on the floor.

"Let's go," she said. "And make damn sure they set the detonators on those things properly! I don't want this place going up until we're well out of range!"

The robed figures finished planting the bombs and scampered back to the elevator. Tim waited until he heard the doors close and counted to ten before sitting back up, grateful that he had been wearing his goggles overtop of his glasses and even more grateful that they had a filter to block out simple curses, like the one Warwick had just used to try to knock him out.

He got up and ran over to Carmilla, shaking her awake.

"Come on!" he said. "They've wired the place to blow! We need to get out of here!"

Carmilla sat up, rubbing her forehead.

"Where the hell am I?" she asked. "What's going on?"

"Short version?" Tim said. "You were brainwashed by a demon-worshipping cult led by our executive vice president of claims in order to get their hands on a hammer they can use to resurrect an extremely unpleasant major demon who will probably wipe out every non-demon he lays eyes on. They've trapped us in the archives with a bunch of explosive devices made of liquid Hellfire that could go off at any moment. I'd prefer to not be here when that happens."

"What?" Carmilla said.

"We need to get out of here!" Tim said. "Is there a way out other than the elevator?"

"Nope," Carmilla said, shaking her head.

"Nothing?" Tim said. "What about stairs?"

"Not that I know of," Carmilla said.

"Seriously?" Tim said. "How can an insurance company be in such brutal violation of basic fire codes?"

"I think this place was built long before fire codes were a thing," Carmilla said.

"Okay," Tim said. "So the only option we've got is to defuse these things before they go off. Do you know anything about defusing bombs?"

"Nothing," Carmilla said.

Tim groaned. "Okay. Don't take this personally, but you're really putting a hole in my boat right now."

"Wait," Carmilla said. "Maybe we don't need to defuse them. We just need to contain them."

"What do you mean?" Tim asked.

"You said they're liquid Hellfire, right?" Carmilla said.

"Yes," Tim nodded.

"Dude," Carmilla said. "These vaults are designed to hold the nastiest demons and curses known to man. If the bombs are made of Hellfire-"

"Then in theory, the vaults should be strong enough to contain it," Tim said.

"Right," Carmilla said. "In theory. We just need to find a vault big and strong enough to do the job."

Tim looked over his shoulder at the open drawer. "Well, that one contained the biggest, nastiest item on the list that I know of. I guess we'll have to take our chances."

"Hurry!" Tim said.

The two of them raced down the aisles, grabbing the devices and wheeling them back to the cabinet.

"How volatile is this stuff?" Carmilla asked, dropping one as she lifted it up to put in the massive drawer.

"I'm not sure," Tim said, racing back with a bomb of his own. "The only way to really know would be to bang them into things with increasing force until they finally blow up."

"Where's your buddy?" Carmilla asked, racing to get the next one. "The fearless vampire hunter who's afraid of ottomans?"

"They grabbed him to use as a human sacrifice," Tim said.

"That makes sense," Carmilla said. "Virgins are always in demand for that."

"He might not be a virgin," Tim said.

"C'mon, dude," Carmilla said. "You've seen the way he dresses, right? The guy was packing a squirt gun, for crying out loud."

"I see your point," Tim said, carefully stacking another one of the glowing blue tubes in the drawer. "We're not exactly buddies. But I'd still rather not see him chopped up by a bunch of fanatics. I kind of owe him one."

The two of them raced up and down the aisles carrying the containers back to the drawer, where they stacked them up in neat rows of glowing blue death.

"Sorry if I hassled you a bit on your first day," Carmilla said. "I just know a lot of people who applied for that job who didn't get it."

"That's okay," Tim said. "In all honesty, I was as surprised as anyone when I got it."

"I mean, I still think it was biased and preferential hiring, which sucks," Carmilla said. "But you're not terrible."

"I take that as high praise," Tim said. "Coming from you especially."

Tim placed the last one of the tubes in the drawer and took a deep breath.

"I think that's it," he gasped.

"Let's close it up," Carmilla said, pushed the drawer closed. "You got the key?"

Tim pulled out the key and locked the drawer. He didn't know if that would make any difference or not but figured it couldn't hurt. Once they had done that, they cranked the gear wheels to roll the massive shelving units back together.

"Okay, let's go!" Carmilla said, running back to the elevator and hitting the call button.

"They probably won't blow it until they're well clear of the place," Tim said hopefully. "Based on what happened back at their lab, anyway."

There was a muffled boom. Tim looked over to see the cabinet was glowing blue and sparking with bolts of electricity. It shook violently and started to vibrate.

"You were saying?" Carmilla yelled over the din.

The units bounced up and down and the floor, glowing brighter and brighter with each muffled bang.

"Okay," Tim yelled. "But it looks like you were right! The drawer is containing it!"

No sooner had Tim said this than there was a crack like lightning and the top of the shelving unit blasted off. A volcanic geyser of blue liquid flame shot into the air, melting the ceiling as a puddle of it began to spread rapidly across the floor. Everything it touched caught fire and started to melt.

"Or not," Tim said.

There was a ding and the elevator doors opened. Tim and Carmilla raced inside and entered 1 on the keypad. The two of them felt a blast of noxious hot air as the doors closed again and they began their ascent.

Tim slumped against the side of the elevator and allowed himself to breathe again.

"So," he said. "I guess being a succubus, you must get tired of guys hitting on you all the time."

Carmilla shrugged. "You get used to it. It's not that much different from what most of the human women I know at work have to put up with day to day."

"Really?" Tim said. "That's kind of dispiriting."

"That's why I prefer to work alone," Carmilla said.

"I do, too," Tim said. "But mostly just because I'm not great with people."

"So how did you hook up with your little sidekick?" Carmilla said. "You know he has quite the rep for pro-human, anti-supernatural causes, right?"

"Yeah," Tim said. "He and my brother do not get along at all. I don't think he's inherently spectrumist. He's got a big chip on his shoulder because his parents were killed by a vampire when he was a kid."

"Yeah?" Carmilla said. "Well, our cult friends are gonna crush his skull with that nifty new hammer of theirs if we can't get to him first."

"We got into their HQ once before," Tim said. "But I doubt we'll be able to sneak in that way again."

"Don't worry," Carmilla said. "I'm pretty sure I can get us in. They may have used mind control on me, but I can still remember most of what I saw while I was there."

"Are you sure?" Tim said. "What if they flash you with the app again?"

Carmilla reached into her jacket and put on a pair of dark sunglasses. "That's why I've got these. Had them made specially. They filter out stuff that the ones in our kits don't even dream about."

"Nice," Tim said. "You'll have to tell me where I can get a pair of those. They're a lot more stylish than the standard goggles."

They arrived at the ground floor and the elevator doors opened. Tim and Carmilla sprinted out of the building to her car. The ground was starting to shake under their feet as they got in and peeled out of the parking lot. Tim looked back over his shoulder in time to see large cracks open up in the pavement and blue flame jet out of them. They had no sooner pulled out onto the street than the entire structure disappeared into a giant blue sinkhole.

"Well, at least it's insured," Tim said as they sped off.

"Hope they got most of that digitized," Carmilla said. "Cause they're not getting it back now."

"Even if we get in and manage to free Stake," Tim said. "There's only going to be three of us and hundreds of them. We'll never make it out."

"No," Carmilla said. "As much as it pains me to admit it, we'll need help."

Tim glanced out the window. "Looks like there's a full moon tonight."

"So?" Carmilla said.

Tim smiled. "I think I know a few people we can call. Well, some of them are people."

28

Stake awoke to find himself chained tightly to a cold metal table.

He blinked his eyes and looked up straight through the familiar glass dome of the headquarters of the Sons of Darkness. If he angled his head, he could see the stands, many of which were full of hooded figures who appeared to be regarding him intently.

He shivered. He glanced down at his body and saw they had taken all his gear and his suit. He was totally naked.

Great, he thought. Not only are they demon worshippers, they're also perverts.

He tried to move, but his arms and legs were stretched out and chained tightly under what looked like some sort of metal pyramid. He looked at it more carefully and saw that it wasn't just decorative—he was actually strapped into a five-bladed guillotine. He could see the blades locked in position near the top, each one designed to drop down between two metal runners and chop off a different appendage. There was one blade for his head and one for each of his arms and legs. He was partially relieved that there didn't appear to be a sixth blade specifically designed to chop off his penis. What else could you expect from demon sex perverts? But it was a short-lived comfort.

"Hello?" he called out. "Let me out of here!"

There was a murmuring through the crowd. He saw a hooded figure approach followed by four of the enormous Serrabluks, one of which was carrying the hammer they had found in the archive. The hooded figure laid a hand on Stake's cheek, which he tried to shake off.

"Don't touch me, corporate devil whore!" he yelled.

The figure lifted off the hood to reveal Warwick, who smiled at him and then turned to address the crowd.

"Sons and daughters of darkness!" she said. "Tonight is the beginning of a new age! The moment we have been waiting for oh these many long millennia! Tonight, we have recovered what we have long sought! The Hammer of Belial!"

The crowd gasped as the massive demon held the hammer up like a prize on a daytime game show.

"Tonight," Warwick continued. "We shall fulfill the prophecy! With the shedding of this virgin's blood, we shall break the seal and unlock the door! Tonight, we shall see the return of our mighty father!"

"I am not a virgin!" Stake said indignantly. "I've had sex lots of times! Way more than you, probably!"

"Nobody believes you," Warwick whispered.

"I'm not lying!" Stake said. "I've had sex like, six times! I don't even count one of them because she turned out to be a succubus who tried to steal my wallet!"

There was a ripple of laughter through the crowd. Stake felt that maybe it was a good idea to try a different tack.

"You won't get away with this!" he said. "My friends are coming to rescue me! I have a whole network! If they get here and I'm still strapped down here like this, they're gonna be pissed!"

"No one is coming to rescue you," Warwick hissed. "You don't have any friends. The only ones you did have, we buried under a thousand feet of solid rock. Now stop interrupting or I'll have one of these Serrabluks fill your throat with something you will not appreciate."

Stake looked uncomfortably at the demon that was standing closest to him, its massive genitals hanging roughly at his eye level. Was it worth calling her bluff on that one? He decided that it was not.

"Tonight," Warwick said, turning back to address the crowd. "We shall finally step out of the shadows and assume our rightful place at the foot of our all-conquering master! Tonight, the mighty Belial shall walk the earth once more!"

"Once more!" the crowd cheered.

"Tonight," Warwick continued, her voice rising in volume and fervor. "The mighty Belial shall purge our enemies and purify the world!"

"Purify the world!" echoed the crowd.

"Tonight," Warwick shouted. "The mighty Belial shall at last be free!"

"Shall be free!" said the crowd.

"Bunch of damn sheep," Stake murmured, shaking his head.

"Step forward, Guardians of the Morningstar!" said Warwick, gesturing to the entrance.

Stake craned his neck to see five hooded figures approach and silently take up a position at the end of one of his outstretched extremities, including one that stepped up behind his head. Stake struggled to free himself but could barely move.

"Mighty Belial!" Warwick intoned, raising her hands and closing her eyes. "We make this offering to purify your passage. With this sacrifice, so shall you be released!"

Sensing that his demise was imminent, Stake started yanking as hard as he could on his restraints. He could feel the skin tear and bones bend as he strained with all his might.

"You can't do this!" he yelled.

"Silence!" Warwick bellowed.

"Psst!"

Stake stopped struggling for a moment and looked up as the figure closest to his head pulled back the hood slightly to reveal a surprisingly familiar face.

"Tim?" Stake whispered.

"Hey buddy!" Tim whispered.

"What?" Stake gasped. "How?"

"Just relax!" Tim whispered. "We'll have you out of here in a second. And we'll find you some pants."

"Let the darkness rise!" Warwick said, turning back to Stake. "Close the star!"

One of the figures standing near Stake's left leg raised an arm to the machine and then quickly pulled off the hood to reveal Tabitha. She raised her other hand, pointing her sidearm straight at Warwick.

"Police!" Tabitha yelled. "Drop the hammer! You're all under arrest for murder, kidnapping and a shitload of other stuff!"

The others quickly pulled their hoods off to reveal Tim, Carmilla, Lonnie and George. Carmilla was holding a spear she had found back-stage while Tim was clenching a spray canister of Demonex, which he pointed at the Serrabluk holding the hammer. Warwick stared at them in confusion for a moment before her expression twisted into one of abject fury.

"Kill them!" she screamed.

The Serrabluk raised the hammer to swing it at Tabitha, but Tim caught it with a spray jet straight to the face. The demon dropped the hammer and went down screaming and clawing at its eyes. A second demon jumped at Carmilla, who sidestepped neatly and speared it in the groin, which it did not handle well. The third one raised a pitchfork to strike George, who transformed into a bat and flew at its face while Lonnie transformed into his wolf form to jump at the fourth.

"We're gonna get you out of here, man!" Tim said, crouching down to unlock the chain around Stake's neck.

"Hurry!" Stake said, feeling his vision clear as the blood began to flow back to his head.

Carmilla and Tabitha managed to free Stake's arms and legs and he rolled off the table and onto the floor. Figures were now jumping down out of the stands to come to the aid of their leader, who had grabbed the hammer dropped by the demon and was lifting it up to try and squash Stake.

"Freeze!" Tabitha yelled. She raised her gun and got a shot off, but it went wide when a spinning demon caught her with its tail and knocked her to the floor.

Stake rolled under the table and out of the way just as Warwick brought the hammer down with a blow that smashed the stone floor like it had been hit by an artillery round.

Tim felt himself grabbed from behind as one of the hooded followers seized him around the midsection and lifted him up as another one tried to punch him in the face. Tim sprayed the second one with Demonex, which worked pretty well on non-demons as well. The hood fell back revealing a man in his sixties who screamed as the solution hit his skin and started to burn. George appeared out of nowhere and grabbed the first attacker by the neck, squeezing tightly enough to knock the man unconscious.

"Thanks!" Tim said.

"It's kind of my signature move," George said, transforming back into a bat and flying into the face of a robed woman running their way with a pitchfork.

Two more Serrabluks came charging out from backstage carrying enormous pitchforks. Lonnie dodged the prongs and jumped over onto the demon's back, locking his jaws around the creature's neck. The demon screeched as Lonnie ripped a chunk of flesh out and spat it onto the floor.

"Ugh," he said. "These things taste terrible."

Tabitha grabbed the pitchfork that the first demon had dropped and braced it against the floor, raising it up as the second one charged forward, impaling itself.

"It's a good thing their brains are a lot smaller than their dicks," she said as the thing sank to its knees and collapsed.

Tim helped Stake back up to his feet.

"I feel kind of naked without my gear or my bat," Stake said.

"I'm not gonna comment on that," Tim said, turning to spray another cult member charging toward them with a knife.

Warwick raised the hammer again and swung it at Stake. He jumped out of the way and it came down on the red seal in the middle of the floor. The seal cracked under the heavy blow. Deep red light began to glow through the cracks.

"I shall free the master!" Warwick said, lifting the hammer up again.

"No!" Tim said, turning and pointing the spray at the wild-eyed cult leader. A hooded figure jumped on his back before he could hit the button, however, and the two of them fell to the floor directly over the seal.

"With your blood, I shall open the gateway!" Warwick said, bringing the hammer down.

"No!" Stake said, throwing himself to the ground to shove Tim out of the way. The hammer came down on Stake's shoulder with a bone--shattering crack and he howled in pain. Blood oozed out of the wound and began to fill in the cracks in the seal, which started to vibrate with a low hum.

"One more blow and Belial shall be free!" Warwick said through gritted teeth. With great effort, she brought the hammer back up over her head and prepared to bring it down one more time.

Tim heard a pop as a bullet punched a neat hole in the arm of Warwick's robe. She made a grunting sound and dropped the hammer, which landed behind her with a thud. Warwick hung in a sort of suspended animation for a moment before staggering backwards against the star-shaped machine. There was a click as she stumbled against the mechanism, releasing one of the blades. She just managed to look up in time to see it fall as it sliced off the top of her head at the bridge of her nose.

Tim tried not to look as she hung there for a second before falling to the floor. Tabitha came running over, the barrel of her semi automatic still smoking.

"Told her to drop the hammer," she said. "Bitch didn't listen to me."

"Stake!" Tim said, rushing to the spot where the vampire hunter had collapsed. "Are you okay?"

"Not really!" Stake wheezed.

Tabitha examined Stake's shoulder, which was horribly misshapen and leaking blood from dozens of puncture points.

"You're gonna be fine," she said. "Medics are on the way!"

"This doesn't look good," Carmilla said, pointing at the seal. The cracks were filling up with Stake's blood and appeared to be starting to widen.

"Get him off the seal!" Tim said.

"We can't move him!" Tabitha said. "His shoulder is pulp! We could send bone splinters into his lungs or heart!"

Tim heard a fluttering sound and looked up to see a bat fly over his head. It circled around and transformed back into George, who knelt down to assess the situation.

"The blood!" Tim said. "It's opening the seal!"

"Well," said George. "We can't have that."

George put his hand down on the floor in the middle of the pool of Stake's blood. As Tim watched, the blood appeared to reverse flow and get sucked up into George's hand like some sort of vacuum pump.

"What the hell?" Tabitha said in disbelief.

George kept going until all of the blood had been sucked up off the floor and out of the crack. As he did so, the vibration slowly reduced to nothing and the red light dimmed until it was gone completely.

"That's incredible!" Tim said.

"Waste not, want not," George said, shrugging.

They lifted Stake up slightly and tucked one of their discarded robes under his head and shoulders to ensure no more blood made its way onto the floor.

"That's the second time you saved my ass," Tim said.

"I know," Stake groaned. "I'm a regular goddamn Han Solo."

Tim looked up to see dozens of police, some plainclothes and some uniformed, swarming through the entrance to round up the fleeing cult members.

"Looks like my task force arrived," Tabitha said. "Finally."

An EMT unit arrived to help Stake, covering him with a blanket.

"You know," he said. "Just because my blood worked doesn't prove anything. I mean, virgin-wise."

"Just take it easy," Tim said. "How many vampire hunters can say they've taken a direct hit from the Hammer of Belial and lived to talk about it?"

"He's a vampire hunter?" George said.

"Yeah," Stake said. "Well, maybe not all of them. Some of them aren't so bad."

The EMT's lifted Stake carefully onto a stretcher.

"Do you know your blood type?" one of them asked.

Stake shook his head. "Uh, actually, no."

George cleared his throat. "It's O Negative."

"You're sure?" the EMT said.

"Trust me," George said, smiling.

The EMTs wheeled Stake towards the entrance as George followed. Lonnie padded over and transformed himself back into human form.

"Well, Tim," he said. "This is a hell of a first case you managed to bag for yourself."

"I guess so," Tim said. "Thanks for all your help."

"What did I tell you before?" Lonnie said. "The SIU sticks together. Maybe for the next one, try to get the boss to assign you to something a little less apocalyptic. Like a nice possessed toaster or maybe even a coffee maker. Something like that."

"Looks like we've got a recent opening for a new claims VP," Carmilla said. "You could always apply for that."

"That's okay," Tim said. "I don't think I'm suited to an executive job. Too cutthroat."

Tim's phone buzzed. He pulled it out of his pocket and answered it.

"Hey bro," came Keef's voice. "I just got your message. I was, uh, entertaining some new lady friends. Couldn't quite make it out. What did you need? Something about a hammer? Do we need one for something?"

"Forget about it, Keef," Tim said. "It's taken care of."

Tim hung up and tucked the phone back in his pocket. Tabitha took him by the arm and the two of them began making their way out.

"Kind of nice when our jobs overlap," Tim said. "Don't you think?"

"Oh yes," Tabitha said. "Now let's make sure that it never happens again."

"I'm going to have so many reports to file over this," Tim said, shaking his head.

"You and me both, buster," Tabitha said. "Do you know that's the first time I've ever fired my weapon in the line of duty? And the first time I've ever killed someone."

"Well, I wouldn't get too worked up about it," Tim said. "Really it was the guillotine contraption that killed her. You just gave her a little push in the right direction."

"I suppose that's one way of looking at it," Tabitha said.

"Did I mention I've been looking at new apartments?" Tim said. "Preferably one with lots of natural light. The kind of thing my blood-sucking brother would tend to shy away from."

"That's good idea," Tabitha said. "It's about time you had your own space. I can help you look. You know, if you'd like a second opinion."

"That would be terrific," Tim nodded.

"We also need to do dinner again," Tabitha said. "My place this time. So there are fewer chances of being interrupted."

"That would also be terrific," Tim said.

One of the uniformed officers called Tabitha over.

"Duty calls," she said, pecking him on the cheek. "I'll talk to you later."

Tim continued up the stairs and through the secret entrance Carmilla had shown them on the way in. The street outside was full of police cars, which had blocked off the streets in all directions. Tim heard a rumble of thunder and looked over to see Volkerps floating towards him on a raging storm cloud.

"Lovecraft!" Volkerps shouted. "What in the name of Asag have you done here? Half our executives and most of the board of company directors are locked up in the back of police cruisers!"

"Sorry, boss," Tim said.

"Somebody told me Warwick was behind the whole thing!" Volkerps roared. "Is she in there?"

"Yes," Tim said. "Some assembly will be required, though. I doubt she'll have much to say at the next company-wide town hall."

"Try not to close any more investigations for a while," Volkerps said. "At least until we've had a chance to do some more hiring."

"Sure thing, boss."

"We'll never hear the end of this from the regulators," Volkerps said, shaking his head. "But screw it. That's for the CEO to worry about. Unless she's locked up in there somewhere, too. We're the SIU. Not a bunch of namby pamby actuaries. Human or not, you did a hell of a job."

"Thanks, boss."

"Keep it up like this, and you could have my job in a couple of thousand years," Volkerps said, winking with three of his eyes.

Tim laughed. "It is important to have goals. Right now, the only one I have is to get some sleep."

"Good idea," Volkerps said. "Maybe take a half day tomorrow. Or hell, take the whole thing. After that, I've got a nice, easy mortgage fraud I'm gonna put you on. Guy takes out huge policies and then fakes his death over and over again so he can keep collecting the payouts. Uses a lot of aliases, but we're pretty sure his real name's Gray."

"Great," said Tim, only half listening. He thought about taking the subway before deciding to spring for a cab instead. He got home to find his brother on the couch with a couple of teenaged girls, both of whom were wearing heavy gothic makeup. All three of them had blood smeared at the corners of their mouths.

"Hey bro!" Keef said, jumping up. "Sorry, I kinda thought you were staying out tonight with, uh, what's her name, so I invited, uh … "

"Kylie," said one of the girls.

"And Kim," said the other.

"Right," said Keef. "Yeah, I invited them over for a, you know, bite." Keef giggled at his own joke. "Hope you don't mind."

"That's fine," Tim said. Tomorrow, he decided, he would go and visit Stake in the hospital and then he would book appointments to view as many new condo units as he could. Maybe Tabitha would like to tag along. And then they could have dinner and talk about something other than demonic cults.

Tim went into his room, climbed up into bed and pulled the blankets over himself, falling almost instantly asleep.

Most people didn't realize it, he thought as he drifted off, but insurance was a dangerous business.

Liked DEMONIC INDEMNITY?

Get the next ebook in the series totally FREE!

INFERNAL NEGLIGENCE

Tim Lovecraft is just getting the hang of working in SIU when he's handed a case involving a homicidal, shapeshifting demon and asked to break in a trainee with an overpowering dislike for humans on the same day.

Nobody said that life in supernatural insurance was going to be easy, but he didn't think it was going to be quite as uneasy (and messy) as this.

JOIN THE MAILING LIST AND GET THE INFERNAL NEGLIGENCE EBOOK FREE AT THE LINK BELOW:

www.craigmclay.com/sign-up/